Praise for
THE PERFECT S[

"Shines a light on topics that many young readers are aware of and eager to discuss." —*School Library Journal*

"[Buyea tackles] topics like racism, immigration, bullying, and family secrets, with a deft hand. . . . Highly recommended."
—*Booklist*

"The characters shine, the plots are engaging, and the issues are addressed in interesting ways that will provide readers with many perspectives and much to consider."
—*Kirkus Reviews*

Praise for
THE PERFECT SCORE

"Buyea confidently mixes humor and heart."
—*Publishers Weekly*

"Readers will be drawn in by the lively voices and eventful lives of these likable and engaging students."
—*Kirkus Reviews*

"A heartfelt look at social interactions in middle school, a pointed commentary on standardized testing, and an entertaining read." —*Booklist*

"Readers will . . . enjoy watching the Recruits fight back against scholastic tyranny." —*The Bulletin*

"Kids will gobble it up because it is pure literary joy."
—*HuffPost*

NOVELS BY ROB BUYEA

The **PERFECT SCORE** Series

The Perfect Score
The Perfect Secret
The Perfect Star

The **MR. TERUPT** Series

Because of Mr. Terupt
Mr. Terupt Falls Again
Saving Mr. Terupt

THE PERFECT SECRET

ROB BUYEA

A YEARLING BOOK

Text copyright © 2018 by Rob Buyea
Cover art copyright © 2018 by Will Staehle
Interior illustrations copyright © 2018 by Penguin Random House LLC

All rights reserved. Published in the United States by Yearling, an imprint of Random House Children's Books, a division of Penguin Random House LLC, New York. Originally published in hardcover in the United States by Delacorte Press, an imprint of Random House Children's Books, a division of Penguin Random House LLC, New York, in 2018.

Yearling and the jumping horse design are registered trademarks of Penguin Random House LLC.

Visit us on the Web! rhcbooks.com

Educators and librarians, for a variety of teaching tools, visit us at RHTeachersLibrarians.com

The Library of Congress has cataloged the hardcover edition of this work as follows:
Names: Buyea, Rob, author.
Title: The perfect secret / Rob Buyea.
Description: First edition. | New York : Delacorte Press, [2018] | Summary: "Told from different viewpoints, five seventh-graders, who face their own personal challenges, are also determined as a group to help two very special people reconcile a long-standing dispute" —Provided by publisher.
Identifiers: LCCN 2018004831 (print) | LCCN 2018011640 (ebook) |
ISBN 978-1-5247-6461-6 (ebook) | ISBN 978-1-5247-6459-3 (hardback) |
ISBN 978-1-5247-6460-9 (library binding)
Subjects: | CYAC: Interpersonal relations—Fiction. | Middle schools—Fiction. | Schools—Fiction. | Nursing homes—Fiction. | Mothers and daughters—Fiction. | BISAC: JUVENILE FICTION / School & Education. | JUVENILE FICTION / Social Issues / Friendship. | JUVENILE FICTION / Family / Parents.
Classification: LCC PZ7.B98316 (ebook) | LCC PZ7.B98316 Pev 2018 (print) |
DDC [Fic]—dc23

ISBN 978-1-5247-6462-3 (pbk.)

Interior illustrations by Leslie Mechanic

Printed in the United States of America

10 9 8 7 6 5 4 3 2 1

First Yearling Edition 2019

To Brenda and Michael—
two of my favorite people
to share secrets with

1

THE RECRUITS

GAVIN

Meggie had this new picture book she kept asking me to read, and I hated it 'cause tucked away inside those pages was the worst sentence any writer person had ever written. The worst! It was the sentence-that-must-not-be-read. I kept trying to steer Meggie toward the other books Mom had bought for her at a yard sale, but she kept going back to the one about the big red dog. I didn't mind Clifford or his girl owner, but if you asked me, there was more wrong with that one sentence than there was with us cheating on the Comprehensive Student Assessments last spring. This particular Clifford book was all about manners, saying things like "please" and "thank you." I was good with that stuff, having been raised to know that holding the door for the old lady behind you was important. But the sentence I couldn't read—especially out loud!—was the one that said *He smiles when he loses.*

I slammed that book shut after reading those words to Meggie the first time. "This is terrible!" I shouted. All the daydreaming and night dreaming I did about football never had me smiling after losing a game. I was gonna win, and if I didn't, I sure as heck wasn't gonna be happy about it.

"Gavvy, don't," Meggie whined. "Read it. Please."

I huffed. "Fine," I said. "As long as you know that what it says in there is wrong. You don't need to smile after losing in order to be a good sport."

"Okay," she agreed. "Just read it."

Meggie didn't care, but that sentence bothered me every time she had me open the book. So I started changing the words to what they shoulda said, like *Clifford shook hands with his opponent after losing the match, but he wasn't smiling*. Or *Clifford hated losing, but he still shook hands after the contest*. Meggie frowned when I made changes, so we finally agreed I would skip that part. The rest of the sentences about being a good sport—stuff like not boasting when you win—were good, so I was fine reading those pages.

When I told Dad about that terrible sentence and how wrong it was, he laughed. "I can tell you this," I said. "In my book it's gonna say, *Gavin smiles when he wins. Gavin's happy winning*."

"You know, it's not just a seventh-grade football team you're joinin'," Dad reminded me. "It's a seven-eight team, which means there might be an eighth grader already slotted for the quarterback position."

"I know. But once the coach sees me outworking everybody else and gunslinging the ball, he'll give me my shot, and that's all I need."

"You'll get your chance as long as you don't go and open

your mouth or whine to the coach. You need to get his attention through—"

"Honest hard work, I know. Don't worry, Dad. I've been listening. I won't let you down. I'm gonna be the hardest-working kid."

Dad nodded. "Good. That's what I like to hear," he said. "And since there's no sense in you wastin' the summer, I brought somethin' home so you can get started outworkin' everybody now. It's in the back of my truck."

I ran over to check it out. "Can we put it up now?" I yelled.

"Yup. Grab ahold of it and follow me."

The tire was heavy, but I put my muscles into it and yanked it over the side of the truck. It bounced off the ground a few times and then fell down flat. I lifted it to my shoulder and marched out to the maple tree in our backyard. Dad met me there with his stepladder.

"Thanks," I said.

"You can thank me by makin' sure you use it."

"I will."

"Good," he said. "Now I need you to lift it up while I tie it in place."

"Is that a tire swing for me?" Meggie cried, leaping off the back porch steps.

"No, I'm afraid not, squirt," Dad said. "This is your brother's new target. He's gonna practice throwin' his football through the middle so he can become a more accurate passer."

"Oh," Meggie said. "So he can throw touchdowns?"

"That's right," Dad said. "So you can cheer for him."

"I'll cheer."

"Me too," Mom said, stepping out onto the porch. The two of them started doing some crazy cheerleader dance.

I smiled and shook my head.

"That should do it," Dad said, securing the last knot.

I stepped back and stood there, staring at my new wide receiver.

"Aren'tcha gonna show us how it works?" Meggie called.

"You've got about twenty minutes before supper's ready," Mom said.

That was all I needed to hear. I ran into the house and grabbed my football. Mom saw me fire a few passes through the tire and then went back inside to finish cooking. Dad and Meggie stayed for the next ten minutes, until Meggie finally got bored and they both headed into the house. But I threw pass after pass until Mom had everything on the table. Wherever the ball landed, that was where I picked it up and threw it from, which made some of the passes nearly impossible to get through the tire, but I knew that was what was gonna help me get better.

I was going to see Coach when Mrs. Magenta's community service program started up again after the Fourth of July. I'd already been looking forward to it, but now I was even more excited. Coach was a football genius. Once I

told him about my new tire target, I knew he'd give me a few tips and maybe even some drills to do.

Principal Allen had made mandatory enrollment in Mrs. Magenta's program one of our consequences for cheating on the CSAs last spring, but it sure didn't feel like any sort of punishment. We were all eager to return to the Senior Center to see our friends, especially after Scott's birthday party, when we'd finally put the pieces together and figured out that Magenta was the daughter Coach had been talking about, and Woods was her mother and Coach's wife. It was a doozy to wrap our heads around. We didn't know why Woods and Magenta weren't speaking to each other. But we wanted to do our best to help make things right between them again—for their sake and for Coach's. Course, I also wondered what Coach would have to say about sportsmanship and smiling after losing. I knew he would agree with me. Randi had reluctantly agreed with me when I'd told her about it the day before.

"It's just a children's book, Gav. Let it go," she said.

"It's a children's book sending the wrong message," I argued. "You're telling me you'll smile if you don't do well at States this weekend?"

Randi caught my pass and stood there. "No," she finally admitted.

"Exactly. If Clifford the Big Red Dog put in half the amount of hours practicing gymnastics that you have, he wouldn't smile after losing—trust me."

Randi laughed. "You're ridiculous," she said.

Now, with the tire target in front of me, I grabbed my football and gripped the laces. I wasn't ridiculous. I was right. I dropped back five steps and rolled to my left. Then I fired a bullet on the run. The ball sailed straight through the tire. Fist pump.

"Gavvy, time to eat!" Meggie called.

"Be right in!" I yelled. I jogged over and scooped up my ball.

After supper I would come back out. If I wanted to be the best, I had a lot of practicing to do. Before things finished up this year, I'd find out I had a lot left to learn about winning and losing and what was truly important.

Randi

I knew firsthand what a strained relationship between mother and daughter felt like. The not-talking-to-each-other stuff. The hurtful words you say and the ones you keep inside. But I also knew what forgiveness and coming together felt like. I'd spent the previous year being afraid of Jane, my high-pressure mother. I never looked forward to being around her. But after things fell apart with our CSAs and my affidavit, Mom and I picked up the pieces and found each other again, and it felt great. I wanted Mrs. Magenta to experience the same thing with Mrs. Woods. Having my mother on my side filled me with a positive energy that had gone missing—and it carried me to my state gymnastics meet.

The arena was huge. There were four competition areas arranged in a square pattern, with large warm-up spaces on the sides. Everywhere you turned there were spectators and athletes and coaches and judges. Music filled the air as a young girl tumbled across the floor. There were other gymnasts performing their routines on the bars and beam and vault. I looked into the stands. That was where I found Mom sitting with Mrs. Kurtsman, Natalie, Scott, and Gav—my personal cheering section. When Scott spotted me looking his way, he jumped to his feet, waving his arms.

"Hi, Randi! Good luck!"

Oh boy. He was getting started early. Too bad yelling in the middle of other girls' routines was not how things worked. I turned away quickly. I didn't want anyone to know I was Randi. I wanted to hide, I was so embarrassed—but I was smiling. I just hoped Mom was up there explaining the rules of cheering to Scott so he knew when to do it and when not to.

Coach Andrea found me, and that helped to settle my nerves. I was scheduled to begin in one hour, so we headed to the practice area. I ran through my warm-up drills and stretches, and talked things over with her. Then it was go time.

First up was the vault. Not my best event, but a solid start would put me within striking distance of an all-around championship for when I got to my strengths on the beam and floor. I sprinted down the runway and exploded off the springboard. *Hands, feet together, point, stick.* A small hop on my landing, but overall not bad—and I had a second attempt. After a good first vault, the pressure was off. On the second try I ran faster and jumped harder, and this time I stuck my landing. That was Gymnastics 101: fly high and stick the landing. I walked away from vault with a new personal best score.

"Woohoo! Way to go, Randi!" My cheering section went nuts.

Everyone knew who I was now, and that was okay. I smiled and waved. Seeing Mom's proud face was the best feeling. I'd kicked butt on the vault, and I wasn't slowing down.

My next event was bars. I chalked my hands and saluted the judges. Then I hopped up, and everything around me faded away as I entered my zone. I felt fast and strong through my moves, and I kept it going for my dismount. *Look. Stick. Yes!* I stuck my landing. Gymnastics 101.

"Woohoo! Yay, Randi!" My cheering section went nuts again.

On to the beam. This had the potential to be my best event, but things went wrong from the start. I didn't realize that the dismount mat was positioned at just one end. So when I mounted the beam, I mounted it facing in the wrong direction. I recognized my mistake as soon as I was up. I froze. I couldn't flip and land where there was no mat. I glanced at Coach Andrea. She told me to add a pivot turn. That put me facing in the right direction for my final maneuver, but it also meant I lost points because my coach had to talk to me during my routine. I knew all this before I took my first step, but I didn't let it ruin everything. The beam was only a skinny four inches wide under my foot, but my balance never wavered. I stepped and twisted and flipped with perfection. My routine took too long because of my slow start and extra turn, so I went over the time limit and was deducted points for that, too, but Coach Andrea gave me a hug when I finished and told me I'd looked beautiful up there. My cheering section went nutso again, but their shouts came to an abrupt end when they saw my dismal score. Maybe Mom would be able to explain to everyone else in the group what had happened, or maybe she was just as confused.

The beam was rotten luck, but I still had one event to go, and I wasn't about to end my day on a sour note. I was destined for better than that. I took a deep breath and refocused. And this time there were no mistakes. My floor routine was nearly flawless. I notched my second personal best score of the afternoon.

After all was said and done, my performance earned me a silver medal for all-around. I was second best in the state. So I didn't win, but I did very well. Well enough that I could still smile when I saw Gavin and the rest of my friends, well enough that Mom had tears in her eyes when she rushed over and threw her arms around me, and well enough that I qualified for Regionals—and that was the first step toward something I never saw coming.

NATALIE KURTSMAN
ASPIRING LAWYER
Kurtsman Law Offices

```
BRIEF #1
July: My Goals
```

Now that school was out, I needed goals for the summer; I'm a goal-oriented person. Here's the good news: I had my first one.

GOALS
- Resolve the strained relationship between Mrs. Woods and Mrs. Magenta.

Writing your goals down makes them real. That's something every expert will tell you. It helps you internalize them. Now, I know what you're thinking. This wasn't just *my* goal; it was something all the Recruits wanted. You're right. But it was up to me to lead the way. For one, I'm the smartest. (Just stating the facts.) And for two, the rest of the Recruits had other things to worry about, other endeavors occupying their time.

Randi had Regionals after her stellar state meet, Gavin had football, Scott had his Grandpa, and Trevor and Mark ... I wasn't certain. Yes, they had changed considerably, but not enough for me to believe that mending relationships had become their top priority. They weren't the next Dr. Phils. So, as you can see, this was up to me. It was my main goal.

Now to the business at hand. I realize you can't make people like each other any more than you can make two people fall in love, but the more you get two people together, the better the chances. Thus, our strategy was born. We had to get Mrs. Woods and Mrs. Magenta together as much as possible, and then, hopefully, they would slowly begin talking. First about the small stuff, ultimately about the big stuff—the hard stuff.

Admittedly, this was a big task. A huge challenge. So huge that all on its own this task could fulfill my requirements for a worthwhile goal. But there was something else that had been on my mind ever since school had ended—before that, actually—and I couldn't seem to shake it. I hadn't decided yet; I hadn't written it down and made it official, but my heart was telling me to go for it.

I wondered, though: *If I do, will I be overstepping my boundaries?*

SCOTT

The good thing about Grandpa living at the Senior Center was that it meant I didn't have to wait for Mrs. Magenta's program to start up again before I could go there. I got to visit all the time.

"Scott!" Grandpa exclaimed when he saw me poking my head into Coach's room. "Get in here. Coach has me on the ropes today." He was referring to their chess match. They went at it every afternoon, always in Coach's room. The familiar surroundings helped Coach stay relaxed and not get as easily confused.

"Who's that?" Coach barked.

"My grandson," Grandpa told him for the hundredth time.

"Well, he can't save you from defeat," Coach mocked.

"Maybe not, but he can take over for me while I use the bathroom. When an old guy's gotta go, he's gotta go." Grandpa got up and sat me in his chair. "It's your move," he said. "Show Coach what you're made of." He patted me on the shoulder and hurried off. He wasn't holding himself like my little brother, Mickey, does, and that was good because it meant he wasn't in danger of wetting himself.

I turned my attention to the game. I looked down and studied the board. I'd had many matches with Grandpa back before his house had burned down, so I wasn't a rookie, but I didn't have the experience Coach did.

"Today, Valentine," Coach said. "I'm not getting any younger."

"I'm not Valentine," I corrected him. "That's my friend Gavin. He's the one you call Valentine. He's really looking forward to seeing you again, by the way. I was with him last weekend at our other friend Randi's gymnastics meet, which was really fun. Randi took second in the state with her overall score. Can you believe it? She goes to Regionals now. She's so—"

"Today, Junior," Coach growled.

"Is Junior my nickname? I've always wanted a nickname."

"Move!" Coach yelled.

I slid my knight forward two and to the right one. "Anyway, at Randi's gymnastics meet, Gavin—I mean Valentine—was telling me all about his new tire target that's he's been firing passes through. He's wondering if you can give him some drills to practice."

Back and forth we maneuvered our pieces, and I kept talking. "Valentine's working hard because he wants to be quarterback. I've seen him throw the ball at recess. He's really good."

Coach moved a pawn. "What position are you going out for?" he asked me.

"Oh, I'm not playing. I'm not very good." I slid my castle across the board.

"But you like the game?" Coach asked.

"Oh yes."

"Tell me what my last seven moves were."

I scrunched my face. "What?"

"My last seven moves. What were they?"

Was Coach confused? I didn't want him to get upset, so I did what he'd asked. I told him what his last seven moves had been. I remembered them all. That was easy. I have a super memory.

"I know your position," he said.

"No, I'm not playing," I told him again. He was confused. Where was Grandpa?

"I didn't forget what you said, Junior. I heard you. Now you need to listen to me. I'm telling you, I know your position."

I didn't interrupt or try to correct him. I let him finish, because people losing their minds can get easily agitated. Grandpa had told me that happened with Coach sometimes.

"Your position is on the sideline," Coach continued, "but it's just as important as those on the field. You're the stats man."

"What's that?"

"You're the guy who keeps track of the game, documenting every play. What was the call? Who got the ball? How many yards? Who made the tackle? All the stats," Coach explained. "During halftime you need to analyze the information and tell the coach about any patterns or tendencies you notice. I can tell from the way you play chess that you're perfect for it."

"But I don't know if there's a stats man on the team."

"There is now. You go and introduce yourself to the coach and tell him I sent you. If you have any problems, you come and find me."

"Who's winning?" Grandpa asked when he got back.

"We thought you fell in," Coach jabbed.

"Missed me, did you? My grandson must be whipping your tail."

"I'm holding my own," I said. I pushed my queen diagonally across the board. "Check."

"Ha!" Grandpa laughed.

Coach sat forward and sneered at me, but he never got to make his next move, because that was when my little brother, Mickey, came tearing into the room, chasing after Grandpa's cat. Smoky was so excited to see Grandpa that he jumped clear over our board. Mickey wasn't so graceful. He tripped and crashed into our table and our chess pieces went flying everywhere.

"What in tarnation is going on here?" Coach hollered.

Grandpa bent down and scooped Smoky into his arms. "My cat just saved you from defeat," he said. "He's special like that."

Boy, hearing that made me feel good, because I was the one who'd rescued Smoky and given him to Grandpa, and then Smoky had saved Grandpa on the night when his house had burned down.

"Gampa, guess what? Guess what?" Mickey squealed, getting back to his feet. "Smoky gets to stay here. Mommy got pamission."

"Really?" Grandpa said. "Did you hear that, Smoky? You get to stay."

Smoky started purring louder than a car engine.

"I see you got your cat," Mom said, entering the room right

on cue. "You get to keep him now, but he has to stay in your room. Or in Coach's when you visit him."

"I had a cat once," Coach said. "An ugly yellow tomcat. A seven-toer. Hector was his name. Just showed up one day and never left. Don't know why; he hated everyone. But he liked me. He was a good cat."

I smiled, partly because I liked Coach's story, but more because he was remembering so much. It had been a good day for his memory. I was super-excited to start Mrs. Magenta's program so the Recruits could help Mrs. Woods and Mrs. Magenta before he ran out of good days.

"Well, c'mon, boys," Mom said. "We need to get going. I told Dad we'd pick up a pizza on our way home."

"Pizza!" Mickey cheered, skipping out the door.

"Bye, Grandpa. Good game, Coach." I waved.

"You're lucky it got cut short, Junior."

That made me smile even bigger. I loved my nickname. I couldn't wait to tell Gavin. Grandpa winked, and I ran to catch up to Mom and Mickey.

Trevor

"How do you think he's doing?" Mom asked Dad at dinner. She was talking about my brother, Brian.

"I'm sure he's fine."

That was Dad's programmed response.

I had the same answer for her when she asked how I was doing. "I'm fine." And I was—sort of, but not really. I wasn't so sure about my brother, though, and neither was Mom.

"You think so?" she pressed.

"Yes," Dad replied.

This was getting old. Before they'd kicked Brian out of the house, we'd rarely had dinner together. This was Mom's new thing. It was her way of trying. I gave her credit, only it wasn't working.

"I'm thinking about driving over to his apartment to check on him," she said.

Whoa. Did my mother really think they could kick my brother out of the house and then go and visit him whenever her heart desired? I understood why she wanted to, but Brian would never go for it. If he wanted to talk to her, he'd answer her phone calls—or call her.

"Dorothy, he's fine. You're not going over there to check on him," Dad said.

"It can't hurt anything. He's my son."

"You are not going over there!" Dad yelled, bringing his fists down on the table. "Your son needs to grow up. Don't forget how he treated Trevor. Or how he flunked out of college while partying our money away. Let him struggle. We're done babying him."

That was the end of that conversation. We finished the rest of our dinner in silence. Then I loaded the dishwasher and went to my bedroom and called Mark.

"Dude," he said.

"Hey."

"What's up?"

"My mom's talking about driving over to Brian's. She wants to check on him."

"Oof. Did you tell her that might not be the best idea?"

"My father did."

"And?"

"She tried convincing him it would be okay, and then he exploded."

Mark let out a long breath. "So they're fighting again?"

I sat on my bed. "Yeah."

"Sorry, bro."

"It'll be one of them moving out next. I can see it coming. The writing's on the wall."

Mark was quiet on the other end. Even though I pretended I didn't care, we both knew that wasn't the truth. This was my fault. I was the mistake. Brian had told me so a thousand times.

"You okay?" Mark asked after a minute.

"Brian's gonna find me, you know. At some point our paths are gonna cross. It scares me just thinking about it."

"Then don't."

"Don't what?"

"Don't think about it," Mark said. "It's not doing you any good. Think about Mrs. Magenta's program that we start next week. Think about football."

Easier said than done, I thought. Mark hadn't seen the way Brian looked at me before driving off in that U-Haul. Mom and Dad had sent my brother packing because of me. Because they'd found out that Brian and his goons bullied me. "Yeah, I guess so," I said.

"Dude, stop sweating it. It's not doing you any good."

"You already said that."

"Well, it's not."

"What do you think Brian will do when we see each other?"

Mark sighed. "I don't know."

I needed a better answer than that. "I've gotta go. Talk to you later."

"Hang in there, bro. It'll get better soon."

I wished I could believe that, but how was I supposed to when I had parents headed for the big *D* and an older brother who hated my guts?

2

A PACT IS MADE

Natalie Kurtsman
ASPIRING LAWYER
Kurtsman Law Offices

BRIEF #2
Mid-July: Mrs. Magenta's Program Resumes

In years past I didn't see many of the kids from school over the summer, but thanks to Mr. Allen that was not going to be the case this year. In fact, it was the first day of Mrs. Magenta's summer program, so our class from sixth grade was all together again.

It's safe to say we broke more than a few rules when we cheated on the CSAs last spring, but the consequence Mr. Allen handed down wasn't anything I'd consider bad. Rather, the word I would use to describe our consequence would be "constructive."

"Hello, and happy summer to all you caring souls," Mrs. Magenta began.

"Mrs. Magenta, are you—"

"Scott!" I snapped. "Quiet," I hissed through gritted teeth.

"That's all right, Natalie. Am I what, Scott?"

I caught my breath. This was it. Our plan was doomed already, and we hadn't even gotten started. It was my fault. I'd neglected to add a very important goal to my list: Keep Scott quiet!

We'd gone over this at his birthday party. We weren't going to let Mrs. Magenta and Mrs. Woods know that we were onto them. Our attempts at getting them together would be better masked if they thought we didn't know about their relationship or their history, if they believed our actions were innocent as opposed to manipulative. But impulsive Scott was about to let the cat out of the bag already. *Here it comes,* I thought. I could hear him now, *Are you Mrs. Woods's daughter?*

Scott cleared his throat. "Are you"—he looked at me and then back at Mrs. Magenta—"a fan of ice cream?"

I exhaled. Thank goodness.

Mrs. Magenta smiled. "Yes, I love ice cream. A little cookies and cream with peanut butter topping is my favorite."

Eww. I grimaced.

"I like cookie dough best," Scott said.

"That's a good flavor, but now let me ask all of you a question," Mrs. Magenta said. "We will be returning to the Senior Center this afternoon, but I'm wondering if any of you would object to our continuing with trips to visit our old friends for our community service when school starts up again."

No hands were raised. If they had been, I would've been on my feet in an instant, yelling, *Objection!* But none of my colleagues were opposed, and that was good, because getting Mrs. Magenta and Mrs. Woods together was going to be much easier to accomplish at the Senior Center than anywhere else.

"Wonderful," Mrs. Magenta said. "I was hoping not. You see, our work at the Senior Center will never really be done. Our friends there will always welcome our company."

"Maybe we can do something more for them, or for the place, like we did at the public library?" Trevor said.

My eyebrows lifted. *How thoughtful—and sincere. Where is this coming from?* I wondered.

"Do you have any suggestions?" Mrs. Magenta asked.

"No. It's just . . . I've been trying to keep my mind . . . It's just an idea that popped into my head, that's all."

"Well, it's a delightful thought," Mrs. Magenta said. "Let's all think about it while we're there this afternoon and see if we can come up with any projects."

"It's a really good idea, Trevor," Scott said, "like the one you had about collecting stuff for my grandpa after his house burned down."

I was in complete agreement. I'd heard that boys change during adolescence, but ever since the CSAs, Trevor had shown what one might call a complete turnaround. It was actually quite astonishing, but I was not to be distracted. Let me be clear: the best aspect of Trevor's proposal was the fact that it had the potential to give everyone else something to do so I could focus on mending a certain mother-daughter relationship.

"Our bus is here," Mrs. Magenta announced.

I reviewed the day's plan in my head. There were three objectives: (1) observe carefully, especially the two parties involved, and especially when together, (2) collect more information, and (3) get Mrs. Magenta and Mrs. Woods together.

"I'm excited to see Agnes and Eddie," Randi said after we took our seats on the bus.

"Me too," I said. Objective number four: spend time visiting with Agnes and Eddie.

The bus pulled out of the school lot, setting my plan in motion.

GOALS

- Resolve the strained relationship between Mrs. Woods and Mrs. Magenta.
- Keep our plan secret, which requires keeping Scott and the rest of the Recruits quiet—but mainly Scott.

GAVIN

I took my seat on the bus, and Scott slid in next to me. This was it. We were off to the Senior Center. "I hope Coach remembers me," I said.

"He will," Scott promised, making it sound like a nobrainer. "Junior was telling him about Valentine and his tire target last week."

"Who's Junior?"

"I am!" Scott squealed. "Coach gave me a nickname, too!"

I shook my head and laughed. It was just like Scott to get wound up over a nickname. "Well, Junior, even though I wasn't sure if we'd get to visit today, I came prepared." I patted my bag. "I have a special memory surprise for Coach and a couple of different poetry books, in case he wants me to read to him."

"What's the surprise?"

"Can't tell you. You'll have to wait and see." Scott scowled. I also had *Clifford's Manners,* but I didn't bother trying to explain that to him.

A few minutes later our bus stopped outside the front entrance. "We're here!" Scott cried. "Let's go!"

The kid's enthusiasm was contagious. That was one of the things I liked most about him. He had all of us excited. We bounded off the bus.

It had been a while since we'd last visited as a group, but Director Ruggelli was cool and didn't hold us up with any big reintroduction. All she said was, "Welcome back. Your friends are eager to see you."

We followed her into the Community Hall, where we were greeted by lots of smiles and waves. I smiled and waved back, but after a quick glance around the place, I saw that Coach wasn't there. Scott had told me his grandpa and Coach had become best buds and that more than likely we'd find them playing a game of chess in Coach's room, so that was where we headed.

"Told you," Scott whispered when we got there and peeked inside.

"Your grandpa gets to keep Smoky here now?" I asked him after spotting the gray cat on his grandfather's lap.

"Yup. My mom took care of that."

"Nice."

"Ready?" he asked.

I didn't answer. I couldn't help it. I was nervous. *What if Coach doesn't remember me? Is this how Woods and Magenta feel every day?*

"Don't worry," Scott said. "Coach knows who you are. And if he doesn't, we'll remind him."

I swallowed. "Okay. Let's go."

In we went, the brave one—Scott—followed by the

chicken—me. That wasn't how things were supposed to be for a football player, but that was how it was. Scott was our Most Valuable Player.

"Scott!" his grandpa hollered, looking up from his game.

"Hi, Grandpa. Hi, Coach."

"Hello there, Valentine," Grandpa said. "Nice to see you again."

Scott's grandfather knew my real name. Was he just trying to help Coach remember me? I sure appreciated that. "Hello, sir," I said. "It's good to be back." I looked at Coach. "Hey, Coach."

Coach's eyes narrowed on me. Did he remember? I wasn't taking any chances. I put my bag down and reached inside. Once I found what I was looking for, I straightened, took a deep breath, walked over, and handed my surprise to him. Scott's trick of using memory objects to help Coach out mighta been his all-time most brilliant idea.

Coach turned the kicking tee over in his hands. He held it up and studied it. "You've got to be ready for anything, Valentine, and we will be. You can count on that," he promised. He was just beginning to pick up steam. "We're going to catch Thomson High sleeping. We're going to start the game with an onside kick."

Coach got out of his chair and started pacing the room, gesturing with his hands and getting into it as he spoke. "We'll line up normal and then shift left when our kicker moves toward the ball. They won't have time to react. One high bounce, and the ball will be ours!" he shouted. Coach swung his arm low as he got near the chessboard, sending pieces flying across the room.

"Nice one," Grandpa ribbed.

"Ah, be quiet," Coach said. "You were losing anyway. I did you a favor."

"You brought a Clifford book!" Scott cried.

He'd gone in my bag when I wasn't looking. "Never mind," I said, grabbing the book from him. "My sister musta put that in there without me knowing."

"Read it," Coach said, sitting back down in his chair.

"You want him to read Clifford?" Scott asked.

"If Valentine's sister wanted me to hear it, it must be good."

"C'mon, Scott," Grandpa said, walking to the door. "Let's give Valentine and Coach time to visit. I need your help with Smoky's litter box."

After hearing that, I think Scott woulda preferred listening to me read Clifford, but he didn't have a choice. "Okay," he grumbled.

I started reading. It didn't take long before I got to that terrible sentence, and when I did, I stopped. I didn't know what to do.

"What'd you stop for?" Coach barked. "Keep reading."

"I can't."

"Why?"

"The next sentence bothers me."

"Bothers you? Let me hear it."

I swallowed. " 'He smiles when he loses,' " I read.

"You don't like that?" Coach asked.

"No," I mumbled. Suddenly it felt silly.

"Me neither!" Coach hollered. "Sportsmanship is important, Valentine, but people today are confused about it. Somewhere along the line that award stopped going to winners, and now it's only ever handed out to the teams that are good at losing. Bunch of baloney, if you ask me."

I loved Coach! I knew he'd hate that sentence.

"I'm not saying sportsmanship doesn't matter, Valentine. It does. You want to be humble in victory and gracious in defeat. But make no mistake about it, if you've worked hard and given your all, then losing hurts. Bad. I hate losing more than I love winning. But, Valentine, it's how we carry ourselves in defeat, how we rise after failure, that tells it all. Because that's when character is revealed."

I needed to think about Coach's words, so I didn't say anything right away, and Coach let me be quiet. He knew I'd say something when I was ready.

"I've been working hard," I said. "My dad helped me hang a tire in our backyard, so now I have a target for practice."

"The good old-fashioned tire, huh? That has helped train many of the great ones. How do you use it?"

I told Coach what I'd been doing, and then he explained a couple of other drills that I could add.

"You know what I like about you, Valentine? You're coachable. You know when to listen. Now grab another book and do some more reading."

Football talk was over, but that was okay 'cause Coach had

given me plenty to think about. I grabbed my Kwame Alexander book. I was rapping out one of his poems when Mrs. Magenta showed up a bit later.

"Hi, boys. How's it going?" she asked. I watched her walk over and place her hand on Coach's shoulder. I held my breath, hoping for Coach to remember her, but he didn't say anything.

"It's going good," I said.

"Well, I'm afraid it's time for us to go. I'll meet you out front." She patted Coach's shoulder and left, but not before I saw the sadness in her eyes.

I packed my things and said goodbye, but Coach didn't say anything. He sat there with a blank face. I wondered where he was, 'cause it sure wasn't there in the room with me. Seeing him glossed-over like that scared me. And it got me thinking. Even though Coach had agreed with me, Randi was right, I was being ridiculous. How could I get all worked up over a silly sentence when Coach was struggling with losing something way more important than any football game? Like I told you, I still had a lot to learn about losing.

Trevor

I was relieved when Mrs. Magenta's program finally kicked into gear, because it gave me something to do so I wasn't stuck worrying about my parents getting divorced and about crossing paths with my brother. I was fine with returning to the Senior Center, but I can't say I was excited. Gavin had become great buddies with Coach, Natalie and Randi had Agnes and Eddie, and Scott had his grandpa, but Mark and I didn't have anyone like that. Maybe that was why the idea of a project had popped into my head. Mrs. Magenta and Scott seemed to like that, so it was a start. We just needed to *find* a project.

When we got to the Senior Center, I had Mark hang back with me. We didn't rush off to the Community Hall with everyone else. We waited so we could talk to Mrs. Ruggelli.

"I've got something you can do for me," she said after I'd finished explaining.

"Really?" I hadn't been expecting that.

"Yes," she said. "I've been wanting to upgrade our TV system, but I don't know the first thing about that stuff. Do you?"

Mark and I looked at each other and then back at Mrs. Ruggelli. "We're not pros," I said, "but I think we can figure it out. It shouldn't be that hard."

"Great," she said. "How about I show you our old system and you can start making plans. Maybe we can go shopping next week?"

Mark and I glanced at each other again, and we both shrugged. "Sounds good," I said.

Mrs. Ruggelli didn't waste any more time. She headed to the TV room. The lounge, they called it. "This is it," she said.

"Dude, you weren't kidding. This is in desperate need of an upgrade," Mark said.

I elbowed him, and Mrs. Ruggelli laughed.

"Sorry," Mark said. "I mean 'dudette.'"

She laughed some more.

We hadn't ever seen this room before because we always spent our time in the Community Hall. It was a nice, large space, but Mark was right. The entertainment system needed serious work. We checked it out, and Mark lost it.

"Mrs. Ruggelli, this equipment is from the dinosaur era."

"I know," she said.

I stood there, taking it all in, assessing the situation. I stared at the ridiculous fat-back TV. It was beyond ugly and looked like it weighed a ton. And that wasn't even the worst of it. Next to the TV there was a VCR. Not even a DVD player, and there were no speakers of any kind.

"Can the old people hear this when they sit in the back?" I asked Mrs. Ruggelli.

"We have to turn the volume all the way up," she said, "and

even then half of them can't hear it, but they don't complain. Guess they're used to it by now,"

"We're going to make this better," I said. "A lot better. I think we should get surround sound."

"That'd be wonderful. Thank you, boys."

"We haven't done anything yet," Mark said. "Thank us when we're done—if we haven't blown the place up."

Mrs. Ruggelli's eyes got big like she was legit worried, but she relaxed after I shoved Mark and told her not to listen to him.

"I should go and check on things in the Community Hall," she said. "I'll leave you two alone so you can make a shopping list."

And that was just what we did. We spent the rest of our visit taking notes and researching different systems on the lounge computer—which was also a fat-back and way outdated. Brian was an expert at all things tech. He'd had a flatscreen and surround sound speakers in his bedroom at home. When he used to let me play video games with him, it felt like we were in a movie theater. Maybe if I'd been older when he'd hooked it all up, I could've helped and learned, but Brian had never wanted me around. Back then I was the annoying little twerp—the mistake—who wanted to dress like him, talk like him, and do everything like him. Now, with the way it stood, I didn't know if I wanted to see him—but sometimes in life, things are out of our hands.

Randi

Natalie and I walked over to the table where Agnes and Eddie were seated.

"Hellc, ladies," Natalie said. "It's nice to see you again."

"Ha!" Eddie scoffed. "'Ladies'! Did you hear that, Agnes? She called us 'ladies.'"

I'd missed these two. I was already giggling, and I hadn't even sat down yet.

"Must you always be so formal, Miss Natalie?" Agnes asked.

"Natalie's always serious," I said.

"That serious face of yours is going to give you wrinkles worse than mine," Agnes warned.

"What she needs is a boyfriend," Eddie remarked. "Playing a little kissy face would give her something to smile about, and then those scowl lines would disappear."

"Edna!" Agnes snapped. "For heaven's sake, the girls just got here and you're already starting in on them. Behave yourself, or they won't want to visit anymore."

I didn't say anything, because I didn't want to cross Agnes, but Eddie's naughtiness was one of the things I liked best about visiting. I wouldn't have been surprised to hear Natalie admit the same thing.

"Well," Natalie said. "I don't know much about playing kissy face, but I did bring a new game for us to try. Dominoes."

"Oh, I like that one," Agnes said.

"Whoever loses needs to kiss a boy," Eddie teased.

I tried holding it in, but my laughter escaped.

"Don't encourage her," Agnes said, glaring at me.

I bit the insides of my cheeks, but then Eddie made a face, mocking Agnes, and the laughter came out again. At least this time Natalie was laughing with me. Poor Agnes just shook her head, which made us laugh harder.

We dumped the dominoes onto the table and got them flipped facedown. Then we picked out our bricks and got started. Dominoes is a good game because you can continue visiting and having conversation when it isn't your turn. Eddie and Agnes filled us in on all the gossip at the Senior Center, which took more than a while, and then Natalie told them all about my state meet and upcoming Regionals.

"That's quite the accomplishment, Miss Randi," Agnes said.

"Thank you."

"When I was your age, I was pretty good at hopscotch and jumping rope," Eddie said, "but my favorite thing to play was kissy face."

"Ugh!" Agnes groaned. "You never stop."

I was laughing again, but Natalie wasn't. Not this time. She'd done a lot of talking, but she wasn't listening. Her mind was elsewhere.

"Heavens, child, who or what do you keep looking for?" Agnes asked. She'd noticed how Natalie kept glancing around the hall.

"Cute boys, of course," Eddie couldn't help but blurt out. I was beginning to think loose lips was something she and Scott had in common.

"Hush!" Agnes scolded. "That's enough." She turned back to Natalie. "How about it, Miss Kurtsman? Who're you searching for?"

Natalie sighed. "Our old teacher, Mrs. Woods," she said.

"You won't see Pearl here now," Agnes said.

"She's never here the same time as her daughter," Eddie added.

Our heads jerked. Natalie and I stared at each other, wide-eyed. "Wait. You know about them and Coach?" Natalie asked.

"We might be old, but we're not off our rockers yet," Eddie said. "We know everything that's going on around this joint. How else are we supposed to run the place?"

"Must be that you girls didn't know," Agnes said. "Otherwise you wouldn't be so surprised."

"We just learned," I said.

"And we need to keep that a secret," Natalie urged. "We can't let them know that we know, so please don't tell."

"You're up to something," Eddie said. "I like it."

"Please don't tell," Natalie pleaded.

"Eddie's right, you're up to something," Agnes said. "I need to know what it is before I make you any promises."

Natalie looked at me again, but all I could do was shrug. What choice did we have? We had to let them in on our plan.

"We intend to fix their broken relationship," Natalie explained.

"When pigs fly," Eddie scoffed.

"What's that supposed to mean?!" Natalie shot back, her voice rising.

"Listen, I know all about getting the boys to love you," Eddie said, "but making those two women like each other again is going to take more than shaking hips and batting eyelashes. You're going to need a miracle."

"Time for us to get going," Mrs. Magenta announced from the front of the room. "Start to wrap things up."

"You girls are playing with fire," Agnes warned. "You shouldn't get involved in their feud. There's more to it than you know."

"We'll tread lightly," Natalie said, "which is why they can't know we're onto them. Will you keep our secret?"

Now Agnes sighed. "I'm not sure I like it . . . but we'll keep your secret—for now."

"And if we see anything that might help you, we'll let you know," Eddie added, leaning forward. "We'll be your insiders, working as your informants. How fun."

"Sometimes you can be such a kid," Agnes said.

"That's what keeps me young. You won't let me get a man, so I've got to do something."

"Ugh!" Agnes groaned and rolled her eyes, but that wasn't enough to get Natalie and me laughing or even cracking a smile now.

We said goodbye and made our way out to the bus. Natalie was feeling discouraged. It was clear this wasn't going to be easy, and we didn't need a crystal ball to see that. But the thing I couldn't shake was what Agnes had said. "There's more to it than you know."

Come to find out, there was more than I knew about a lot of things. Seventh grade was a year of secrets and discoveries.

SCOTT

Our first trip back to the Senior Center was a whopping success. Everyone was happy and feeling good after seeing all our old friends again. The only one who seemed a little quiet was Natalie, but that was because she was busy thinking. I was thinking about something, too.

"What's an onside kick?" I asked Gavin. "Coach said it's a great way to start the game against Thomson High."

"Do you know what a regular kickoff looks like?"

"No."

"Then it's too hard to explain," Gavin said. "It's complicated."

"But I need to know these things if I'm going to be Stats Man."

"Stats what?"

"Stats Man," I said. "It was Coach's idea. After I played chess against him, he told me I would be the perfect person to be in charge of keeping the statistics and analyzing the information for our team."

"Really? He told you that?"

"Yessiree," I said, sitting up tall, feeling important.

"And you want to do it?"

"Yeah!" I exclaimed. "I'm going to be the best at it."

Gavin chuckled. "Then here's what you need to do. You've got to start watching the preseason football games on TV and watching clips on the computer. You've got to learn the basics, and then I can help you understand the more complicated stuff. Think of it as your homework assignment."

"I can do that," I said. "You've got a deal." We shook hands. This was going to be so much fun.

Our bus stopped in front of the school, and I hopped up and used the seat backs to swing myself down the aisle. When I got to the steps, I was feeling so excited that I jumped all the way over them, but that was a bad idea, because I ate dirt.

"Scott, what're you doing?" Natalie yelled. She grabbed me under the arm and helped me to my feet. "Are you all right?"

I'd skinned my hands and knees, but I was fine. There was only a little blood. I brushed the sand off my legs and the pebbles from my palms. "I'm okay," I said. "Guess I'm not good at sticking my landings like Randi."

"No, you're not," Natalie agreed.

"Not the smartest thing I've seen you try," Gavin said, stepping off the bus behind me. "Keep that up, and you'll be on the injured list, forget the sideline."

Natalie gave him a funny look because she didn't know what he was talking about, but I did. "Never mind," Gavin told her.

"Never mind," I repeated.

She scowled at us. "We don't have time for this nonsense. Let's go."

Boy, she meant business, and when Natalie meant business, there was no fooling around. She marched us over to a nearby grassy area at the side of the school, away from everyone else, where the other Recruits were already waiting for us.

"Okay, listen up," she said. "After today one thing is obvious: helping Mrs. Magenta and Mrs. Woods fix their broken relationship is going to be much more difficult than I had anticipated. We can't possibly get them together if they're never visiting the Senior Center at the same time."

"What're we going to do?" I asked.

"I don't know yet, but I'm not about to give up because of one obstacle."

"You don't have to do this all by yourself, you know," Trevor said. "We're here to help. We can start thinking, too."

Natalie stopped. She stood there looking at Trevor, but he was no match for her, so he was the first to look away. "Okay. You're right," she said. "If any of us comes up with an idea, we need to let each other know."

"But how?" I asked. "How do I let everyone know if I have an idea?"

"Good point," Natalie said. "Since not everyone owns a cell phone, I'll need your home phone numbers."

"My mom won't let me have a phone because she says I'll lose it like everything else," I explained.

"And she's probably right," Natalie agreed.

"Why do you even need one?" I asked.

"Find me a lawyer who doesn't have one," she snapped.

I had to think about that.

"Now, as I was saying," she continued, "I'll need your home phone numbers. When I get to the office, I'll make up an emergency phone tree. The document will tell each of us who to call if something comes up. I'll pass it out the next time we meet. But remember, it's for emergency purposes only."

We took turns giving Natalie our numbers. This felt really important and secretive, and it got my brain fizzing. Then I got one of my best ideas. "There's something else we need to do," I urged.

The Recruits looked at me. "What now, dude?" Mark asked.

"This is a top-secret mission, so we need to make a pact. Otherwise we might not succeed," I explained.

"What kind of pact?" Trevor asked next.

"A blood brother and blood sister pact." I wiped the blood from my knee onto my hand and held it out.

"Whoa, dude," Mark said.

"Absolutely not!" Natalie cried. "That is the most disgusting and unsanitary thing I have ever seen."

"Calm down, Kurtsman," Gavin said.

"The blood pact will unite us and make us stronger," I explained. "It's necessary."

"No way," Natalie objected.

My shoulders sagged. "Without it we'll fail."

"Scott, you're the only one bleeding," Trevor said. "So how about we use our spit instead. That's still part of the body."

"It might not be as strong, but I think it'll work," I said.

That was all it took. The guys didn't hesitate. Trevor spit on his hand, and then so did Gavin and Mark. And once they did, Randi followed. She did it the best. I bet that was because she had to spit on her hands all the time at gymnastics.

"C'mon, Kurtsman," Gavin said. "You're the last one."

"You're serious?"

"Yes. C'mon."

"Close your eyes, and it won't be that bad," Randi said. "You can do it."

"I can't believe this," Natalie whined. She turned her hand over and did the wimpiest spit in the history of the world. It dangled from her lips like a spider's web, and then it swung back and stuck to her chin. "Eww!" she shrieked.

"Dude, that's nasty," Mark teased.

"Now you look like a football player and not any fancy lawyer," Gavin joked.

"Eww!" she shrieked again.

"Natalie, it's okay," Randi said, trying to calm her down.

Trevor grasped Natalie's wrist and helped her wipe the spit from her face onto her palm.

"Hands in," I shouted.

Natalie squeezed her eyes shut and stuck her hand into the middle with the rest of ours. We took turns mushing our spits together.

"Eww," Natalie whined.

"Team on three," I said. "One. Two. Three."

"Team!" we shouted.

That sealed it. We were bound together for eternity. I don't want to brag, but the pact was a good thing, because we really needed each other in the months ahead.

3

FLEA FLICKERS,
GLOSS-OVERS,
AND ALARMS

Randi

The ride to gymnastics was a quiet one. Not because Mom and I couldn't talk to each other like before, but because I was busy thinking. There was this tiny nagging thought that had been bothering me, and after seeing Eddie and Agnes, it started bothering me even more.

A hypocrite is a person who says one thing and does another. Not like saying you'll be right home, and then running errands instead. More like a person who lectures during the day about nutrition and how late-night snacking is unhealthy, but then spends the evening on the couch with a bag of chips, watching TV. That's being a hypocrite. That's not the kind of person I wanted to be, or the kind of person I liked. But I couldn't stop thinking that maybe Mrs. Woods was one.

At our parent-teacher conference the previous year, Mrs. Woods had told Jane that she was putting too much pressure on me and that it was going to ruin our relationship. It was true, but come to find out, Mrs. Woods had done no better with her own daughter, Mrs. Magenta. At least my mom had apologized and we were supertight now. That was more than Mrs. Woods could say.

Eddie had told us there was more to their story than we knew. Well, I wanted to know the rest of it, because I hoped it would make me feel different about my old teacher. I didn't like feeling this way about Mrs. Woods.

"You're quiet today," Mom said.

"Busy thinking, I guess."

"Yeah. About what?"

"Nothing, really."

Mom laughed. "I know how that goes. If you decide you want to talk about nothing, let me know."

I smiled. I'd done enough thinking for now, so I reached out and turned up the radio. Next thing I knew, Mom and I broke into the best car karaoke ever. We sang for the rest of the ride, belting all the way until Mom stopped in front of the gym.

"If gymnastics doesn't work out, maybe you and I will become the next big mother-daughter duo," she said.

I laughed and kissed her on the cheek. "Better hope gymnastics works out," I said. "We didn't sound *that* good."

Mom chuckled. "Love you. Have a good workout." I hopped out of the car and ran inside while Mom left to run a couple of errands.

Practice was all about getting ready for Regionals, which was only a few weeks away. I had my routines down, so I was just working on perfecting every nitpicky detail. The only exception was on vault, where Coach Andrea was helping me with a new skill—one with increased difficulty. If I could master it in time for the competition, I'd have a better chance at getting a higher score.

"Okay, Randi. You've got this," she encouraged from the side, where she stood ready as my spotter.

I pulled in a deep breath and exhaled slowly. Then I sprang out of my stance, attacking the runway.

"That's it!" Coach Andrea cheered. "Don't slow down."

Over and over again I sprinted down the runway and exploded off the springboard. I worked and worked at my new maneuver. I felt great. Coach Andrea was even more pumped than I was. "I can't wait to see the looks on the other gymnasts' faces when they see you flying and twisting through the air."

What I didn't know then was that my new skill wasn't going to only launch me through the air. It was also going to catapult my destiny—and Mom's—in a whole new direction.

SCOTT

The second I got home from the Senior Center, I went straight to the computer. I had homework to do. I planted my butt in the chair and got started researching football.

The first thing I looked up was the kickoff. It was easy to find information because the kickoff is the first play in every game. After watching several video clips, I noticed that the guys on the field didn't have to line up exactly the same every time. There were different ways of doing it. I ran to my room and found an old notebook so that I could begin taking notes. Since I was watching highlight videos, I also saw that the person catching the ball ran it back all the way for a touchdown. So I didn't study only the kicking part but the return part, too.

Once I was satisfied with my knowledge of the kickoff and kick return, I looked up Coach's special play—the onside kick. The runbacks for touchdowns were exciting, but these onside kick things were full of suspense. In this play, instead of being blasted deep, the ball was kicked across the ground, soccer-style, and you never knew which way it was going to bounce.

Guys from both teams would go sprinting and jumping and diving to get it, because whoever came up with the ball got to keep it. What I noticed after studying several of these clips was that these plays always occurred late in the game, when there was very little time left. Coach was talking about doing this on the very first play. Now I understood why he'd said that we would catch Thomson High sleeping. I took more notes, and then I began studying other highlight plays. This was loads of fun.

"Scott, time for dinner," Mom called.

"Okay, be right there." I'd come across a play called the flea flicker. The weird name made me curious, so I started the video. The quarterback handed the ball off to his running back in a normal way, but after running forward a few steps, the running back stopped and pitched the ball back to the quarterback, who then threw a deep pass down the field. The idea was to trick the defense into thinking it was a run play, so that your wide receiver could sprint past everybody and be left wide open for the pass.

"Scott!" Mom called again.

"Coming!" I yelled. I shut down the computer and hustled into the dining room.

"What were you doing?" Mom asked.

"Studying the flea flicker," I said.

"Mrs. Harris does the booger flicker!" Mickey exclaimed.

"Ha ha!" Dad and I laughed.

"Excuse me?" Mom said.

"Mrs. Harris does the booger flicker," Mickey repeated.

"Mrs. Harris, your pre-K teacher?" Mom asked.

"Yup."

"I could see that," Dad said.

"Roger!" Mom snapped, giving him the look, which made me laugh more. "I hesitate to ask, but what exactly is the booger flicker?" Mom said.

"Mrs. Harris picks her nose when she thinks no one is watching," Mickey explained, "but I always see her. And then she inspects the booger ball on the tip of her finger like this"—Mickey demonstrated—"and then she flicks it across the room at one of the kids. Like this." More demonstrating.

"Ohmigoodness!" Mom cried.

"Can't say I'm surprised," Dad said. "She is kind of gross. I'm more surprised that she doesn't eat it."

"Roger!" Mom snapped again. "You're not to repeat that, Mickey. Mrs. Harris is a nice woman."

Mickey had already had me cracking up, but then I laughed even harder when Dad got in trouble.

"Scott, why don't you tell us about the flea flicker," Mom suggested.

I wasn't convinced that she really wanted to know about it, but I was eager to explain the play. I moved the peas and carrots around on my plate, lining them up in position. This was perfect because I didn't like my vegetables anyway. I designated two carrots to be my quarterback and running back. Then I demonstrated how the flea flicker worked, using a pea to be the football. When I tossed the pea (football) back to the quarterback so he could throw it deep, I loaded it up on my spoon and told Mickey to catch.

He opened up wide, and I launched the pea. It flew from my spoon before Mom could say anything, and stuck in Mickey's nostril.

"Ah!" he squealed.

"Let's see that booger flicker now," Dad teased.

"I don't think so," Mom warned. She reached over and plucked my pea from Mickey's nose. "Honestly. Sometimes I can't help but wonder what dinner would be like with daughters at my table instead of crazy boys."

"Girls are gross," Mickey said.

"It'd be boring," I added.

Mom chuckled. "You're probably right," she said.

"That was a fascinating demonstration, Scott, but what I'd like to know is why you were watching this football stuff to begin with," Dad said, turning serious.

I sat up straight. "Because I'm going to be the stats man for this year's football team."

"Really?" Mom said. "And where did you come up with that idea?"

"Coach told me I was the perfect kid for the job after I played him in chess."

Mom and Dad exchanged looks.

"You're the fat man?" Mickey asked, confused.

"No, the stats man," I repeated. "I'm the guy on the sideline keeping track of all the plays and what happens on them. Coach said I'll be good at analyzing the information and helping the coaches make decisions."

"Sounds like a terrific idea to me," Mom said. "It'll be fun going to your football games this fall."

"Don't worry, Mickey. They have snacks there," I said.

"Cupcakes?"

"Maybe."

"Yum!"

"Better keep studying so you can do a good job and impress the coach with how much you know," Dad said.

"I will." That was going to be no trouble at all. With my photographic memory I could remember stuff after reading it once. I was going to be the best stats man.

GAVIN

"Gavin, guess what? Guess what?" Scott yelled, running to me as soon as I got out of Dad's truck. He was hopping up and down with excitement. The kid was really wound up, but then again, when wasn't he?

"I don't know. What?"

"I have a surprise," he said.

"Whaddaya mean?"

"I brought a surprise for Coach. And you."

I stopped. "It's not a snake or some crazy thing like that, is it?" With this kid you never knew what to expect.

"No. This is better."

"Really?"

"Really!" he exclaimed.

"Okay. I can't wait to see what it is." I hoped I didn't regret saying that.

"I can't wait to show you," he said.

Well, turns out *wait* is what we did. Our bus was late, so we ended up standing around outside the school for close to an hour. I shoulda known then that this wasn't gonna be a typical day at the Senior Center.

Since we got there later than normal, Scott's grandpa and Coach were hanging out in the Community Hall with everyone else. They were passing the time playing cards and munching on a bowl of mixed nuts.

"We didn't think you were coming," Grandpa said. "Where've you been?"

"Our bus was late picking us up," Scott explained, grabbing a handful of nuts.

"The bus was late?" Coach repeated. "Probably those darn kids from Thomson High messing around again. They're the hooligans who let all the air out of our tires so that we got to the game late and didn't have time for any of our pregame warm-ups."

It amazed me how Coach could remember things like this in such detail with the right trigger. I always got excited when it happened 'cause I loved hearing his war stories. "What did you have the team do?" I asked.

"The boys warmed up on the sideline as best they could, and then we hit Thomson High with our own surprise—"

"You started with the onside kick, didn't you?" Scott interrupted.

"That's right, Junior. It was the perfect play. We caught them off guard and recovered the ball and had all the momentum from the get-go. All that bus nonsense and no warm-up garbage was forgotten after the first play. We blew them out."

"I know what the onside kick is," Scott said. "I've been studying. I'll show you."

So here was his surprise. He grabbed a second handful of nuts and lined them up in formation. Scott was so excited that he actually demonstrated several different versions of the onside kick. I won't lie. I was impressed. The kid was going a mile a minute, but he definitely needed a lesson on *X*s and *O*s so he could do this stuff on paper. At this rate he'd be drawing plays in the dirt to show our coaches what he meant.

"Told you he was smart," Grandpa said to Coach.

I waited for Coach's response, but he never said anything. When I inched closer, I saw he was wearing that glossed-over look again. He was gone. Must have been that Magenta was watching, 'cause she showed up and helped him back to his room.

"That's been happening every so often," Grandpa said. "When it does, it's better to have him in his own room because he's less likely to get confused. When he's confused, he can get angry."

Me and Scott played cards with his grandpa for the rest of our visit, and after Magenta returned, she rounded us up 'cause we were "out of time." That was the exact word I couldn't get out of my brain—"time." How much *time* did Coach have left? We needed a special play now, before it was too late.

Natalie Kurtsman
ASPIRING LAWYER
Kurtsman Law Offices

BRIEF #3
Early August: A Business Meeting

Today's objective: Get the story from Agnes and Eddie.

"Good afternoon, ladies," I said, taking my seat at the table. Randi sat next to me.

"Uh-oh," Eddie said. "This feels like a business meeting today, Agnes. Natalie's got that serious look in her eyes again."

I dumped the dominoes onto the table and spread them around with my hand. "Instead of referring to this as a business meeting, how about we think of it as a working game day?" I suggested.

"I'm game," Eddie said, then smirked. For an older woman she could be remarkably witty.

"Okay," Agnes agreed.

We selected our beginning set of dominoes, and then Randi placed the first brick down because she had the highest double. Play proceeded with each of us taking a turn. I didn't rush the conversation, but after two rounds I decided I'd waited long enough.

"Being the smart women that you are, I'm sure you already know what I'm going to ask," I began.

"She's trying to soften us up, Agnes. Don't fall for it," Eddie said. She winked at me, and Randi chuckled. This was the game Eddie was having fun playing, not dominoes.

"Go ahead, Natalie," Agnes said. "Never mind her. Ask your questions."

Agnes was a taskmaster. Between the two of us, we'd keep this meeting on track.

I glanced around the room, making certain there were no eavesdroppers. Since we'd arrived late, both Coach and Mrs. Magenta were present in the Community Hall; we had to be careful. I leaned forward and spoke in a hushed voice. "Before we left last time, you warned us that there is more to Mrs. Woods and Mrs. Magenta than we know. We'd like to know what we don't know."

Agnes and Eddie let out long breaths.

"Their story is a deeply sad and painful one," Agnes whispered. "I know you girls desperately want to hear it so that you can help these two women, but Eddie and I don't feel it's our place to tell."

"Ugh," I groaned. I sat back, disgusted. I played my next domino—with some authority.

"I realize that's not what you wanted to hear," Agnes continued, "but I trust you can understand how we feel, because you're two very smart young ladies."

"It's your turn," I snapped at her.

"Don't get nasty, Natalie," Eddie said. "That doesn't fit you. And it won't help you, either. Just because you can't get Pearl and Olivia together here doesn't mean you're out of hope. You need to figure out how to bring them together at your school, that's all."

"We can do that," Randi said. "But don't you think knowing their story would help us do a better job?"

"No," Eddie was quick to say. Gone was her usual foolishness. "Forget the story. The past is the past. Stop going after it. Pretend you don't know there even is a story and just do your best to help them like you had planned all along. The story will come to you on its own, when it's ready."

Like you said yourself, Natalie, better to appear innocent than manipulative. Agnes and Eddie are keeping you innocent.

"Let me ask the two of you a question," Agnes interjected. "Who's the lucky one in that family?" She nodded to her left, and I glanced and saw Mrs. Magenta helping a confused Coach back to his room. I saw the sadness in Gavin's face as he watched his old friend walking away. "Coach is losing his mind," Agnes continued, "which is a terrible shame, but also a small blessing. He's free from the burden of painful memories. On the other hand, Mrs. Woods not only carries the burden with her every day, but she's also watching her husband slowly slip away. She's the strongest woman Eddie and I know, but how much more can she possibly endure?"

"You kids gave her new life last year," Eddie said. "Pearl told us all about you long before you showed up with Olivia's program. Don't give up on her."

I won't say I was happy leaving the Senior Center that afternoon, but I understood, and I respected their wishes. Maybe

Agnes and Eddie didn't make the best informants, but they were good friends for not airing Mrs. Woods's dirty laundry.

When we arrived back in front of school, I pulled the Recruits together and passed out copies of the emergency phone tree document I had created. "Start thinking of ways to get Mrs. Woods and Mrs. Magenta together in school," I said. "If anyone comes up with an idea, initiate this phone tree by calling the person after your name."

"We're running out of time," Gavin said. "This is serious."

We stood there looking at one another. I saw a mix of sadness and worry and doubt in my friends' faces. It was time to lead. "We'll come up with something," I said, providing the optimism that was needed. "Trust in one another. We're a team."

"Hands in," Scott ordered. "One. Two. Three."

"Team!" we shouted.

Trevor

After the day's visit to the Senior Center, everyone was quiet and down in the dumps. I couldn't tell you what had happened because I wasn't there to see any of it.

We were late getting to the center, so when we finally arrived, Mrs. Ruggelli didn't waste any time. She found Mark and me and told us to get in her car.

"Where're we going?" Mark asked.

"To Best Buy so you can get what you need to start on this project."

Mark punched me in the arm. "Dude, did you hear that? We get to buy a TV today."

"I heard," I said, punching him back.

We hopped in Mrs. Ruggelli's car, and away we went. It didn't take us long to get there. We parked and went inside.

"I need to use the restroom," Mrs. Ruggelli said. "Start without me. I'll find you when I'm done."

"Okay," we said, and nodded. We headed for the TVs and had three different people ask us if we needed any help before we even got there. It was kind of annoying, but nothing compared to what was about to happen.

"Dude, we should get one of those new curved ones," Mark said, pointing to the biggest and baddest TV on display. "Those things are the bomb. The old farts would love it."

"Yeah, and those TVs cost thousands of dollars." I pointed to the price tag. "I don't think Mrs. Ruggelli wants that. We can get this large flat-screen for way less and still have money to buy what we need for a surround sound system and movie player."

"And a popcorn machine," Mark said.

"You're starting to sound like Scott."

He punched me in the other arm.

We studied the various flat-screens and quickly narrowed down our decision. It was either the Sony or the Samsung.

"You boys need some help?" a voice behind us asked.

My skin tingled. This was no store worker. I turned. The voice belonged to Chris, my brother's number one goon and my biggest tormentor. His sidekick goon, Garrett, was missing.

"What's wrong? Can't even say hi?" Chris shoved me.

I closed my eyes like a little kid, hoping that would make the bad thing disappear. "Yo, I'm talking to you, punk." He shoved me again—harder.

"Can I help you with something?" It was Mrs. Ruggelli's voice. "Is everything okay here, Trevor?" she asked, walking toward us.

I nodded.

"Who's this, your new babysitter?" Chris jeered.

I felt the heat rising up my neck and into my cheeks. I glared at him.

"No, I'm not," Mrs. Ruggelli responded. "And for your information, this tough-guy act you're trying to pull just shows how much growing up you've got left to do. These boys are way ahead of you in that department. I'd say you're the one in need of a babysitter."

"You're the one in need of—"

"Leave us alone," I said, finding my voice and stepping forward. I wasn't about to let him bully Mrs. Ruggelli. No way. I took a second step forward, and Mark was right beside me. That was when I realized we were almost as tall as Chris now, and I think he realized it, too.

"Losers," he spat as he turned and walked away.

"Who was that?" Mrs. Ruggelli asked.

"No one important," I said. "Which of these TVs do you like better?" I pointed to our two options. The last thing I wanted was to talk about Chris.

Mrs. Ruggelli was cool and didn't push it. She picked a TV, and then Mark and I carried it to the front so we could pay for it along with the other things we had in our basket. I'd thought our excitement with Chris was over, but I was wrong. The second we tried walking out of the store, the alarm blasted. The security man stopped us and had to check everything in our bags to determine what was triggering the alarm. He couldn't identify the item, so we were asked to empty our pockets. Seeing the way Mrs. Ruggelli looked at us—like she thought we'd stolen something—hurt. But it burned to see Chris laughing as he snuck past security and the alarm.

"Found it," the officer said. He pulled some lightweight electronic device out of Mark's hood. "Not sure how that got in there," he said.

"Me neither," Mark responded, but that was a lie. We both knew how it had gotten there.

I stared out the store windows and spotted Chris running across the parking lot. He pulled two different video games from under his shirt before getting in my brother's car. When he yanked the passenger door open, I saw the look on Brian's face. In that instant I went from worrying about crossing paths with my brother to worrying about him.

4

THE END
OF SUMMER

Randi

The Regionals brought together the best girls from six different states. It was insane. The arena alone made it clear that
this was a mega event, but add to that the parking people, the
ticket and admissions people, the concessions, and the building, and there was no mistaking that this was serious business.
A lot of the girls participating in the competitions throughout
the year tried their best but were also just having fun. The
Regionals were different. The girls walking around had that
eye-of-the-tiger thing Gavin loved to talk about from those
Rocky movies. These girls weren't about fun—just about winning. I could have let that intimidate me, but I didn't. Instead it
got me psyched. I was ready. I belonged here. I had prepared.
My body tingled with nervous energy.

First up in my rotation was the bars. I loved the bars, but
I had too much adrenaline surging through my veins. Right
off the bat I forgot to do my basic kip and went straight into a
pull-over. I knew it as soon as it happened. A missed skill was
an automatic deduction, but I didn't let that slow me down. I

flew high through the air and nailed my landing. I ran off the mat and high-fived Coach Andrea. "Gymnastics 101."

"Fly high and stick your landing," she said. "Great start."

It wasn't my best score ever, but I still posted a strong one. There were a couple of other girls who made mistakes and scored low, but none were crying like I sometimes saw at my regular meets. We still had three events to go, so no one was about to quit. No way.

"Composure," Coach Andrea reminded me. "It's a long day. Don't get too high. Don't get too low. Stay focused."

"Got it," I said.

And I did. After bars I matched my personal best on beam and I delivered another flawless routine on floor, which earned me the highest score of all the gymnasts. With one event left, I was in the top five all-around scores. I couldn't have hoped for a better day. After every routine my group in the bleachers went nutso.

"If people didn't know who you were before this, they do now," Coach Andrea said. "And I'm not saying that because of your fan club. You've been awesome today, Randi. I'm very proud of you."

Coach Andrea wrapped her arm around my shoulders, and I glanced up at my section. Mom gave me a thumbs-up, and my friends cheered wildly. The guys stood behind my mom and Mrs. Kurtsman with their shirts off. They had painted a different letter from my name on each of their chests. Mark was the *R*, Scott was the *A*, Gav was the *N*, and Trevor was the *D*. Last in line, wearing a plain white T-shirt (for obvious reasons) with an *I* painted on it, was Natalie.

"Randi, listen," Coach Andrea said. "If you choose to do

your regular vault, you will almost definitely finish in the top five."

"You mean if I play it safe."

"Yes. Safe, and maybe smart," Coach Andrea said.

"Smart because if I mess up on the harder one, then I could get a bad score and drop out of the top five."

"Exactly."

"Or I could nail the harder one and potentially get a medal."

Coach Andrea smiled. "It's your decision."

I glanced up into the stands again. When I saw Gav, I thought of Clifford, which I know sounds weird, but I suddenly realized that the sentence Gav had a problem with would be better if it made it clear that Clifford had given his best effort. Then his smiling after losing would be somewhat understandable. If I didn't try the harder vault, I would always wonder.

"I'm going for it," I said. I'd be able to smile afterward no matter the outcome.

"Let's do it!" Coach Andrea exclaimed.

When it was my turn, I saluted the judges and stepped onto the runway. I took my mark, and then I shot out of my stance, sprinting with all the power I could muster. I exploded off the board, and everything after that was a disaster. I landed on my hands and knees.

Awful! But I still had my second attempt, so I picked myself up and walked back to my starting point. I saluted the judges and stepped onto the runway for my second, and final, vault. *I can do this,* I told myself. I flew down the track, hit the board, and soared through the air. My form might not have been perfect, but I added the extra twist and stuck my landing—and then I smiled like never before.

I didn't get the highest score, but I had attempted the most difficult vault of the afternoon. In the end, I won four event medals and scored well enough that I finished standing on the podium in third place for all-around. When I tell you that this was the happiest day of my life, I'm not exaggerating. When your mom cries tears of joy and pride, it's hard to explain just how that makes you feel inside. After the awards ceremony my friends gave me hugs and congratulations, and Coach Andrea picked me up off the ground, she was so happy.

"Randi, I can't believe you didn't tell me about your new vault," Mom said.

"I wanted to surprise you."

"Well, you did. If you keep this up, that scholarship will definitely happen. We can win this thing next year."

I stiffened. That was Jane talking.

"Sorry," she said. "I didn't mean that." She grasped my hand.

I exhaled. I hoped my winning didn't suddenly encourage Jane. The funny thing was, with Jane, I had always been scared of failing. I never would've tried the harder vault. But with Mom, I wasn't afraid anymore.

My friends gave me more hugs and said goodbye. I thanked them for coming, and then Mom and I went back into the arena to watch some of the younger girls from my team who were getting ready to compete. We stopped and celebrated with dinner out and ice cream on our way home. I didn't want the day to end, and once we finally made it home, it didn't. I found a surprise waiting for me. The letter was addressed from school.

Our destinies had changed course with the arrival of a

letter just before the start of sixth grade, a letter informing us that Mrs. Woods would be filling in as our long-term substitute, a point that I had forgotten until I spotted this envelope.

This time around the letter contained lots of boring general information, but there were two paragraphs at the end that did matter. The first paragraph thanked Mrs. Woods for her year of service, and the second introduced the permanent new hire for the sixth grade. In other words, Mrs. Woods was no longer teaching at Lake View Middle School.

A while later our phone rang. It was Natalie, enacting the emergency phone tree. The letter was a big deal, but it wouldn't ultimately change my life. The letter that would was still yet to come.

Natalie Kurtsman
Aspiring Lawyer
Kurtsman Law Offices

BRIEF #4
Late August: Phone Tree Emergency #1

Mother and I spent the day inside an arena watching Randi soar to new heights in her gymnastics. She was nothing short of amazing. I do believe that if I had been any sort of serious athlete, I would've been envious of her, especially when she stood on that podium with all those medals draped around her neck and that large trophy in her hands. But such was not the case; I was far from being a serious athlete. Perhaps someday, but for now my prowess resided in my brain, and when I made it home later that evening, I discovered that it was time for me to put my skills to the test.

The envelope was from school. It was reminiscent of the one that had come the previous summer. I asked Mother if I could open it, and she agreed. To the average student or community member, the contents of the letter would've seemed unimportant.

"Not much here," Mother said after reading it. (Case in point.)

For me (not your average anything) this letter presented a serious problem, one that potentially marked the end of the road. I was not accustomed to failing, but we'd been racking our brains and still hadn't come up with a way to get Mrs. Woods and Mrs. Magenta together in school. Now I'd learned that our efforts were all a waste of time because Mrs. Woods wasn't even going to be at Lake View Middle School. This devastating news required immediate implementation of the emergency phone tree.

I quietly slipped away to my bedroom, careful not to make Mother suspicious, and called Randi at once. "Did you get the letter!"

"Hi, Natalie."

"Did you get the letter?" I repeated. I didn't have time for greetings or small talk.

"If you're talking about the one from school, yes. I just read it."

"This is serious, Randi. How are we ever going to get Mrs. Woods and Mrs. Magenta together if we can't do it at the Senior Center or at school?"

"Natalie, we just got the news. Calm down and give yourself time to think. We'll come up with something."

We kept telling ourselves that, but so far we had nothing. "We need to carry out the phone tree," I said. "We need everyone focused on this so we can come up with a plan as soon as possible. You heard Gavin; we're running out of time."

"I'll call Trevor."

"Good. . . . And, Randi, you were great today."

"Thanks," she said.

After we hung up, I sat there looking down at the phone I held in my hand. I had another call to make, and it wasn't to one of the Recruits.

This thought had been swimming around in my head all summer; it surfaced only every so often. Whenever that happened, I always told myself it was a silly idea and pushed it back under. But things had changed this afternoon.

Following Randi's awards ceremony, she and her mom had stayed at the arena to watch some of Randi's teammates compete, so Mother had volunteered to give Gavin a ride home. (Trevor and Scott had gone with Mark.) Gavin had very politely thanked Mother for the ride when we'd pulled into his driveway, and then he'd turned to me and said, "See you later, Kurtsman."

"Goodbye," I'd responded.

Mother had waited before leaving, to make certain he got inside. As I'd been watching Gavin walk toward his house, Mrs. Davids had suddenly stepped out onto their front porch and waved to us—a gesture of thanks. Gavin's little sister had been under her arm. That was the first time I saw the woman who couldn't read English. She was very pretty. And the little girl by her side was adorable. Gavin's sister shot an arrow through my heart when she smiled and waved at me; all at once that silly idea that had been swimming around in my head jumped clear out of the water, yelling at me. It was no longer just a thought. This idea had morphed into a goal.

I knew the phone number. I had looked it up earlier but hadn't had the courage to call then. That little girl had changed everything. I hit the numbers and let the phone ring. Gavin's mother answered.

"Hello, Mrs. Davids. This is Natalie Kurtsman."

GAVIN

Kurtsman was in the dumps over the letter about Woods not being around. I agreed that the news stunk, but I was still psyched about the start of school 'cause that also meant the start of football. Being so close to the thing I'd been wanting for as long as I could remember had me feeling restless. I was having a hard time sleeping at night. Not even my audiobooks could do the trick.

It was our final visit to the Senior Center before seventh grade kicked off. I was excited to see Coach and take any last-minute advice he had for me. He'd already shared so much wisdom, but I wasn't going to be surprised if he'd saved something important for that afternoon. If my team coaches turned out to be half as smart as him, then I'd be on my way to the Hall of Fame after my rookie season.

Course, I wasn't the only one feeling excited. Scott was so pumped about his role as stats man that he was determined to learn as much as he could about the game. To tell you the truth, when I first heard about the idea, I didn't think it stood a chance. But Scott's brain was incredible at absorbing information, and between his research and his sessions with Coach, he'd turned into a mini-encyclopedia of football plays. Just like for every other visit we'd had over the summer, he came ready to talk about some new plays. But we only had a few minutes to talk shop 'cause Trevor and Mark were done with their project, and the afternoon's big event was the unveiling of their newly renovated TV lounge.

Scott didn't waste those precious minutes. He jumped right in with Coach. When that kid had his mind set on doing something, he was unstoppable. He didn't even take time to talk to his grandpa first.

"Coach, I want to go over—"

"Junior, never mind plays," Coach said, holding up his hand. "It's not how many you have in the arsenal that matters but how well you can get the boys to run the ones you do have. You understand?"

I did.

Scott nodded. "Better to be great at a few than poor at a lot," he said.

"That's right!" Coach hollered. "You're ready. You're both ready." He gave his assistant a nod.

"Sit down, boys," Grandpa said, taking over. "Coach and I would like to give you something before this football season starts." He pulled a bag from behind the chair and passed it to Coach.

"Junior, every stats man needs one of these," Coach said, handing Scott a deluxe clipboard. It was the kind that opens so you can store your notebook and pens inside. It sure was fancy.

"And a hat," Grandpa added, sticking a brand-new Lake View Middle School cap on Scott's head. It was yellow, with a black emblem of our Warriors mascot on the front. I'd have to help him adjust it so it didn't look dorky, but that could wait till later. I wasn't gonna ruin the moment.

Just saying thank you wasn't enough for Scott. He gave his grandpa a hug, and then he hugged Coach like it was Christmas morning. That was a play that caught Coach off guard and had me and Grandpa laughing.

"Gavin," Grandpa said, handing me a shoebox. "This is for you."

"Thank you," I said.

I held the box on my lap and opened it. I didn't see anything at first 'cause tissue paper covered up whatever was in there. I moved the paper, and then I found it. I lifted out the hand towel. I knew exactly what it was for.

"A quarterback can have a great arm, Valentine, but he also needs to be able to grip the ball on those bad-weather days," Coach said.

"What is it?" Scott asked.

"My quarterback towel," I said. "I tuck it inside my pants so that it hangs down in front of me like this"—I showed him—"and then I can wipe and dry my hands before taking the snap," I explained.

"Oh," Scott said. "What's *EW*?"

I looked to where he was pointing and saw the letters *EW* embroidered at the bottom of my towel. "I don't know. What's *EW*, Coach?"

No response. Coach's eyes had glossed over.

"Maybe it stands for 'Everyday Winner,'" Grandpa said, patting me on the shoulder.

I nodded. That was a nice try, but probably not the real answer. "Thank you," I said again.

"You boys are welcome," Grandpa said. "Coach and I are looking forward to coming to your games."

"We'll make you proud," Scott said. "Wait till you see Gavin scoring touchdowns with the plays we've been going over—"

"I hate to break up your party," Magenta interrupted, "but it's time to gather in the lounge for Trevor and Mark's big reveal."

"See what we got," Scott said, showing off his presents.

"Very nice," she replied. But the second Magenta saw what I was holding, she gasped. Shaky fingers covered her lips. She glanced at her father, but Coach's eyes were still glossed over. Then she looked back at me with glassy eyes and gave me the softest smile. "You've got to get to the lounge now," she said, her voice cracking. "I'll stay here with Coach."

I rubbed the letters on my towel.

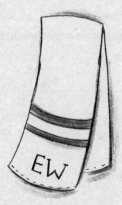

"Let's go, boys," Grandpa said, placing one hand on my shoulder and the other on Scott's, nudging us forward. "Mrs. Magenta will keep an eye on Coach. He'll be okay."

I followed Grandpa and Scott out of the room. I wasn't worrying about Coach. It was Magenta who had me confused. What was the story with my towel? 'Cause I was pretty sure *EW* didn't stand for "Everyday Winner."

Trevor

We still weren't done with everything in the lounge, but we were finally ready to share our improvements with everyone at the Senior Center. When you only get a few hours here and there, a project like ours can take a while—especially when things happened that you weren't counting on. Like when we were all set to mount the speakers and found out we needed to predrill holes for the screws, but we didn't have any drill bits. That forced us to make a trip to the hardware store with Mrs. Ruggelli. There were a few of those headaches along the way, but we didn't let it stop us. Mrs. Ruggelli was so impressed with what Mark and I had accomplished that she got a sign made—COMMUNITY THEATER—to hang on the wall outside the room.

"You boys make a great team," she said. "You've transformed this dinky TV lounge into a theater. The residents are going to love what you've done."

She was right. You should've heard the old folks when they came in to check the place out for the first time.

"Well, by golly, that's a TV that I can see!" one old guy exclaimed.

"Is that what that man's voice has always sounded like? I could never hear it before," someone else said.

"Did he change his hair color?" the woman wearing the lime-colored nightgown asked.

"No," Eddie answered. "His hair has always been white. I've seen pictures of him in the tabloids. The old TV made it look pink, that's all."

Mark looked over at me and we laughed.

After we had everyone settled, I gave them the rundown on things. I showed them how the remotes worked and explained the surround sound to them. I realized this could be confusing, especially to older people, so we had typed up directions and had them posted on the walls and even stuck on the backs of the remotes. When I got done talking, Mark turned the volume up as a demonstration, and then everyone got really excited. "Whoa!" they squealed, and giggled.

Next we showed them the cards we'd laminated that listed all of the TV stations, similar to what you see in hotel rooms. That seemed like a silly thing, but the oldies thought it was great. And last, we showed them the movies we had stored in their new cabinet. Boy, did their eyes light up then. We explained these were DVDs, not tapes anymore, and pointed to the DVD player.

"Put one in," someone yelled from the back.

"What do you want?" I asked.

"Anything," several voices answered.

I looked at Mark and shrugged. He grabbed one of the old John Wayne flicks we'd gotten on sale and popped it in. The oldies loved it.

"Guys, this is awesome," Randi said, coming over to us. "I can't believe you knew how to do all this."

"We still need to get a popcorn machine," Mark complained, "but don't tell Scott. I'm not sure he could handle that."

"I don't think you need to worry about Scott," Randi said, pointing.

The kid was sitting crisscross applesauce like a kindergartner in the middle of the floor, completely fascinated by the black-and-white western. I scanned the room. The oldies were in heaven. I spotted Gavin standing against the far wall, and he gave me a thumbs-up.

"Look how happy they are," Natalie whispered. "If we could just find a way to do that for Mrs. Woods and Mrs. Magenta . . ."

"We will," I said. Don't ask me where that positive attitude came from, because I sure didn't have it when talking about my parents or my brother, but I wanted to say something to make Natalie feel better. I didn't like seeing her sad.

She looked at me. "I hope so."

Leaving that afternoon, Mark and I felt really good about what we had pulled off. Mrs. Ruggelli was right; we did make a great team. It was like Mr. Allen had said in his speech at the beginning of sixth grade last year, "If you want to do well in school and in life, you've got to surround yourself with the right people. In other words, choose your friends wisely." Back then that had been stupid principal talk and nothing more, but I couldn't stop thinking about his words now. I'd chosen wisely, but Brian hadn't. What was he doing hanging out with Chris? And why did I even care?

SCOTT

I was up before the sun on the day that football started. I knew a lot about the game now, but not much about how sign-ups and practice worked, so I called Gavin and got a ride with him. I didn't want to go alone. Mom had the same advice for me she always did. "Stay out of trouble and be a good boy." I gave her a quick hug, grabbed my deluxe clipboard, and ran out the door.

There was already a bunch of kids in the gym when Gavin and I walked in. Trevor and Mark must've gotten there right before us, because they were at the end of the line. We joined them.

Mark's eyes almost popped out of his head when he saw me. "Dude, you're playing football?"

"No. I'm here because I'm going to be the team's stats man," I explained. "It was Coach's idea."

"Cool," Trevor said.

Gavin pulled the brim of my Warriors cap down, but I saw all the guys smiling after I fixed it. This was going to be the best season ever.

"Name?" the big coach said when it was my turn at the registration table.

"Scott Mason," I said. "What's your name?"

The big man studied me. "A jokester, huh? We'll see if you're laughing when I get done with you." He wasn't smiling. "I'm Coach Holmes, and that's Coach Frazier," he said, pointing to the man operating the scale. "What grade are you in, Scott Mason?"

"Seventh."

"Got your forms?"

I opened my deluxe clipboard and pulled out the necessary permission and information papers. This present that Coach and Grandpa had given me was already working out great.

"Hop on the scale," Coach Holmes said. Coach Frazier recorded my weight, and Coach Holmes snickered. "What position you trying out for, lightweight?"

"Stats man," I answered.

"What?"

"I'd like to be the team's stats man," I said. "I'll keep track of all the plays we run and help you and Coach Frazier analyze the information. I'm very good at that."

"Ha!" Coach Holmes slapped the table. "You hear that, Frazier? Kid wants to help us analyze the stats. Ha!"

Coach Frazier laughed along with him. I stood there waiting, because I was going to be the stats man, and that was it. Coach Holmes wiped his face and turned back to me. "We could use a water boy," he said. "And with muscles like yours, I'd say that's the perfect job for you. See those bottles over there? Go fill them up in the locker room and get them out to the field in time for practice."

"Yes, sir," I said, using my best manners. "But I'm the stats man, not the water boy. That's the perfect job for me because of my brain. Coach Woods said so."

"Yeah, whatever. I don't know any Coach Woods. Now get outta here!" he barked.

Even though filling water bottles wasn't in the stats man job description, I didn't complain, because something told me I didn't want to get Coach Holmes mad. I hustled, and I was doing pretty good until I got the bottles filled and had to lift them. Water is heavy! One gallon weighs eight pounds. I don't know how many gallons I had, but it took me three trips to get all of the bottles out to the field. My sneakers and socks were soaking wet by the time I got done, but the good news was that I didn't miss much of practice. I was finishing my last trip when Coach Holmes blew his whistle. "Give me two lines behind Nicky and Adam!" he shouted.

Nicky and Adam were two of the eighth graders. Coach Holmes blew his whistle again, and the team started jogging down the field. When they reached the end, they turned the corner and came back down the opposite sideline. Coach Holmes was waiting for them. He showed the guys how to break off into lines every five yards so that everyone was spread out and we looked like a team.

Nicky and Adam were at the front and led the calisthenics and stretching, and then Coach Holmes took over with his whistle again. He put the team through something he called "dynamic warm-up." That included high knees and shuffling and bear crawls and more. I was loving it. After the dynamic warm-up the guys were sweating and breathing heavy, so Coach Holmes gave them a quick water break.

I was ready. I passed out the bottles. "Nice job out there, boys. Keep it up," I said. It was important for coaches and managers and the stats man to encourage the team. I gave a few high fives and pats on the backs. I ran a good water break, until only two players remained.

"This water is warm," Nicky growled. "You suck, water boy."

"You're screwing up on day one," Adam sneered. He grabbed my cap and tossed it on the wet ground.

Nicky stomped on it and spit water in my face. Then they chucked the bottles over my head and ran back to Coach Holmes, laughing.

That wasn't funny, but the worst part was when I saw that all the water was gone, so I had to trudge back to the locker room and refill the bottles, which took time. I was more upset about that than I was about Nicky and Adam.

But I've always been fast. So even though it sounded like I had a swamp in my sneakers, when I got back to the field, I saw that Coach Frazier had just started working with the linemen—that was where Trevor was—and Coach Holmes had the skill players in two lines. One line was paired with Nicky and one with Adam. The guys were told to run different passing routes so those two could practice throwing the ball. Coach Holmes had already picked his quarterbacks. I watched, and after a few minutes I knew the first piece of advice I had for Coach Holmes was to put Gavin in there. He was definitely better than these eighth graders, and I wasn't saying that just because he was my friend.

"Dude, where've you been?" Mark asked when I finally joined them after practice. We were outside waiting for our rides.

"Coach Holmes and Coach Frazier had me giving them a hand with the cones and balls and stuff."

"Giving them a hand, or doing it for them?" Trevor said.

"It's okay. It's only day one," I said. Things would change once I got the chance to show the coaches my skills.

Mark's dad pulled into the parking lot, and he and Trevor left, so it was just Gavin and me waiting when Coach Holmes and Coach Frazier came walking out of the school.

"Hey, Coaches. Great practice today," I said.

Coach Holmes chuckled. "What's your name again, kid?"

"Scott Mason."

"He's the one who wants to be our stats man," Coach Frazier reminded him.

"Oh yeah. The water boy," Coach Holmes said. "Okay, Stats Man. Tell me what you saw out there at practice today."

He asked for it. "Nicky completed thirty-five percent of his passes when the receivers were on his right and twenty-five percent to his left. Adam was about the same. They need to get much better throwing to their left before I'd call one of those plays."

Coach Holmes and Coach Frazier looked like Dumb and Dumber standing there with their mouths open. I almost laughed. Coach Frazier even scratched his head.

I smiled. "I told you I'm good with numbers and analyzing information. That's why I want to be the team's stats man. I can help you."

"Help me?" Coach Holmes scoffed.

"Yes. I can give you the data to help you make decisions. We've got a good group, and I know it's only day one, but the data suggests that Nicky and Adam need lots of work. They'll make fine backups, but you should put Gavin in at quarter-back. He's better."

"Is that right?" Coach Holmes sneered. He stepped closer. Then he leaned forward, his eyes narrowed on Gavin. "You're Gavin?"

Gavin nodded.

"Gavin what?" Coach Holmes growled.

"Gavin Davids."

"Davids," Coach Holmes repeated. "Your mother is that woman from Mexico. She used to bartend at Coleman's." Coach Holmes wasn't asking a question, so Gavin didn't say a word. "I was hoping she got smart and went back to where she came from." Coach Holmes got even closer, so his face was only inches from Gavin's. He growled something else, but his voice was too low for me to hear it.

"Dad, you ready? Let's go." It was Nicky. Adam was with him.

Coach Holmes straightened. "I'm coming," he said. He glared at Gavin and me, and then he turned and left with his kid, and Coach Frazier left with Adam.

My ride and Gavin's ride showed up right after that, so we left without talking about what had just happened.

It was only day one. Things would get better.

5

SEVENTH-GRADE
KICKOFF

NATALIE KURTSMAN
ASPIRING LAWYER
Kurtsman Law Offices

BRIEF #5
September: Baby on Board

It was official, the start of school—in my case, the beginning of seventh grade. Same as always, I made certain that Mother drove me there early. This day was all about first impressions; I had several of them to make—four, as a matter of fact. That was because seventh grade meant we had a different teacher for each major academic class: English language arts (ELA), math, science, and social studies.

To be frank, there was no eccentric teacher like Mrs. Magenta, and no one even remotely close to Mrs. Woods. My teachers were normal, which on the one hand was fine, but on the other was boring. The only exception was Mrs. Yazmire. To be clear, Mrs. Yazmire was normal, but her present condition wasn't anything I had prior experience with in the classroom. It was hard to believe she was still four weeks away from her due date. Either she was going early or she was going to pop. While the uncertainty of her situation provided some excitement, I did not like the thought of her water breaking and labor commencing in our classroom; I was interested in law, not medical school.

Aside from meeting the people responsible for my education this year, the only other thing we accomplished was an overview of each course syllabus. I realize I risk sounding like Scott when I say this, but it was a day of boring teachers with super-boring agendas. Unfortunately, I didn't have anyone to commiserate with until lunch, because my friends all had different schedules. Not surprisingly, the administration had decided to place the CSA cheaters in as many different classes as possible to avert any potential problems this year. None of us Recruits were together. I wasn't happy about this, but I couldn't argue that it wasn't fair.

Needless to say, day one of seventh grade was utterly underwhelming. A letdown of this magnitude would've had me in the dumps had I not had my personal goals to keep me challenged. The day's most important first impression was scheduled to occur after school. We had chosen that time to meet because that was when Gavin would be preoccupied with practice.

I had two objectives going into the meeting: (1) meet and greet, and (2) share my vision and plan with Mrs. Davids. Unlike with Mrs. Woods and Mrs. Magenta, I needed Mrs. Davids on board to accomplish this goal. No keeping secrets from her, though I did anticipate keeping this secret from everyone else.

GOALS

- Resolve the strained relationship between Mrs. Woods and Mrs. Magenta.
- Keep our plan secret, which requires keeping Scott and the rest of the Recruits quiet—but mainly Scott.
- Teach Mrs. Davids how to read English.

Trevor

Sixth grade was not an ordinary year, and that's putting it mildly. Mrs. Woods and Mrs. Magenta were special; there was no other way of saying it. I wasn't stupid enough to expect the same thing out of seventh grade, but I also wasn't going back to my old ways. I'd tolerate school, if only because Mrs. Woods had taught me that I could do better. And "tolerate" was the right word, because believe me, by the end of that first day, I'd had enough and was more than ready to get away from my teachers.

Every single one of them had to ask me, "Oh, are you Brian's younger brother?"

"Yes," I answered truthfully.

"How's he doing?"

"He's fine," I lied through my teeth.

What else was I supposed to say? As far as all these teachers knew, my brother was a college graduate. And why shouldn't they think that? My brother hadn't been the best student when he was in school, but he had held his own. It wasn't until college that Brian had gotten in with the wrong crowd and blown his opportunity—and Dad's money. He came home a different person—sad and angry—and it only got worse after he met Chris at his gas station job.

Now my parents were sad and angry and fought. All. The. Time. The first day of school might have sucked, but the morning at home on my first day sucked more. Mom and Dad's screaming match was a big one. One of their worst. And it started with me.

"Trevor!" Dad yelled from his bedroom.

Huh? What? I rolled over.

"Trevor, get in here!"

Huh?

"Trevor!"

I threw my covers off and swung my feet to the ground. "Coming." *What is his problem?* I got up and stumbled into his bedroom, still rubbing my eyes. "Yeah?" I mumbled.

"Don't 'yeah' me. Can you explain this?" He pointed to the small wooden box sitting on his dresser.

"Explain what?"

"Do you see what's missing?"

"No," I said. I'd never looked in the box before. How was I supposed to know what was missing?

"Three hundred dollars! Three hundred dollars has disappeared!" my father yelled.

"And you want me to explain that?" I said. I glanced at Mom, looking for help. I saw the hurt in her eyes.

"Well, it's gone somewhere," he said.

"You think I took it?"

"I've already had one son turn out bad. Maybe you're getting an early start," Dad said.

"Steve!" Mom snapped. "That's enough. He didn't take it."

"Here we go again," Dad said, "always babying your sons. Look where that's gotten us."

"Don't blame your stupid money on us!" Mom shouted. "You've been married to your job, chasing the almighty dollar and missing out on your kids for the last twenty years. Look where that's gotten us!"

"And you should talk! It's not like you've been around for these boys, either!"

That was my cue. I wasn't sticking around. I walked into my bedroom and put my headphones on and cranked the volume. I tried not to think about my brother or my parents' constant fighting, or what a jerk my father was, but that was impossible. Blasting music into my brain didn't keep the word "divorce" out of my head, and there was no way to forget about Brian, especially when my teachers kept asking about him. I had hoped to find my escape on the football field that afternoon, but Coach Frazier's constant yelling only reminded me of home.

"Trevor!" Coach Frazier hollered. "Trevor!"

What I heard was my father, yelling my name that morning. Blaming me for his missing money. I still couldn't believe he'd done that.

"Trevor! Over here!" Coach Frazier barked.

I came to, remembering where I was.

"A lineman has to be able to focus," Coach Frazier yelled. "Otherwise you'll be forgetting the snap count and jumping offside, or worse—forgetting the play and getting our guys killed."

"Sorry, Coach."

"I don't have time for 'sorry.' Pay attention!"

I tried, but my mind wandered to Mom and Dad and Brian. I stared off into the distance and saw Gavin running laps on the track. He wasn't the sort of kid to talk back or smart-mouth, so what was he doing out there? What had happened?

"Trevor!" Coach Frazier hollered. "If I have to yell your name one more time, you'll be on the track with him!"

I got down and fired out of my stance on Coach Frazier's count, and then I went back to the end of the line. "Go!" Again and again we drilled it. "Go!" Coach Frazier never stopped barking. "Go! Butt down! Eyes up! Stay low! Go!"

The yelling. The shouting. It was too much. *Stop!* I needed to get away. *Stop!* I looked the other way and spotted Scott struggling with the practice bags, dragging them across the ground from the equipment shed to the sideline.

"What was that?" Coach Frazier screamed at the kid doing the drill.

I took two steps away from the back of the line and broke into a run.

"Trevor!" Coach Frazier yelled after me. "Trevor!"

I didn't stop. I never even slowed down. I ran until I had ahold of a bag.

"Trevor, what're you doing?" Scott asked.

"Helping," I said. *Getting away,* I thought. I gripped the handle on the bag and pulled it to the sideline. Then I jogged to the shed and grabbed the next one. By then Gavin was right behind me. We got the bags out to the field for Scott, and then we returned to our groups.

"You done being a Good Samaritan?" Coach Frazier asked.

"Just being a team player, Coach."

"How about being a team player with the rest of the linemen? You're the ones who need to work together to get us into the end zone. That stupid water boy isn't getting us there."

There was plenty I wanted to say to Coach Frazier, but I kept my mouth shut. He didn't know Scott like I did. Stats Man would prove him wrong all on his own before our season was over.

NATALIE KURTSMAN
ASPIRING LAWYER
Kurtsman Law Offices

BRIEF #6
September: A Meeting with Mrs. Davids

By the time I made it to my parents' office, I had only a few minutes to get things organized before Mrs. Davids arrived. I didn't want to leave her waiting, because I got the feeling she was already uneasy about our meeting. Why? I didn't know. But time would tell; it always does.

"Hello, Mrs. Davids," I said, greeting her at the entrance.

"Hi, Natalie."

"Please, come inside." I held the door for her. "I've got us set up in the conference room. It's a quiet space."

"Are your parents here?" Mrs. Davids asked.

"Yes, but they're both on the phone with clients. Did you want to see them?"

"Oh no. Don't bother them. I was just wondering."

I smiled and led the way down the hall. I noticed Mrs. Davids shooting glances all around the office as we walked.

I stopped outside our room. "Here we are," I said. "After you." I followed her inside and closed the door behind us, sensing that Mrs. Davids would want that. "Have a seat," I said, gesturing to a chair at the table. Mrs. Davids was clearly showing signs of anxiety, but I didn't mention it. A lawyer needs patience; the client needs to feel relaxed in order for anything meaningful to transpire. "Here's some water," I said, placing a cup in front of her. This was something Mother always did.

"Thank you," she said, grasping the cup and taking a sip. Nervous people always go for the water as soon as it's offered. Besides that, I could see the cup shaking in her hands. I attributed that to Mrs. Davids being out of her comfort zone, nothing more. But a good lawyer knows enough to follow up on all observations. All leads. Not simply shrug them off, which I did—and that was a mistake. What can I say? I was more concerned with getting started.

Teachers often begin the school year with pre-assessments, so that they have an idea about where their students are in their learning. It's important to know what your student doesn't know. With this in mind I decided to administer my own version of a reading pre-assessment, but not before asking one key question: "Mrs. Davids, just out of curiosity, are you able to read Spanish?"

She shifted in her seat. "Yes, and I can write, but not that well," she admitted. "It's been years since I've done much reading."

I smiled. "That's okay," I said. "If you can read another language, then you should be able to pick up on English in no time. You'll see." I slid a paper across the table. "Let's get started. Please read these letters for me. I'm just trying to get a sense of what you already know so that I can determine how best to proceed."

Mrs. Davids studied the paper. Then she swallowed and slid it back to me. "Thank you, Natalie, but I don't think this is a good idea. I should go." She pushed back in her chair.

"Of course it's a good idea," I said, springing to my feet. The time for patience was gone. I had to convince her or this could be documented as a failure. "Mrs. Davids, we can do this. If you can't read English, you're at a huge disadvantage. I understand this might be embarrassing, but nobody needs to know. It will be our secret."

"What about your parents?"

"I'll have them sign an attorney-client confidentiality contract with me. We'll all be sworn to secrecy by lawyer oath. You have nothing to worry about."

She hesitated, which meant she was contemplating. "Mrs. Davids, I'm not doing this for me. I want to help you. I want you to be able to read to Meggie at bedtime."

That did the trick. Those last words brought a weak smile to her face. She wanted that, too. Mrs. Davids reached out and pulled the alphabet paper back, and, after a deep breath, she began making her way down the list.

GAVIN

"How was football?" Mom asked when I got home after my first practice. "How was football?" she asked after my second practice. "How was football?" she asked and asked and asked.

"Great," I lied over and over and over.

"No concussion?"

"Mom, we aren't even wearing full pads yet. You can't get a concussion if you aren't hitting at practice." I thought I was telling the truth about that at least but turns out I was wrong.

"When do you start the hitting?"

"Next week."

"No concussions, *Niño*," she reminded me.

"No concussions," I said.

I wanted to tell her she could stop worrying, 'cause Coach Holmes wasn't going to play me. The guy hated my guts. "Your kind is supposed to play soccer," he'd hissed in my face after Scott had opened his mouth and told him to put me in at quarterback. And just in case it still wasn't clear how he felt about me, he was going out of his way to show me.

Our football field sat on the top of a knoll in back of our school. Coach had said it was good luck to find seagulls on your field. There were never seagulls on ours. I could've used them that afternoon.

I was playing catch with Mark before practice, just throwing the ball around like a bunch of other guys. Coach Holmes came out and blew his whistle to get things started, and I sailed one more tight spiral so that he could see my arm. I wasn't the only one to throw a pass, but I was the only one he went after.

"Pablo!" he yelled.

We all looked around. Who was Pablo?

"Yeah, I'm talking to you," Holmes said, pointing at me. "I blew the whistle because I wanted the balls put away and you guys lined up. Give me a mile on the track for not being a team player."

I'd already spent so much time on the track you'da thought I was on the cross-country team, but I didn't gripe. I never said a word. Whining and complaining wasn't gonna help anything. I put my helmet on, buckled my chin strap, and started running.

I finished my mile pretty quick and ran back onto the field and joined the skill drills, but Coach Holmes had other ideas. "Give me another mile, Pablo. That one wasn't fast enough."

I was onto him. He was trying to get me to lose my temper and say something stupid so he'd have a reason to treat me like dirt. I wasn't falling for it. I smiled. Then I turned around and jogged back to the track and ran the second mile—and I ran it faster.

Holmes loomed on the sideline, away from the rest of the

team, waiting for me when I finished. "Our sissy water boy is taking too long. Go get the bags," he growled.

I made one step in the direction of the equipment shed, and Holmes lost *his* temper. He couldn't take it that I wasn't fighting back. (But I was. Just not the way he wanted me to.) He grabbed me by the front of my jersey and yanked me close. He held me there, huffing and puffing in my face like the big bad wolf. "That's your kind of work, Pablo. Cheap manual labor is all your people are good for, Pablo. Better get used to it, Pablo." He shoved me.

I didn't give him the chance to do anything more. I took off for the bags. I'd given up telling myself that things would get better. I'd been dreaming about football all my life, and it felt like it had become the worst thing I could imagine— turns out, I was wrong about that, too. The hope that I'd get my chance to shine was gone, but what wasn't dwindling was my determination. Coach Holmes wasn't going to break me. I made Trevor, Mark, and Scott swear not to say anything to anyone, 'cause that would only make it worse. And I never mentioned a word of what was happening to Mom, not to Dad when he asked about practice, and not to Randi or Kurtsman when they asked about football.

"It's going great," I lied to everyone. I lied 'cause I was going to handle things on my own, like a man. I lied 'cause I didn't want to disappoint anyone—especially Dad.

The only one who didn't grill me about football was Meggie. Maybe she didn't know any better. Or maybe she did. All she ever asked was, "Gavvy, can you read this book to me?"

"Okay." I always said okay. "What book tonight?"

Megs had one of her Mudge stories. Our public library

didn't charge you when stuff was overdue and that was good, 'cause Magenta was the one who'd sent me home with these Mudge books at the end of last year. I liked this big blockhead dog a heckuva lot better than Clifford. Meggie loved all dogs, though. Matter of fact, she was beginning to ask about getting one, but I didn't see Mom and Dad going for that. Megs wasn't worried. She figured Santa would bring her one if Mom and Dad didn't. The girl was always so positive about things—and that was something I needed more than anything else those days.

When we finished the story about Mudge visiting the farm—which was my favorite one—I gave Megs a kiss good night.

"Gavvy, Mommy and I stopped at a tag sale today. I got this for you." She handed me the book she had hidden under her pillow.

I flipped through the pages. There were a lot of pictures. Not like picture book stuff but cool cartoons and pencil drawings.

"When I saw it, I thought of you because it's got sketches inside like you make. The lady at the tag sale said it's called a graphic novel."

"Thanks, Megs." I gave her another kiss on the head and went to my room. I'd started reading the newspaper over the summer 'cause that was the one thing I always saw my old man reading. Truth was, I was also imagining seeing my name and picture in it for football. Not anymore.

I kicked the paper under my bed and sat down with the book Meggie had just given me—*March: Book Two*. It was the story of a real guy, John Lewis. And you know what he did? He fought against much worse circumstances than what

Coach Holmes dished out—and he did it through peaceful protest. They called the things he did nonviolent civil disobedience. That was what I was doing. And I gotta tell you, even though the things in his book were different, they were also the same.

Graphic novels don't take as long to read. I finished the book that night. And when I got done, I flipped through it again. It got me drawing my own cartoon—a quarterback dropped back to pass, but he was holding a soccer ball instead of a football.

Randi

Mom and I agreed with Coach Andrea that I should take a short break from gymnastics. I had earned it, plus my body needed it. I would benefit both physically and mentally from the time off. Not to mention, this would also give me a chance to get adjusted to seventh grade. So that was the plan, but the plan went out the window before it even got started.

The letter that changed the course of everything, the one that altered my destiny, sat waiting for me after school. I grabbed the mail when I got off the bus, before heading into the house. As I walked up our front path, I thumbed through the stack of envelopes out of habit, not expecting to find anything. The third one was from a place I'd never heard of—Elite Stars Camp—and it was addressed to me. I hurried inside, threw my stuff down, and tore it open. It wasn't a typed letter but a handwritten note.

> *Dear Randi,*
>   *Congratulations on your outstanding performance*
> *at Regionals. I was in attendance and saw it firsthand.*

*You should be proud. You dazzled on the floor and
the beam, and flew on bars, but that is not why I'm
writing. After I saw you attempt the more difficult
vault, when you very easily could have played it safe,
I knew I would be contacting you. True, your vault
didn't end perfectly, but your fearless attitude and
willingness to go after it were the most impressive things
I saw all afternoon. You have what it takes to make
a champion—the un-coachable attributes. I'd like to
invite you to our Elite Stars three-day camp. This camp
runs from Friday afternoon to Sunday afternoon and is
reserved for special invitees only. There will be multiple
sports represented but only a small number of athletes
per sport, which allows for individualized attention
and instruction. I have enclosed a brochure with more
information. I hope to see you in the near future.*

Yours in gymnastics,
Ally Merot

Coach Andrea and Mom and my friends had all told me
how awesome I'd been at Regionals, but they were going to
say that no matter what, so I only half-believed them. I all-
the-way believed it after reading Ally's note.

As soon as Mom pulled into the driveway, I ran outside,
waving my letter in the air. I was telling her all about it before
she even got out of the car.

"Randi, I'm so excited for you," she said, hugging me. "This
is the break we needed. What an incredible opportunity."

I flinched when she said "we" but let it go. "I want to do it,"
I said. "Can I?"

"Let's go inside and talk. We've got a lot to discuss. And I need to make sure we can afford it."

The first thing Mom did was call Coach Andrea to tell her the news. Coach Andrea was thrilled. She'd heard of this camp and agreed it was something I should attend if we could make it work.

Mom and I talked about it over dinner and into the night. We were long past the question of whether I was going or not. I was definitely going. We spent most of that time talking about how awesome the experience was going to be.

That was where my talking about this incredible opportunity ended, though. I kept the news to myself. I didn't mention it to Natalie, because I didn't want her to think I didn't care about our mission with Mrs. Magenta and Mrs. Woods. And I didn't tell Gav because the last thing I wanted to do was brag about gymnastics when he wasn't having the best football experience. How did I know that? Because he hadn't told me anything about football practices yet, and when I asked him, I got the kind of answer you give when you don't want to talk about something. "It's great," was all he ever said. No, it wasn't. Did he forget who he was talking to?

Somewhere along the way we found ourselves keeping more secrets than just our plans for Mrs. Magenta and Mrs. Woods. I didn't know how to feel about that. I just hoped destiny was looking out for us.

SCOTT

I had four different teachers this year, and that meant four folders and subjects to try to keep organized. That also meant four different people to lose papers for. Luckily, the deluxe clipboard that Coach and Grandpa had given me was exactly what I needed. I stored everything my teachers gave me throughout the day inside it. I was supposed to take my papers and put them into the right folders after school, but the problem was, I never had time because I had to get to practice. I just crammed it all in my backpack to sort later. The reason I had to have an empty clipboard was in case I needed it at practice. So far I hadn't, but I could've used some extra muscles and extra hands.

Coach Holmes and Coach Frazier were confused. They still thought "stats man" meant "equipment boy." I was responsible for the water bottles, cones, med kit, pinnies, and all the practice bags. We had blocking dummies, hitting shields, and more. Some of the bags were superheavy. I couldn't even lift them, so I had to drag them. It always took me too long to get all the stuff out to the field. I hated missing any part of practice, but I wasn't hating it as much as Gavin. He did more running than anything else. Coach Holmes wasn't even giving him a chance at quarterback. He wasn't giving him a chance at anything. You didn't need to be the stats man to see that.

Even though football hadn't been what I was hoping for, I was still excited about going to see Grandpa and Coach. I hadn't seen them since football had begun, so that night was my first chance to tell them all about it. I wished Gavin could come with me, but I was going with my family. We were bringing pizza and salad so that we could have dinner with Grandpa, and we had invited Coach to join us. After-school programs like Mrs. Magenta's weren't starting for a few weeks, so that everyone—teachers and students—had a chance to get used to a new school year.

When we made it to the Senior Center, Mom and Dad began setting out paper plates and drinks and other stuff in the Community Hall, where there was more space. I liked helping, but Mickey and I didn't stick around. We raced to get Grandpa and Coach. Running in the halls is a lot of fun, but they never let you do that stuff in school, so we always did it at the Senior Center. Mickey thought he was faster than me— and he wasn't!—so I had to show him. We burst into Coach's room on two wheels.

"Whoa!" Grandpa exclaimed. "No running in here, you wild men."

"Smoky!" Mickey squealed. He scurried over to the chair and started petting the kitty.

"How's football, Junior?" Coach asked, eager for answers.

"Yes, how's it going?" Grandpa asked.

I had thought that we would talk about football at dinner, and I had thought I'd be ready to tell them all about it—until they asked. Grandpa picked up on my hesitation.

"What's wrong?" he said.

I sighed. "It's not great," I admitted. "Coach Holmes hasn't given Gavin a chance at quarterback. He has his favorites, and Gavin isn't one of them."

"That's too bad," Grandpa said.

"If you can't win the coach, win the team," Coach said.

"What does that mean?" I said.

"If you can't win the coach ... win the team," Coach repeated, more slowly this time. "You need to pour your heart out at practice in every drill, every sprint, and every play, no matter your position or your role. When the team sees how hard you work, they'll start supporting you and quietly making noise. But only if you're a team player and not a loner. You've got to work hard, but you also need to encourage your teammates. If Valentine does that, then he'll win the team and Coach Holmes won't be able to keep this up."

Boy, I wished Gavin were with me. This was one of Coach's classic pep talks. He already had me feeling better.

"I'll tell him—" I started to say.

"Can we go eat?" Mickey interrupted. "Mommy got ice cream!"

"Oh boy," Grandpa said. "That sounds good. Let's leave Smoky here for now."

"You've got to eat pizza first," Mickey reminded him. "Pizza!" he yelled, running out the door.

"Wish I still had that energy," Grandpa said.

110

"You want to race?" Coach challenged. "See what we've got left?"

I could've hugged my brother. He'd gotten them moving along before they could ask how football was for me. I've never been good at lying, but I didn't want to have to tell Grandpa and Coach or anyone else the truth. They didn't need to worry, because I was going to win the team, too—like Gavin—and then things would be great for both of us.

6

A STICKY
SITUATION

NATALIE KURTSMAN
ASPIRING LAWYER
Kurtsman Law Offices

BRIEF #7
Mid-September: Extra! Extra!

Something of importance finally occurred during our second
week of school.

"As I'm sure you can see, I'm due to have a baby in the very
near future," Mrs. Yazmire said, stating the obvious.

"You mean she's not just fat?" Tommy whispered behind me.

Snickering followed. I shook my head in disgust. Were boys
programmed to be this stupid? Seriously. Thankfully, Mrs.
Yazmire didn't hear his idiotic remark.

"I'm telling you this because I'll be going out on maternity
leave," she continued. "The school will be hiring a long-term
sub to fill in for me while I'm away."

My hand shot into the air.

"Yes, Natalie," Mrs. Yazmire said.

"Do you know who our substitute will be? Has the person
been hired?"

"It's not finalized yet, so I'm not at liberty to say, but I should be able to tell you very soon."

"Not finalized" was all I needed to hear. "Not finalized" meant there was still a chance. I marched to the main office straightaway after class.

"Hi, Natalie," Mrs. Lane, our secretary, said. "What brings you here?"

"I was hoping to see Principal Allen," I said.

"Oh. Is he expecting you?"

"No, but I have a bit of an emergency."

"I know he's busy. Is there something I can help you with?"

"No."

I didn't mean to be so short, but it was imperative that I see Principal Allen right then—not later. Time was of the essence.

"I wouldn't normally do this," Mrs. Lane whispered, "but let me see what I can do." She rose from her swivel chair and went and knocked on Principal Allen's door.

Thanks to last year's fallout with the CSAs, I'd made a name for myself and had a reputation among the office staff for being a go-getter. Simply put, they liked me—and that clearly had its advantages.

"Natalie, how are you?" Principal Allen asked, suddenly coming out of his office. Mrs. Lane was right behind him. She winked.

"I'm doing well, thank you. And you?"

"Me? Guess I can't complain. But never mind me. How can I help you?"

"I was hoping to meet with you for a few minutes," I said. "It's an emergency."

"Of course. Everything okay?"

114

"Yes," I replied, following him back to his office.

"Have a seat," he said, gesturing to a chair. He sat on his desk. "So, what's so urgent?"

I got right to the point. "I just came from ELA. Mrs. Woods is the perfect person for that long-term sub position. Please tell me you're offering her the job."

"I did offer it to her. She turned it down."

"What! Why?"

"You'd have to ask her that."

I felt like I'd been punched in the stomach. True, that had never happened to me, but I imagined that finding it hard to breathe and feeling nauseous would be the result. *She turned it down,* I thought. *My perfect plan is ruined—again.*

"I'm sorry, Natalie, but rest assured, we're going to hire a very capable person. Don't worry."

I nodded.

"You should head to your next class," Principal Allen said. "And I have to get this office cleaned out. Wanted to do it last year when I took the job, but I never found the time. You wouldn't believe how much stuff is crammed in here, taking up precious space. Stuff that was left over from the previous principals and that we don't need anymore."

I glanced at the boxes he was referring to. "What's that?" I asked, pointing to an open box piled high with stuff.

"Looks like issues of the old school newspaper."

"School newspaper? I didn't know Lake View Middle had one."

"Used to," Principal Allen said. "But from what I understand, the interest wasn't there to keep it going. Mrs. Yazmire was in charge of it until a few years ago."

"Maybe Mrs. Woods can revive it," I said, springing forward from my chair. "She could volunteer. Where do you think Mrs. Ma—"

I was about to say, *Where do you think Mrs. Magenta gets her passion for volunteering from?* but I stopped myself before that came spilling out. I didn't need Mr. Allen to know I had an ulterior motive for getting Mrs. Woods to the school. If I continued to act as eager as Scott did, that would be certain to raise suspicion. I recomposed myself. "What do you think?" I said, speaking in a calm voice.

"I guess it's worth a shot," Principal Allen said. "I'll ask her."

"Thank you. Please let me know what she says. I would love to be involved in the school newspaper. So would many others, I'm certain."

"I'll keep you posted. Enjoy the rest of your day, Natalie."

"You too. Thank you for your time, Principal Allen."

I left his office with newfound confidence. I wasn't giving up. I was going to get Mrs. Woods and Mrs. Magenta together yet. My only concern was how long it would take before Principal Allen was able to contact Mrs. Woods and ask her my question, but that wasn't anything I had to worry about, because it wasn't only during school that something of importance occurred, but afterward as well.

Randi

Natalie was in her take-charge mode at lunch. Something was up.

I sat next to her at our table. "What's going on?"

"We need the guys here first," she said. "Then I'll explain."

"They're in line to buy food, so they'll be a few minutes."

"Ugh," she groaned. "Why don't they bring their lunches to school? It's so much easier—and healthier!"

I chuckled. Natalie took out her perfect little triangle sandwiches with the crust cut off, and her yogurt and carrot sticks. It's what she brought every day. You couldn't have paid the guys to eat a lunch like that.

"Here they come," she said. "Finally." She stood and waved her arm, trying to get them to hurry up.

"Dude, what's the deal?" Mark said. "Why are you freaking out?"

"If you guys would hurry up and sit down, I'd tell you."

"Whoa. Pushy," Mark joked.

"Sit down," Natalie ordered.

They did. You didn't mess with Natalie when she meant business. She leaned forward and began explaining. "I think I've found a way for us to get Mrs. Woods here, and if we do that, then we can work on getting her together with Mrs. Magenta."

"What way is that?" Gav asked.

"Principal Allen is going to ask her if she'd consider volunteering to be the adult overseeing our school newspaper."

"We have a school newspaper?" I asked.

"We used to, and now we're bringing it back from the dead," Natalie answered.

"Who's *we*?" Mark asked.

"Us."

"Sounds fun!" Scott cheered.

"Dude, are you listening? She wants you to *write* for the paper," Mark said. "Still think it's gonna be fun?"

"That's not necessarily true," Natalie shot back. "There are many roles to fill at a newspaper besides writing articles. But we can decide on all of that at our first meeting."

"When's that going to be?" Gav asked.

"I don't know yet," Natalie admitted. "Soon, I hope. But first we need Mrs. Woods to accept Principal Allen's offer. In the meantime I'll be meeting with Mrs. Yazmire so she can give me pointers before she goes out on maternity leave. She used to help with the paper. And remember, once we do get the paper up and running, we'll need to figure out how to get Mrs. Magenta involved, but that should be the easy part."

"Great work, Natalie," Scott said.

"Yeah, great work, Natalie." Trevor mimicked in a high-pitched voice.

It was silly teasing, so we giggled, but it was super-funny when Scott grabbed Trevor and pulled him into a headlock and started giving him a noogie.

"Yeah, get him," Mark encouraged.

"Yeah," Gav joined in.

Trevor didn't stand a chance against Scott, but we cheered for our underdog.

"Not the hair," Trevor cried, wrestling his way free—but not before his face had turned beet red.

Gav and I high-fived Scott.

"Dude, your hair? Gimme a break. Who do you need to impress?" Mark asked.

"No one. Shut up," Trevor grumbled.

Call me crazy, but I thought I saw him glance at Natalie when he said that. And I thought I saw her quickly look away. *No way.*

The bell rang and brought an end to the boys' horseplay. It also saved me from feeling bad about keeping my big news a secret. It would've been fine if going to the Elite Stars Camp hadn't meant missing Gav's first-ever football game. The worst part was, he wasn't going to have any idea why. I just hoped his game went well so that he would be in better spirits and then I could explain everything to him after I got back.

Unfortunately, destiny doesn't always play out the way you want it to.

BRIEF #8
Mid-September: Serendipity

At the conclusion of our first session, Mrs. Davids and I had agreed to meet at the public library for our future lessons. I suggested the library for several reasons: (1) we could find a quiet study room downstairs where we'd be left alone, (2) it contained all of the resources and materials I'd need to be an effective teacher, and (3) it was also home to the children's room, and that offered a much better space for Meggie than my parents' office. (Meggie was going to be with us during each of our sessions.)

I walked to the library directly after school and got set up at a table in one of the study rooms. There still wasn't a permanent librarian working in the children's room, so it was quiet when I arrived. Mrs. Davids and Meggie showed up shortly after me.

"Hi, Meggie. I'm Natalie," I said, and smiled. She was

wide-eyed, staring at the room full of books. "I thought you'd like this place." I took her by the hand and led her on a tour. "This is the room we cleaned and painted last year when we were coming here with Mrs. Magenta's program." I glanced at the throw rug on the floor but didn't mention the secret beneath it.

"Can I look at the books?" Meggie whispered.

"Yes, of course. You can look at as many as you want," I said. "There's only one rule: when you're done with a book, you need to put it on that cart over there." I pointed. "I'll teach you how to put the books back on the shelves when we're done."

She was all smiles.

"Your mom and I will be in that room right back there." I pointed in a different direction. "If you need anything, come and get us."

"Okay," she said, finding her voice and skipping off.

"Thank you," Mrs. Davids said.

I nodded. "Let's get started."

We walked into the study room and sat down. I pulled out the alphabet paper and we began reviewing the basics. Then I got Mrs. Davids practicing with blends and reading short words. She was a quick learner. I wondered why she hadn't done this before, but I didn't ask.

Meggie was a good girl. She left us alone, and we were able to make excellent progress, but eventually she came in to show us what she'd found.

"Mommy, look at these," she said, referring to the stack of books she was hugging.

I had to smile. It was cute to see her that excited.

Meggie plopped the books onto the table and went through them one by one, showing her mom different pages and explaining to her what each story was about. She had one about a bear who ended up with baby geese, and the geese thought the bear was their mother. Meggie found that one especially funny. We laughed with her. She had another about crayons who took turns complaining to the boy who owned them. That one was fun, too. And then she had one about a wedding.

"Tell me about yours and Daddy's wedding, Mommy," Meggie said. "I never heard about it."

"Maybe later, *mija*. We need to get going. Our time is up."

It was an abrupt end to our meeting, which I attributed to the time of day.

"Can we take these home?" Meggie asked. "Gavvy can read them with me."

"Not today. I don't have a library card," Mrs. Davids said.

"I can check them out for you," I offered.

"Yay!" Meggie cheered.

"Thank you, Natalie," Mrs. Davids said. "That's very nice of you."

"Your mom will be reading these books to you in no time," I told Meggie. "But remember, our meetings are—"

"Compidental," Meggie said, finishing my sentence.

"That's right, confidential," I said. Was I worried about her spilling the beans? Not in the slightest. It was much harder keeping Scott's lips zipped about things.

We got our stuff together, and then I showed Meggie how to work the self checkout kiosk. I was beeping one of her books when I heard someone behind me say, "Hello, Miss Kurtsman."

To say I was startled would be a gross understatement. I

don't know how to accurately describe what I felt when I saw Mrs. Woods, so let me just say that I was a mix of elated and dumbfounded. This was serendipity.

"Mrs. Woods, what're you doing here?" I said.

"The library still hasn't hired a full-time children's librarian, so I've been volunteering some."

I wanted to ask her about the school newspaper, but I waited. *Mrs. Davids and Meggie first,* I told myself. "Would you be able to help Mrs. Davids get a library card?" I asked.

"Of course," Mrs. Woods said. "Good to see you, Mrs. Davids. I hope Gavin is well. Just need your driver's license," she said.

Mrs. Davids sighed. "Hello, Mrs. Woods. I'm embarrassed to say this, but I do not have my license with me."

"That's okay," I said. "We can do it next time."

"Thank you," Mrs. Davids said, gathering up the books and quickly whisking Meggie away.

"Bye, Natalie," Meggie called.

"Bye."

In hindsight, I should've given that moment more thought, but I was still flummoxed by Mrs. Woods's sudden presence. She was the one who had my focus now. It would be much easier for her to turn down the newspaper gig if Principal Allen did the asking, so I wasn't taking any chances. I was going to offer her the job myself. After all, Mr. Allen and I had discussed the possibility. I was merely acting on his behalf—not exactly the truth, but close enough.

"Mrs. Woods, I have the perfect volunteering opportunity for you," I said.

Randi

Mom picked me up from school on Friday afternoon, just after lunch. We had a three-hour drive to get to the Elite Stars Camp. Check-in started at four o'clock, and we didn't want to be late. I quietly disappeared from Lake View Middle School without mentioning to any of my friends a word about where I was going. Would they even notice I was gone? I hadn't stopped stressing about missing Gav's first game, but as soon as we reached the camp, Gav and the rest of the Recruits slipped from my mind.

The camp was being held on the campus of an old boarding school. The school was no longer operating, but the buildings were still beautiful and well kept. Check-in for gymnasts took place in the lobby of the dorm where we were staying, but there were several other camps also arriving.

I finished registering before my roommate, so that meant I got to choose which bed I wanted. I picked the one by the window, but I'd switch if that made her upset. I wasn't going to make a stink about it, because I knew I'd be spending most of my time at practice anyway. Mom helped me get things situated, and then we walked to the gym. Parents were allowed to stay and watch our first workout, but after that they had to leave. Mom said she'd hang out for the first half, but then she needed to get on the road. She had a long drive back. It was kind of crazy. Just last year I'd been ready to run from Jane, and now I was nervous about being away from her.

Once we warmed up, my nerves were quickly replaced by excitement. All the girls were talented, and being together pushed us to be better. Our first session that evening flew by. I loved every minute of it. I learned a lot. The girls I met were super-nice, and so were our coaches, especially Ally. I was spent by the time we finally turned in for the night, and psyched for the rest of camp and how much more I was going to learn.

I had no idea.

GAVIN

Scott told me what Coach had said about winning the team. His advice made sense. The only problem was, I didn't know how to do that if I never even got the chance to play. Instead of being excited for our first game, I woke up worrying on Saturday morning. Holmes couldn't keep me off the field for all four quarters, could he?

I planned on being the first one to the gym on game day, 'cause part of winning the team was working the hardest—in every aspect—but Scott beat me to it. Matter of fact, he'd already been there for a while by the time I showed up. He was busy spraying Windex all over our helmets, inside and outside, giving them a good shine.

"What're you doing?" I asked him, even though I could see.

"Winning the team," he said proudly.

"With Windex?" I teased.

"Yup. I had something else when I started. I used it on the inside of Nicky's and Adam's helmets, but then the nozzle stopped working. It was an old can and the label was worn off. This Windex was the only other thing I could find."

"Well, it's doing the trick. The helmets look awesome."

Scott beamed when I said that. The kid was so proud. The best part was that most of the guys thanked him and told him the same thing when they rolled in and saw what he'd done for them. I smiled inside 'cause I knew Scott was winning the team. The junky part was that "most of the guys" didn't include Nicky and Adam.

"Hey, water baby," Nicky said. "What're you doing here so early?"

"Cleaning helmets so we look sharp out there today."

"'Bout time you did something useful," Nicky said. "Keep up the good work, and I might let you wash my jock."

Adam laughed. "Ha ha ha! Good one."

"Yeah, too bad the sissy probably doesn't even know what a jock is since he wears panties."

"Ha ha ha!" The sounds of those two cracking up over their stupid jokes filled the air. My muscles tensed. I felt the heat rising in my neck and face. I was this close to losing it, but brawling in the locker room with Coach Holmes's prized boys wasn't going to help anything. Besides, the other thing I heard was silence. No one else was laughing along with them. The locker room was changing. Scott was winning the team.

Stats Man finished with his last helmet and then quietly left to do his other jobs while the rest of us got our gear on. After we were suited up, Coach Holmes gathered us in the team room and took a few minutes to talk game plan.

"If you protect Nicky, we should have plenty of guys

reaching the end zone. He's our best player, so take care of him!" Coach Holmes barked.

"Protect Nicky." It was all about Nicky. Our best player. Whatever. Holmes did a lot of yelling after that, and I did a lot of not listening. I could stop worrying, 'cause I'd just gotten my answer. I thought for sure there was no way I was getting into the game. Turns out, I was wrong. And that was all thanks to our stats man.

"All right, boys. Helmets on," Coach Holmes hollered. "Give me two lines behind Nicky and Adam."

That was when things got exciting.

"Ah! What the hell!" Nicky yelled. "What's all over my helmet?"

"Mine too!" Adam cried.

"I'll kill that little twerp!" Nicky screamed. "Dad!" His voice was changing. There was something new in it—panic. "Dad!" he screamed again.

"What's the matter?" Coach Holmes said.

The guys around me started mumbling and whispering, wondering what was going on. None of us knew.

"That little punk sprayed my helmet with Stickum!" Nicky cried.

"Mine too!" Adam whined.

Oh, man. He'd done it again. Chalk this up as another one of Scott's classic brilliant terrible ideas. Stickum was the stuff wide receivers and running backs sprayed on their hands and gloves so they wouldn't drop the ball. It was ultra-wicked sticky. That musta been what was in the old can he had thrown out. Whoa! This was crazy bad for Nicky and Adam, but I loved it.

"Take the helmet off. Let me see," Coach Holmes said. "We don't have time for this."

"Ahh!" Nicky yelled louder. "I can't take it off. It's going to rip my scalp!"

"We'll deal with it later, then. We've got a game to play."

"No!" Nicky whined. "It's ripping my hair. Ow. My skin. Ow!"

Coach Frazier was trying to help Adam but was having no luck. Superstar Nicky was on the verge of tears. Go ahead, ask me if I was feeling sorry for them. No way!

"Argh!" Holmes growled. "Get into the coaches' room. Both of you. Frazier, take the team out to the field."

I grabbed Scott and shoved him to the front. "Lead us out," I whispered. Knowing him, he'd want to stay back and make sure Nicky and Adam were okay. It wasn't a good idea. They'd never believe the Stickum had been an accident. I'd have to make sure Scott was never alone with those two losers after this.

I tried.

Randi

Everyone was hanging out in the quad area outside the dorms on Saturday night. We had finished a full day of workouts, and to celebrate, the coaches had a bonfire and an outdoor movie going. There were even concessions and different camp merchandise for sale. All the campers from the various camps were out and about, mingling. It was chilly, so I chose to wear my hoodie, the one that had my home gym on the front and my last name on the back.

I was standing in line to get some food when I heard someone behind me say, "Hey, what're you doing wearing his sweatshirt?"

"Shut up," someone else hissed.

I looked around but couldn't tell who they were talking to.

"Hey, Cunningham. What're you doing in his sweatshirt?"

"Shut up," the other voice hissed again.

Cunningham? Are they talking to me? I wondered. Slowly I turned around.

There was an older high school boy smiling at me. The

friend standing next to him had his hand over his mouth and was snickering.

"Excuse me?" I said.

"Little man here thinks you're cute," the high schooler said, nudging a younger boy who was beside them, "but we want to know why you've got his sweatshirt on."

"His sweatshirt? This is mine."

"'Cunningham' is his last name, too," the first high schooler said.

"Oh," I replied.

"You could marry him and not even have to change your name," the snickering friend added.

I shook my head. I saw what was going on. The high schoolers were teasing the younger boy. They were obnoxious, especially the snickering one, but the boy with my last name was kinda cute, especially with the way his face was turning red. "Whether I change my name or not is up to me, not the person I marry," I told the high schoolers.

"Whoa, you're messing with a tough one," the first high schooler said to the younger boy. "Good luck with her." They paid for their candy bars and left. Guess they'd had their fun.

"Do you have to put up with those two all weekend?" I asked the boy.

"Yeah, but they're cool. They were just giving me a hard time because . . . What're you here for?"

"Gymnastics," I said. "And you?"

"Wrestling."

"Is your last name really Cunningham?" I asked.

"Yeah."

"What's your first?"

"Kyle. How about you?"

"Randi."

"It's nice to meet you, Randi Cunningham."

"Nice to meet you, Kyle Cunningham."

We shook hands and got our snacks. Popcorn for me, nachos for Kyle. Then we walked over to a bench and sat down. We ate and chatted about our different sports. He was younger than me but didn't look it. He was also easy to talk to, especially for someone I'd just met.

"My dad's one of my coaches," Kyle said. "He was a high school standout when he wrestled. Everyone knows him and remembers him . . . and wonders if I'll be as good as him. . . ." His voice trailed off.

"That's a lot of pressure."

"There are banners hanging in our gym with the names of past champions and record holders. I see my dad's name every day at practice. Tom Cunningham. It's up there more than anyone else's."

"Did you say 'Tom Cunningham'?"

"Yeah, why?"

"That was my dad's name, too," I said.

"What do you mean 'was'?"

"My dad left when I was a baby," I explained. "I've never known him."

"Oh. Sorry."

"It's okay. My mom said he was a jerk."

"Where did he go?"

"I don't know. My mom doesn't say much."

Our conversation that up till now hadn't slowed one bit suddenly stalled. A crazy idea burst into my head. I turned and looked closely at Kyle. He was doing the same with me. We studied each other's features. His eyes were my eyes. His nose and chin and the shape of his face looked like mine.

"You don't think?"

"Gross," I said, shaking my head.

"I know. I was thinking you were hot. I mean, you still are hot, but if you turn out to be my half sister, that's gross."

"Eww. Stop it."

We laughed together.

"Do you really think—" he started.

"No way," I said. "Do you know how crazy that would be?"

"Yeah. But . . ."

We grew quiet again. It was crazy, but it was also possible. Kyle and I exchanged addresses and promised to write to each other if we discovered anything after we did some sleuthing back at each of our homes. Texting would've been much easier but was out of the question. We didn't want our parents to know what we were up to, and his mom was always checking his phone to make sure he wasn't doing anything inappropriate. What was one more secret to keep, anyway?

Going to sleep that night, I didn't know if I was supposed to be excited or scared. Digging into the past meant bringing up the father I didn't know, the man my mom wanted to bury and forget.

GAVIN

After we hit the field without Coach Holmes, Nicky, or Adam, football became everything it was supposed to be. We received the ball to start the game. Coach Frazier was more than a little freaked about his son and being the one calling the shots, but never fear, Stats Man was there to tell him what to do, and that started with putting me in at quarterback. Frazier didn't like it, but he had no choice. I got the nod. I wanted to hug Scott.

I knew all the plays. Even though I hadn't run them in practice, I'd rehearsed all of them with my pretend teammates in my backyard, and I'd gone over them in my head countless times. I stepped into the huddle and took charge. I was ready. I'd been ready for a long time.

After every play I smacked my linemen on their shoulder pads and a few times on the butts. "That's how to block!" I praised them. "Keep it up!"

"Way to run hard!" I encouraged our backs.

Part of being QB and the leader is getting those in the

huddle to believe in themselves and each other. We marched the ball down the field. And then Stats Man got Frazier to dial up our first pass play.

I rolled to my right and spotted Mark running a shallow drag across the middle. I threw a perfect ball that he caught in full stride and took all the way to the end zone—my first career touchdown pass. I ran down the field with my arms in the air. It was the best feeling, one I had thought I'd never experience and had almost given up on.

As I jogged to the sideline, I looked into the stands and saw my mom and dad and Meggie waving. I saw Grandpa, Coach, Magenta, and even Woods. They weren't together, but they were there cheering us on. Could something like football help unite them? Was it that simple? Hard to say, 'cause we didn't give them much to cheer about after that. Holmes and Nicky and Adam came running out of the gym and joined the team.

"Your day is done, Pablo. Your kind will never be the star," Holmes hissed.

That was it. My game was finished. I didn't see the field again. Nicky and Adam got the call and didn't play that great, but they had excuses, and the team still hung on for a 7–6 win. We were 1–0 to start the season, but I felt like we'd lost.

Mom and Dad were thrilled for me, though. I hadn't just played; I'd shined out there. The fact that I'd gotten benched seemed like it was just so the other guys would get a chance to play. In my parents' minds I was the starter. It was all fair. But nothing was fair when dealing with Coach Holmes. Mom and Dad might see the truth as the season wore on, but I wasn't gonna say anything. I wanted to handle this on my own. Like a man.

The only one to ask me about something other than football that night—you guessed it—was Meggie. "Gavvy, want to read with me?"

"Okay." I followed her into her room and sat on her bed. She plopped down next to me with a new stack of books. "Where did these come from?" I asked.

"The library."

"The public library?"

"Yup. Mommy took me there," Megs said, all proud.

"Really?"

"Yup. I saw your hungry caterpillar drawing on the wall."

I smiled. "How come you haven't asked me to read these books until today?" I asked her.

"I've been reading them by myself," she said.

"You can read them?"

"I make up the words when I don't know them. Want me to read to you?"

"Yeah," I said.

She opened the first book and began telling me a wedding story that went along with the pictures. Meggie could read more than I'd expected, which made me feel both proud and relieved. She wasn't going to struggle like me. She was also really good at adding in her own words. Tell you the truth, the ones she came up with were better than the ones in the book. I liked her story better. Maybe she'd grow up to be a writer.

"Do you remember Mommy and Daddy's wedding?" Megs asked when she closed the book.

"No. They got married before I was born, goofball."

"Oh. But did they ever tell you what it was like?"

I sat there thinking, and realized I'd never heard them

talking about it. "No," I said. "It's not the sort of thing a boy asks about, I guess."

"Well, I'm gonna ask Mommy tomorrow," she decided.

"You do that," I said. "Good night, Megs." I messed her hair.

"Good night, Gavvy."

I turned off her light and walked down the hall to my room. A wedding wasn't the sort of thing a boy asked about, but Meggie's question got me wondering why there weren't any pictures of the big day anywhere in the house. It was probably 'cause hiring a photographer cost too much money.

The thing I couldn't explain was why Randi woulda missed my game. I'd spotted Kurtsman with her parents, but Randi was a no-show. Some best friend.

Trevor

I was missing football practice because Mrs. Magenta's program got started up again, and I can't believe I'm going to say this, but I was happy about it. Happy about restarting her program—and even more happy to be missing football.

Yeah, I loved football, but I didn't love Coach Holmes. And I wasn't the only one feeling that way. Who wants to play for a guy that is all about his son? I was sick and tired of hearing about how great Nicky was. Gavin was better, plain and simple, and I'm not just saying that because he was my friend. The rest of the guys were beginning to talk. At first it was only the seventh graders coming to his side, but since our game, I'd been hearing some of the eighth graders mumbling the same thing. If I were Gavin, I would've been fine with missing practice, but he wasn't.

"This only gives Holmes a reason to keep me on the bench," he said when we were on the bus. "It's not helping."

"It's not helping me, either," Scott complained. "Who's

going to get the equipment out and keep the stats? I'll never win over Coach Holmes this way."

"You need to stop worrying," Gavin said. "I already told you, this could be a good thing for you. Maybe after some of the other guys have to help with the equipment, they'll start to appreciate you more."

It was funny how Gavin could see missing practice as a potential good thing for Scott but not for himself.

"Dude, you shouldn't be worrying, either," Mark told Gavin. "I hate to break it to you, but if leading our team down the field for our one and only touchdown doesn't help your case, nothing will. Face it, Coach Holmes has it out for you. You're a threat to his precious Nicky, so he's going to keep you off the field, and there's nothing you can do about it."

"I can win the team," Gavin said. "That's why I need to be there. I've got to keep working hard."

"You're already working harder than everybody else," I said. "Mark's right. Coach Holmes has it in for you."

"We could miss our blocks on purpose and watch precious Nicky get creamed," Mark offered. "That would be fun."

"Sabotage!" Scott exclaimed.

"No!" Gavin snapped. "Don't you dare. My problem is with Holmes, not Nicky."

"Nicky's a punk, and you know it," I countered. "He deserves to get flattened."

"No," Gavin said, leveling his eyes at me. "I'm getting the spot fair and square."

"Fine. Have it your way. But just so you know, it's definitely not fair."

The bus came to a stop outside the Senior Center, and we filed off. It was time to forget Coach Homes and football and focus on the task in front of me. I had a job to do.

It was nice seeing the old people, and even nicer to hear them calling Mark and me "the TV Boys" and thanking us for the new theater all over again. But I needed to find Mrs. Ruggelli. The last time we'd visited, she had mentioned getting a new computer for the place. We needed to make that happen. Mark was in on this with me. We had to get Mrs. Ruggelli to make another trip to Best Buy. Not only did I want to get a computer for the Senior Center, but I had all of my savings with me to buy something I needed. I'd thought about taking some of Dad's money, but I wasn't a thief, even if he didn't believe me—and neither was my brother. I was going to prove it. I was going to catch our crook red-handed.

SCOTT

The guys kept telling me not to worry about missing practice, but I couldn't stop thinking about it, especially since Coach Woods started talking football as soon as Gavin and I walked into his room. "Heckuva game, Valentine," Coach said. "That was a beautiful pass you threw for that touchdown."

Gavin shrugged. "Thanks. That was Junior's play call."

Coach winked at me, and Grandpa patted me on the shoulder. Gavin walked over and started petting Smoky.

"What's the matter?" Grandpa asked him.

"Nothing," Gavin lied.

"He's mad about not playing much," Coach said. "And he should be."

Gavin looked up.

"I'd be concerned if you weren't upset," Coach continued. "Good sportsmanship doesn't mean giving up and not caring. You were the better quarterback, but it'll take more than one good showing to change your coach's mind. Why was he late getting out to the field with those other boys?"

My eyes got big, but Gavin didn't tell on me.

"Ah, never mind," Coach said, waving his hand. "Doesn't matter."

I sighed, and Grandpa smirked. "You can tell me later," he whispered.

I nodded. I couldn't fool Grandpa, and that was okay. I knew he'd get a kick out of my story, but he would need to keep it our secret.

"Valentine, things like this have a way of working themselves out," Coach went on. "That's one of the beauties about sports. Good things happen to people who work hard."

"My dad likes to say that," Gavin said.

"Well, it's true. You've got to trust that and keep giving your best. How was practice today?"

"We're missing it right now," I exclaimed.

"What!" Coach yelled. "That's not okay. You're not going to win the spot that way. We've got to do something about that. Where's that teacher of yours?"

"You mean your daughter?"

Grandpa's eyebrows jumped, and Gavin's head yanked in my direction. Gavin shot me a hard look. *Oops.* The words had fallen out of my mouth before I'd even realized it.

"Olivia," Coach said. "Where is she?"

Gavin looked at me again, and we both got wide-eyed. Was Coach remembering? There was no time to waste. I ran out of the room and down to the Community Hall.

"Mrs. Magenta, your da—I mean, Coach wants to see you. He's asking for you," I said.

"He is?" Her face lit up just like mine does around cupcakes.

Natalie and Randi also perked up, but I didn't have time to explain. I ran with Mrs. Magenta back to Coach's room.

"Olivia," he barked as soon as we got back. "These boys can't be missing football."

"I know. I feel bad about that, too, but there's no other way."

"Sure there is. You need to start bringing them after they're done with practice. Some call it happy hour, but we'll call it visiting hour. That's the perfect time of day for slowing down and catching up, anyways."

Mrs. Magenta's hand flew to her mouth the way I'd seen it happen before. Her eyes turned glassy. What had Coach said that had made her do that?

"Yes, visiting hour can be special, too," she repeated. "But I'm afraid the school won't be able to arrange for a bus to get us here. They'll never approve that."

"Our parents can drive us," I was quick to say. "It wouldn't have to be everyone. Just the Recruits. The others could still come after school."

"It's settled, then," Coach said. "We'll see you after practice from now on."

Mrs. Magenta smiled.

I was already thinking about Mrs. Woods. She was always here in the evenings. Natalie would be so excited when she found out what had just happened. Now we'd be able to start getting everyone together for visiting hour. It was like Coach had said, good things happen to people who work hard, and the Recruits had been working hard.

7

SPIRIT WEEK

Randi

Keeping all these secrets seemed harmless at first, but now it was beginning to bite back. Gav was mad at me, and I couldn't blame him. I'd missed his first-ever game, and on top of that I'd given him no warning or explanation why. To make matters worse, it sounded like he was incredible in the first quarter, leading the team to their only touchdown, but then he never stepped onto the field after that. Trevor and Mark played a lot, but not Gav. That made no sense, and I was dying to ask him what was going on, but I couldn't. I already knew his answer: *If you care so much, why didn't you come to my game?*

So instead of talking, we spent the week with silence growing between us. My silence was full of explanations and truths, and his was full of misunderstandings and hurt feelings. We'd gone down this road the year before (after Natalie had entered the picture and she and I had become friends when Gav couldn't stand her), and I'd hated it then. I couldn't do it again. Keeping quiet and avoiding each other was just making it worse. But Gav wasn't going to cave and start talking. And why should he? I was the one who'd messed up. I needed to break the silence.

I had myself ready to do it. I'd visualized the event like it was the bars or vault, but things went wrong before I even got to my approach.

GAVIN

At first I was so mad at Randi for not coming to my game that I swore I was never talking to her again. Just seeing her made the anger boil inside me. I'd gone to both of her stupid gymnastics meets, and then she blew off my game like it was nothing. She hadn't even said sorry. It didn't make sense. The Randi I knew wouldn't do that. And then it hit me. I coulda kicked myself. I wasn't mad at her anymore. I was mad at me. Something had to be going on, but she wasn't talking. Neither one of us was, and that had to change. I needed to tell someone about football 'cause it only kept getting worse. I needed my best friend. And she needed me. I was putting an end to this. Enough with the secrets.

I was hanging out in the cafeteria before the start of school, waiting for everybody else to show up. When she got there, I was gonna say something to Randi about the way I'd been acting, but she didn't give me the chance. She never even sat down. She dropped her bag and ran to the bathroom first thing. Her bag was sitting next to our table, where it shoulda been safely out of the way, but "safely out of the way" didn't exist with Scott.

The kid came waltzing into the cafeteria with his nose buried in his notebook. Naturally, he tripped on her bag. His arms and legs went flailing in all directions. By some miracle he managed to land sprawled out on our table instead of on his face. Randi's bag tumbled across the floor and spilled open.

"Way to go, Junior," I said.

"I didn't see it."

"No kidding. Believe it or not, it's hard to see where you're going when you've got your face in a book."

"I'm studying plays. I've got a good one," he said.

I got down on the ground and started picking up Randi's things. That was when I saw the picture.

Randi

Knowing that Kyle could be writing to me, I made sure I was the one to get the mail after school. If Mom saw a letter for me, she would start asking questions. Go ahead, call me paranoid, but it's a good thing I was playing it careful, because Kyle's first letter showed up soon after camp. I didn't have any news for him yet. How was he so fast?

I hid the envelope in my bag and didn't open it until I was in my room later that night, after Mom had gone to bed. It wasn't much of a letter. More of a note, really. It was what he'd sent with his note that made my heart thump like it did before my routines. *This was the only one I could find,* part of his note said. *Will keep looking for more.*

He'd included two pictures. One of his dorky wallet-size school photos—the kind you have too many of and don't know what to do with—and the heart-thumping one of him and his dad that looked like it had been taken after a wrestling event recently. I didn't even know if Mom had any pictures of my father still in the house, but if she did, then this was a picture I could compare it to. It was time to start digging.

I hid Kyle's note and pictures in my bag, where Mom wouldn't mistakenly find them. She didn't, but Gav did—and I didn't even know it.

GAVIN

The picture was of some kid—a guy!—named Kyle. There wasn't any Kyle at our school, so Randi musta met him somewhere else. This wasn't just some guy! *Last weekend was crazy,* I had time to read. That was why she hadn't been at my game. She'd been with her boyfriend! I knew there was a lot that Randi wasn't telling me, but I didn't see this coming. What a traitor! Anger surged through my veins like it did when I was with Coach Holmes. I crammed the papers back in her bag and split.

"Where're you going?" Scott called.

I was out of there. If Randi had a new guy, that was fine by me, but I wasn't gonna waste my time with her.

Too bad going to classes didn't help. I sat behind my desk just getting madder all morning long. I wanted nothing to do with even seeing her, so I skipped lunch. I hid in the bathroom, and then I wandered the halls. I'm not sure how or why, but I wound up at Magenta's room. She was busy showing tangrams to her math class, but that didn't stop her from dropping everything and rushing into the hall the second she spotted me outside her door.

"Gavin, what're you doing here? Is everything okay?"

I shrugged. That was the only answer I could give her.

"Oh, Gavin." She gave me a quick hug, and it didn't even bother me. "Tell you what, you can come and sit in the back of my class until you have to go, but do you have any other free periods today?"

"I have study hall during sixth period," I said.

"That's perfect. My class will be at specials during that time. Come back then, okay?"

I nodded.

"Good. C'mon."

I followed her into the classroom and took a seat where she pointed. I pulled out my journal and sketched quietly until it was time for me to go. And then I went back during sixth period like she'd said.

"Gavin, I normally work on my art during this time. Would that be all right with you? You're welcome to join me."

"That sounds great," I said.

Magenta put on some soft music and got set up at her easel, and I sat down with my journal. She painted while I sketched. Working side by side with her made my art feel more serious, and I liked that. The best thing Magenta did, though, was not ask me what was wrong. She was smart enough to know that if I wanted to talk about something, then I'd talk about it. And that wasn't happening right then. Maybe later. But I did have a couple of questions for her. It took me most of the period, but I finally got the nerve to ask.

"Mrs. Magenta," I said.

"Yes?"

"Do you think there's any chance that I could maybe . . . keep coming here for my study hall?"

She smiled. "I'd like that. Let me see what I can do."

I sighed. Magenta was the best. I really wanted to ask her about the quarterback towel Coach had given me, but I couldn't find the courage. It seemed like the longer you waited to talk about something, the harder it got to ever bring it up, sorta like with me and Randi. Magenta and Woods had gone so long not communicating that they had a concrete wall between them. The only way I knew to break it down was to get them together so that they could start hammering away.

"We're about out of time," Magenta said. "I need to go and get my class from specials."

"Okay." I packed up my stuff, and then I asked her one more question. "Mrs. Magenta, what're you doing after school?"

NATALIE KURTSMAN
ASPIRING LAWYER
Kurtsman Law Offices

```
BRIEF #9
Early October: Poker Face
```

I remembered Mother telling me the single most important rule—the cardinal rule—for a trial lawyer: the poker face. No matter the circumstances, you must never let the jury see you rattled, not even by a sudden drastic turn of events. It was imperative to remain composed and appear to be in control.

It was one thing to hear Mother tell me these things, but it was quite another to put her advice into practice. The truth is, one can read, listen, and study about such things all their life but never actually master how to apply that knowledge. So how, then, does one learn the poker face? In my case it was by getting thrown into the fire. Much like the kid who gets tossed into the pool and has no choice but to swim.

We convened for our first official newspaper meeting in Mrs. Yazmire's classroom after school. I'd gotten the okay from her before she'd gone out on maternity leave. Our meeting was advertised on the morning announcements, and I had even hung a few posters throughout the hallways, but the only students who attended were the Recruits—minus Gavin.

Admittedly, I was slightly disappointed by the low turnout, but I remained optimistic. We could always gain additional people by publishing an exciting product—and I could personally guarantee that our newspaper would be nothing short of amazing, because I was in charge.

It was Gavin's absence that annoyed me. I'd gone to his stinky football game, and he couldn't be bothered to attend our newspaper meeting? He knew how important this was to our overall mission. So much for a pact.

Natalie, he must have a good reason for not being here, I thought.

He'd better.

"Hi, Mrs. Woods!" Scott cheered when our former teacher walked in. He actually ran up and hugged her. We laughed, and I forgot all about being peeved. What can I say; it was Scott.

Mrs. Woods hugged him back. She was genuinely happy to see us. And she was genuinely surprised by who arrived next; so was I, though I didn't show it. I carried on as if nothing monumental had occurred, but let me be clear, the chain of events that followed made everything else possible.

Gavin finally showed up—and Mrs. Magenta was with him! Instantly the room went silent. This, of course, was not us acting normal. On the contrary, our frozen bodies and stunned expressions were dead giveaways that we were onto them.

Poker face, Natalie! Do something!

"Hi, Gavin," I said. "I was beginning to wonder where you

were. I see you've gone and recruited Mrs. Magenta to give us a hand. Great thinking. Thank you for coming to the first meeting of the newly resurrected school paper, Mrs. Magenta."

She smiled at me, but there was no such exchange of pleasantries between her and Mrs. Woods. We had finally cleared a major obstacle and brought mother and daughter together. Now the hard work was just beginning.

"Okay, everyone, listen up," I continued. "Our mission is simple: we're going to create the best newspaper Lake View Middle School has ever known—"

"What's it called?" Scott interrupted.

"I don't know yet, so start thinking about names. We also need to decide on our various roles—"

"What various roles?" Scott interrupted again.

I didn't mind; I was glad he was excited. "Well, for example, we'll need a sports reporter," I said.

"That's me!" Scott cried. "That's me!"

We laughed. "Okay," I said, "you've got the job. We also need someone to add art. I thought you might agree to that, Gavin. And maybe Mrs. Magenta can help you?"

They nodded.

"We'll also need a photographer and more writers," I continued. "I'll be responsible for taking your work and formatting and editing the final paper. Of course, I'll also write an editorial for each edition. And Mrs. Woods will be here to assist whoever needs it and to help with getting the copies made when we go to print."

Once I got all of that out of my mouth, I realized how ambitious it sounded, and maybe daunting, but Scott's excitement overruled any of our concerns.

"I'm going to write the best sports report ever!" Scott cried. "And it's going to help Gavin and me win the team."

"Win the team?" I repeated.

"Never mind," Gavin said, nipping that in the bud. He gave Scott a look that meant, *Zip it.*

Whatever. I didn't have time to worry about any of that, because we needed to proceed. "Does anyone else have ideas about what we can include in our first edition?"

"Maybe a story about our after-school program with Mrs. Magenta?" Trevor suggested.

"Super idea," Scott said.

"Yes, it is," Mrs. Woods agreed.

I would've replied, but I couldn't get my mouth to say anything. I settled for smiling and nodding.

By the end of our first meeting, we had a plan, and we had a deadline established. Most important, we had Mrs. Woods and Mrs. Magenta in the same place at the same time. Now we just had to get them together more often. Easier said than done, but we'd managed this much, so there was hope for us yet.

SCOTT

Seventh grade finally got into a routine after the first month of school, and that was a good thing because I do better with routines. My deluxe clipboard was holding all the papers my teachers kept passing out, even though I didn't need them. I read that stuff once and had it memorized. Classes were easy, but that was a good thing, too, because that meant I got to put my energy and attention on more important matters, like Mrs. Woods and Mrs. Magenta, football, and my sports article— nothing was easy about those projects.

Fixing the relationship between Mrs. Woods and Mrs. Magenta was turning out to be the hardest puzzle I'd ever worked on. And even though Mr. Allen had agreed to let us start visiting the Senior Center after practice, that didn't fix football. I was happy that I wasn't missing practice, but practice still stunk.

Coach kept giving Gavin and me the same advice: win the team. We were trying, but it wasn't making a difference.

"I never said it would happen overnight," Coach said. "You're not quitters, are you?"

We shook our heads.

"Boys, some things in life are worth fighting for."

"What did you have to fight for?" I asked him.

Gavin elbowed me. "That's kinda personal," he whispered.

I didn't mean to be nosey, but I wanted to know.

"I'm fighting now, Junior. . . . I'm fighting now."

Grandpa squeezed my shoulder. I wished Mrs. Woods and Mrs. Magenta could've heard Coach talking. I wanted to solve their family puzzle now more than ever.

Coach's words stuck with us, and we kept fighting, but Gavin still wasn't seeing the field and Coach Holmes never wanted my stats and analysis. And that was too bad. I could've told him not to run the option against the Knights because Nicky didn't know how to carry out the fake. He got hit and fumbled. The Knights recovered the ball, and we lost. I could've told Coach Holmes not to run that bootleg play to the left like he had against the Hornets—the one that cost us the game. We'd had a man open down the field, but Nicky can't run to his left and still throw. After winning our opening game, we'd dropped five in a row, and we hadn't managed a touchdown since Gavin's pass to Mark.

Coach Holmes blamed everything on poor blocking, but that wasn't true, and the other guys on the field knew it. Maybe Gavin and I weren't winning the team, but Coach Holmes was losing them. And so was Nicky. I heard it in the locker room.

"It was the same garbage last year," one returning player grumbled.

"I'd hoped it'd be better this season, but it's even worse," said another. And I saw it during practice when Nicky was on the ground and no one bothered to help him up.

That was the stat I wanted to give Coach Holmes. That was the one I wanted to put in my newspaper article, but I couldn't. Being a sports reporter was hard.

I'd never struggled to say what I thought before. Just the opposite. I blurted stuff out and realized my mistake afterward. But with writing, I got to see my words and erase them before they were printed, so that kept me from saying what I maybe shouldn't. It also kept me from getting much written. My article was due to Natalie at the end of the following week, and I still didn't know what to write. I wanted to do something that would make Coach Holmes happy, so that he might give Gavin and me a chance, but the only thing I could think of was a feature on Nicky, and I couldn't come up with that many fake sentences.

It was a nice change on Monday when practice wasn't all about Nicky. Instead Coach Holmes was making a huge fuss about it being Spirit Week. "You boys need to lead the charge. I expect all of you to be participating. Tomorrow is face paint day. That means I expect to see all of you with your faces prettied up. If you don't have face paint, use your mother's makeup. No excuses. Spirit Week needs to get all the students fired up. We've got a big game Friday night. Here. Under the lights."

The guys started hooting and cheering. Playing under the lights was going to be awesome.

"That's right," Coach Holmes barked. "Get excited. Playing under the lights is special. And if you want the stands to be packed, then you've got to get serious about Spirit Week and get everyone else psyched."

More hooting and cheering.

"After a big victory on Friday, we've got the annual Halloween dance on Saturday night. A great Spirit Week and a great victory mean a great turnout for our dance, and that's got to happen, because the Halloween dance is the number one fund-raiser for our athletics booster club. I'm the president of the booster club, so I expect you boys to get the job done!"

"Yeah!" we yelled. "Woot! Woot!"

I cheered because I'd just figured out what I was going to write for my article. I was going to give the best report ever on the Halloween dance to show what great work the booster club did for all our sports programs.

"Woohoo!" The guys kept it going.

We were psyched just like Coach Holmes wanted. It was the best speech he'd given all year, and that was because it was finally about something other than Nicky. Too bad he didn't see that, because by the next day it was back to Nicky this and Nicky that.

At practice on Wednesday—team jersey day—Spirit Week turned ugly. I wished I had a jersey, but Coach Holmes had forgotten to order me one. I was bummed, but at least I found an old Warriors jersey in the equipment shed. The thing was ancient, but I wore it with pride.

"Hey, dork," Nicky said, smacking me on the back. "Nice jersey. We need to put your name on it." He laughed and jogged off. Once again he was the last one out to the field, and that was starting to rub guys the wrong way—Gavin especially.

I could tell that Gavin was mad from the way he was running drills. He always ran hard, but he was catching the ball hard, slapping the leather in his hands after pulling in each pass, slamming the football on the ground when he brought it back to the starting point. When it was time for the team's first water break, he came over and didn't even bother getting a drink.

"Turn around," he told me.

I felt him rip the tape off my shoulders. I looked at the strip he held. *LOSER*. "We need to put your name on it," Nicky had said. I tried, but I didn't like that kid, and I don't say that about people. Gavin wadded the tape and threw it on the ground. Then he jogged back onto the field.

I should've seen trouble coming when Nicky and Adam decided to hang around after the rest of the guys had gone back to practice. Adam threw his water bottle at me, knocking my clipboard to the ground. "Nice catch, loser," he sneered.

I bent down to pick it up, and Nicky stomped on my hand.

"Ow!" I yelled.

"What's wrong?" he said, playing dumb.

"My hand!"

"Oh, jeez. Sorry. I didn't realize," he said, twisting and grinding his cleat into my knuckles and fingers.

That hurt really bad. I couldn't stop my eyes from getting wet. I cradled my hand while they laughed and high-fived. I watched them put their helmets on and start toward the field. The first football drilled Adam in the face mask, and the second walloped Nicky in the ear hole.

"Ah!" they both cried.

"Nice throws!" I blurted, real loud. I couldn't stop myself.

"You better say that was an accident!" Nicky yelled, holding the side of his head.

"It was no accident," Gavin answered. "I hit my targets, unlike some of us."

"You don't belong here," Nicky spat. "You . . ."

I'm not even going to tell you what he called Gavin, because it was horrible, and I don't say or repeat those things.

"Hit the track, Pablo!" Coach Holmes bellowed. "You're not a team player."

Not a word to his son about what he'd just said. Nicky should've had his mouth washed out with soap—two bars!

I saw the team quietly congratulating Gavin on his double pass. He'd won the guys, but I knew he'd never win Coach Holmes. I wished there was something I could do with my article to help him.

Trevor

It was another pretend-family dinner. I've got to give her credit, Mom stuck to her guns. She kept making the three of us sit down at the table together, but it was a lost cause. In the beginning Mom was serving up fancy meals, some of my favorite things, and Dad's, too, but lately we'd been having the stuff that came in boxes. Trying less was a step closer to throwing in the towel. Did Dad even notice—or care?

You didn't need to be a rocket scientist to see that Mom was exhausted, and not from work but from worry. The more she and Dad fought, the more concerned she became about me. Instead of checking on me once a day to ask if everything was okay, she was doing it two and three times now—not including all the texts she was sending me. And though she never mentioned Brian, I knew my brother was constantly on her mind. She wore his name in the bags under her eyes.

If we'd picked through our food in silence that night, ignoring the obvious like we always did, then I imagine nothing would've happened. But my father asked for it when he said, "What's wrong, hon? You seem upset tonight."

"Nothing," she answered. "Just tired, I guess."

"You look lost in thought," Dad pressed. "What're you thinking about?"

Like I said, he asked for it.

"Brian!" my mother snapped. "Brian's on my mind. He's on my mind every day. I worry about him working the night shift at that crummy gas station. I worry about him in that apartment all by himself, trying to make ends meet. And with the holidays coming up, I'm worrying more, and I can't help it. Thanksgiving will be here before we know it. How am I supposed to just sit here and pretend all is well?"

"We've been over this, Dorothy. I know that this time of year is going to be difficult, but if we can stay strong, then he'll see that we aren't going to bail him out again."

"I didn't realize staying strong meant staying away."

Dad fell silent. I glanced at Mom and then across the table at him. That was when I first saw he was struggling with this as much as my mother. My father talked tough, but he had more gray hair than I ever remembered seeing. And he had the same bags under his eyes.

"You know what?" I said. "You guys should go out on a date tomorrow night."

Their heads snapped. They looked at me with surprised faces.

"On a Thursday?" Mom said.

"Sure," I said, trying to play it cool. "We're gonna have a short practice because our big game is Friday, and teachers aren't giving homework since it's Spirit Week, so I'll have Mark come over, and he and I can hang out and have pizza."

This idea came out of nowhere, but I suddenly saw how perfect it was. If my parents went out, then Mark and I could get the video surveillance camera that I'd bought at Best Buy installed without them knowing. *C'mon, Mom,* I prayed.

"Where would we go?" she asked.

"I'll figure that out," Dad said. "It'll be date night, just like old times. I'll make the reservations."

Mom peeked at him. When I saw her slight smile, I breathed a sigh of relief. Maybe they weren't ready to give up.

8

THE HALLOWEEN DANCE

GAVIN

So far seventh grade had been nowhere near as good as sixth grade had been, but it wasn't all bad. There was something I'd started looking forward to—study hall with Magenta. She got it worked out so that I was able to hang with her and do art three times a week. When we got together, all the bad stuff with football and Randi left my mind.

"Mrs. Magenta, whatever happened with the painting you entered in that contest over the summer, the one with the little girl picking black-eyed Susans?" I asked her.

She stopped, with her brush midair, and looked at me. "You remembered. How sweet of you."

"Well, I kinda forgot for a while, but I remember now. I loved that painting."

She smiled. "My piece finished as runner-up."

"Wow!" I exclaimed. "That's awesome."

"The better news is that I had a gallery pick up my name after seeing my work, and now they're selling my stuff."

"Whoa! I'm so happy for you, Mrs. Magenta! You're living the dream."

She chuckled. "Thanks, Gavin—for saying that and for encouraging me. Now it's my chance to return the favor."

"Huh? What do you mean?"

"You've got real talent. Your sketches and cartoons are unique . . . but they'd be better if they came from your heart. Stop worrying about people not liking your stuff. If you put your heart into your work, people will connect with it. It took me a long time to understand that, but it's the truth. Trust me."

To explain, Magenta showed me her newest creation, a set of four paintings that told a story when put together. The first in the sequence showed a little girl holding hands with her dad as they walk on a spring day. The next showed the same pair, looking older, walking through a summer field of wildflowers. Following summer, we see them in the fall, looking older still. And last, the set finishes with the pair in the winter. The dad is an old man and the girl a grown woman.

There was no mistaking that this was Magenta and Coach. There was no mistaking that this came from her heart. "It's beautiful," I said. It was sad, too. But I never let on about knowing. "What're you working on now?" I asked.

"A different set. Same concept." She showed me the first. It was a little girl with her mom. "Not sure how this one will end yet," she said.

It was Magenta and Woods in that painting. I never thought I'd be the one to spill our secret plan, but I couldn't take it. Her paintings connected and pulled at my heart strings. I sighed and opened my mouth, but before any words came out, Magenta stopped me.

"We're about out of time," she said. "You'd better pack up your things and get going so that you're not late for your next class."

Saved. I gathered my stuff and got ready to leave. I still hadn't asked her about my special quarterback towel, either. *Next time,* I kept telling myself.

"Good luck in your game tonight," Magenta said. "I'll be there cheering you on. And have fun at the dance tomorrow."

"Thanks," I said. "See you later."

She gave me a small wave, and I walked out the door.

We won our big game under the lights. I didn't get to play quarterback, but Holmes did put me in with about four minutes to go, after we had things wrapped up. Us winning had put him in a generous mood. I got to play tight end. That wasn't a position that I'd ever practiced, but I didn't care. By then Adam was in at quarterback, and I did my best to block for him. Better him than Nicky. Not *much* better, but better.

I got to go out for a pass on one play. Maybe Adam forgot it was me, or maybe he didn't have time to think about it, but either way, he threw it in my direction. It wasn't a perfect pass, but I jumped and made an acrobatic one-handed grab, and then I rambled for twenty more yards before getting knocked out of bounds. The team went nuts. Holmes didn't like that, so he took me out, but I was smiling.

After the game Coach Holmes rounded us up in the locker room and told us how proud he was. Then he presented the game ball to Nicky, which was a joke. Mark had rushed for more than one hundred yards and scored two touchdowns. He deserved the recognition.

"Last thing. We have a bye on the schedule next week," Holmes said, "so you boys have Monday and Tuesday off. No practice."

The team erupted in cheers.

"When we come back on Wednesday, we start preparing for our Thanksgiving showdown against the Titans. We'll have two weeks to get ready for our biggest game of the year. They're our rivals and they think they're better than us, so we want to kill 'em!" Holmes hollered.

The guys hooted and cheered again, more about not having practice than about the Titans, but we let Holmes live in his world.

I knew Holmes had only stuck me in 'cause it was a home contest and he didn't want anyone from school asking him why I wasn't getting to play. But it wasn't him they asked. It was me.

"*Niño,* did something happen with Coach Holmes that you're not telling us about?" Mom asked later that night, after we were home and I'd showered.

"No," I sorta lied. Nothing had happened. He just hated me.

"You're sure?" Mom pressed.

"Yes." I'd made it this far. I could make it one more game.

Dad's eyes narrowed. He wasn't buying it, but he sighed and said, "Okay. But if you change your mind, you can come and talk to us."

I laughed, acting like that was funny, but who was I fooling? I mighta cracked, but Meggie saved me—again.

"Gavvy, will you read to me before I go to bed?" she asked.

"Okay," I said, happy to escape the football questions.

I followed my sister. "Mommy and I got new books," Megs said, showing me her stack.

"You went to the library again?"

"Yup. I like it there. I like all the books. I sit under your hungry caterpillar in the reading nook and look at them."

That made me smile.

"The librarian gave me something for you, too."

"She did?"

"Yup. Here it is."

Megs handed me an audiobook and its matching hardcover. I traced the letters in the title with my finger. *ECHO* by Pam Muñoz Ryan. "You said the librarian gave this to you?"

"Yup."

"What's her name?"

"I don't remember. She's not always there, but she's very nice. She loves books. She even smells them."

It had to be Woods. *Why this book?* I wondered.

"Let's read this one," Megs said, handing me one of her picture books called *The Other Side*. "I got it for us because the girl on the cover has a tire for swinging and not for football."

I chuckled. Then I sat back and cuddled next to my sister. I read her the story about the two girls, Clover and Annie, and the fence standing between their houses, separating black and white, and then I tucked her in.

"Gavvy, I know the fence is still there at the end of the story, but I think Clover and Annie already knocked it down by being nice to each other and becoming friends."

I smiled 'cause my little sister was one smart cookie—and 'cause she was like me. She didn't just listen to the stories, but she was a thinker about them, too. "You've got a smart brain in that head of yours, Megs," I said, borrowing the words Woods had told me last year.

"Gavvy, are there still fences like that?"

I took a deep breath and thought about the one Holmes had put between us. It wasn't coming down anytime soon. "Yes," I said. "There sure are."

"I'm going to knock them down by being nice to people," Megs said.

I smiled again. "You're going to make the world a better place," I told her. I rubbed her head and said good night, and then I went to my room.

I put the *ECHO* audiobook on and sat down with my pencils. As I listened, I drew from the heart. I sketched me standing outside a fence. Could things with football get any worse? Maybe not, but it wouldn't be long before I learned that football wasn't everything.

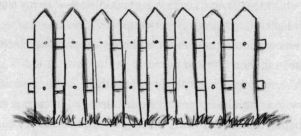

Randi

I scoured the house, searching high and low whenever Mom wasn't around, but I couldn't find a single picture of my father. She must've thrown all of them out. I had to write to Kyle, explaining the situation. Maybe my possible dad had a picture of me there? I pulled a random cookbook off Mom's rack so that I'd have something hard to write on. I was hurrying because I wanted to get this done before Mom got home, but people make mistakes when rushing. I dropped the book, and as it crashed to the ground its pages flopped open—and a single picture fell out. This was destiny at work.

It was a photo of my father and baby me making cookies. I studied it. Was this the same man that was in Kyle's picture? They were years apart, but I thought so. My heartbeat quickened. I grabbed the cookbook and raced to find pen and paper, an envelope, and a stamp. Once I had everything, I sat down and scribbled my note to Kyle. I told him the news and urged him to find a younger picture of his dad so that I could know for sure. I sealed the envelope, ran and stuck it into the mailbox, and was back inside just before Mom pulled into the driveway. Everything was still secret—from Gav, too.

I'd thought I was going to talk to Gav weeks before, but that never happened. Something else did—and I still didn't know what. He'd stormed out of the cafeteria, and things had been even worse ever since. He was avoiding me, sitting as far away from me at our lunch table as he could, never making eye contact. Natalie asked me about it, but I told her not to get involved. Thankfully, destiny took over and had us run into each other at the Halloween dance—literally run smack into each other.

I was hurrying out of the gym to go to the bathroom, when Gav came rushing around the corner, headed in my direction. Our bodies slammed. The collision knocked Gav sideways and sent me to the ground.

"Sorry," we said at the same time. Even though ramming into him hurt, I smiled.

He gave me his hand. "Are you okay?" he asked, helping me to my feet.

Everything I wanted to say to him came spilling out then. "Gav, I'm so sorry. I missed your first game because I was away at the Elite Stars Camp. I got a special invite because of my performance at Regionals. I didn't know how to tell you because I knew football wasn't going well. . . . I'm sorry."

"That's why you didn't tell me?"

"Yes," I mumbled.

"I've been making up all kinds of stories in my head trying to explain why you'd do that."

"I'm sorry," I said again.

"Randi, best friends don't keep secrets like that from each other."

I hugged him. It was a quick one, but I was so relieved to hear him call us best friends.

"So how was the camp?" he asked.

"Amazing." I told him all about the girls, the coaches, the practices, and the food, but I didn't mention Kyle. That was a secret I needed to keep for now.

"That sounds awesome."

"It was," I agreed.

"Well—"

"Gav, what's going on with football?"

"What do you mean? Football's good."

"No, it isn't. I was at last night's game. You didn't get in until you guys were way ahead, and you were playing tight end, not quarterback. What's going on?"

He looked down. "Coach Holmes hates me."

"What? Why?"

He shrugged. "There's too much to explain," he said. "Season's almost over anyway, so it doesn't matter."

Gav was wishing away the thing he'd been wishing for all his life, and it made my heart ache for him. I didn't know what to say, so I stepped closer and hugged him again. This wasn't a quick one but a hug packed with feelings. When I felt him squeeze back, it made everything around us okay again.

"We really need to get Mrs. Woods and Mrs. Magenta to do this," I whispered.

"We will," Gav said, letting go. "Kurtsman's on it."

I chuckled. "And Trevor, too. Have you noticed her acting weird around him?"

"Kurtsman? You're crazy. C'mon. Let's go inside."

I wasn't crazy. Maybe I'd noticed it because I was having similar feelings about someone else. "I need to use the bathroom first. I'll meet you in there."

I headed for the locker rooms with an extra bounce in my step. I felt better now that we'd broken our silence, though I still wondered what Gav wasn't telling me. Guess he had his secrets, too. We'd get to that other stuff later, I told myself—maybe when destiny said so.

I walked past the boys' locker room door and down the hall to the girls'. It was dark because the overhead lights had blown.

I didn't take long to pee because I wanted to get back to the dance. I'd told Natalie I'd make it fast. I washed and dried my hands and was just coming out of the locker room when the boys' door banged open. Two guys jumped out, laughing their heads off. They had their backs to me, and I could barely see their outlines in the dim light. One shoved his friend, and they laughed harder. They weren't fighting, just carrying on the way stupid boys do.

"That was awesome!" the first one said.

"You think he's okay, right?" the second one asked.

I stopped. I heard worry in his voice.

"Who cares? Water Boy's getting what he deserves."

I stepped back and pressed myself against the wall, where I could stay hidden. I held my breath so that I could hear better. I didn't move a muscle.

"No, for real. He fell kinda hard."

"For real, who cares?" the first one balked. "Nobody likes that sissy anyways. Let's go."

They disappeared around the corner. I stayed there, re-playing their words in my head. Something had happened inside that locker room. Someone was hurt. I waited until I knew those two weren't going to see me coming behind them, and then I ran to find help.

SCOTT

Coach Holmes had started the Halloween dance as a fund-raiser for the booster club a few years back. Maybe he wasn't the best football coach, but he had scored a touchdown with this event. It was the talk of the school. I couldn't wait.

My favorite thing about the dance was that you had to dress in a costume. I wore my Gryffindor stuff. Natalie and Randi waltzed in as cowgirls. Gavin made a funny hippie, but Trevor and Mark would've won my vote for awesomest costumes. They showed up as Batman and Robin. Everyone looked terrific. The only costumes I didn't like were Nicky's and Adam's. They came in wearing scary horror-movie masks.

It was fun seeing the different costumes, and I made sure I got to see all of them, by volunteering at the admissions table. Coach Holmes had decided to let me work that spot because of my knack with numbers. What he didn't know was that the real reason I wanted to be there was so I could get a good estimate of how much money the dance raised. I was going to include that in my article for the newspaper.

I spent the first hour sitting behind the table alongside Mrs. Woods. I hadn't even known she was coming, but she'd volunteered her time because she'd heard this was an occasion not to be missed. She was great at keeping things organized, so I was glad she was my partner. After most people had arrived, she told me to go inside and have some fun, and that's what I did. It was incredible. There was a haunted house on one side of the gym, and as soon as you exited it, you got in line for a chance to put Mr. Allen under in the dunking booth. It cost one dollar to do both.

The dance floor was packed with bodies, and the concessions table just outside the gym had these huge cookies and brownies. I would've volunteered to work that station if I'd known about it. I spent five dollars on the brownies to show my appreciation, and that made me so thirsty, I had to spend another five dollars on drinks so that I could wash the brownies down. I asked the woman serving me how much she had sold, and she told me almost two thousand dollars' worth. My eyes got big. Between that and the inside attractions and admission, Coach Holmes was looking to make close to ten grand. He was going to love my article. I was going to make him sound like a hero. I was going to win him over yet.

I went back inside the gym, but I didn't last long, because those sodas I'd guzzled had me needing to pee so bad that I would've been dancing even without the music. I ran into the locker room. The urinal was out of order, so I ducked into one of the stalls. You know you have to go bad when the sound of your pee stream hitting the toilet water echoes off the walls.

This is where my memory of things gets a little fuzzy. I remember it going pitch black when the lights turned off, and the sound of my peeing stopped because I started missing my target. When that happens, you shoot in the dark until you hit the bowl again, and then you don't move. I found the water after swiping my stream back and forth a couple of times, so I didn't make that big a mess.

Feeling blind, I used my hands to find my way out of the stall after I was done. I would've gone to the sink to wash, but I couldn't see, so I skipped that. I kept one hand on the wall and inched my way along.

"We'll help you," a voice said, startling me. I squinted, but I couldn't see who it was.

"Yeah, *stick* with us," a different voice said.

I remember the word "stick" sounding funny, and then I remember getting sprayed with a wet mist. It burned my eyes, and when I yelled, it got in my mouth and burned more. I jerked and twisted and tried to get away, but whoever was there grabbed me. I fought harder, but I couldn't move.

The last thing I remember is falling.

Trevor

Randi grabbed Mark and me. "Someone" —heavy breathing—
"needs help" —heavy breathing—"in the boys' locker room."

Mark and I looked at each other, puzzled.

"Dude, slow down," Mark said. "What're you talking about?"

She answered in one run-on breath. "I think it's Scott. Quick!"

We bolted.

It was pitch black when we burst into the locker room. Mark found the light switch and flipped it on.

"Scott!" I called.

No response.

"Scott!"

Still nothing. Talk about making your heart race. Mine took off, beating faster than it had when I'd been on the dance floor. I hurried around the corner.

Randi's panicked words had scared me, but when I found

Scott, scared went to another level. Terrified was more like it. He lay on the ground by the showers—unconscious.

"Go get help!" I screamed.

I knelt by Scott's side while Mark ran off. I didn't know what to do. I'd never felt so helpless. "We're here now, buddy. We've got you," I whispered.

Mark wasn't gone more than a couple of minutes, but those were some of the longest minutes of my life. Scott didn't start stirring until Mark got back with Mr. Allen. I let out a sigh of relief. Mr. Allen got down on the ground next to me. "What happened?" he asked.

"I don't know. We came in here and found him like this." But I did know. His hair was stuck to his forehead and his cheeks were tacky, too.

"Scott, are you okay? Tell me your full name," Mr. Allen said. "Do you know where you are?"

When Scott couldn't answer those questions, I got even more worried. When he rolled to the side and started vomiting, terrified went to a level I couldn't even measure. This was serious. Mr. Allen grabbed his phone and called 911.

Natalie Kurtsman
ASPIRING LAWYER
Kurtsman Law Offices

BRIEF #10
Halloween: Concussed

The doctors ran a bunch of tests, and they all came back with good news. Scott's skull wasn't fractured and there was no internal bleeding. But he did have a serious concussion. It was unclear how long Scott had been unconscious, so only time would reveal the severity of his injury. The one thing the doctors did promise was that Scott had a long road to full recovery. He couldn't remember simple stuff, like the fact that he'd been at a Halloween dance.

GAVIN

The best the doctors could figure, Scott had fallen in the locker room and hit his head on the shower wall on his way to the ground. Everyone supposed he had slipped on water, which mighta been true, but I knew he'd had help falling.

He wasn't supposed to be out of my sight. I could take anything Coach Holmes dished out, anything Nicky and Adam wanted to say or try, but they'd crossed the line by hurting Scott. They were dead meat.

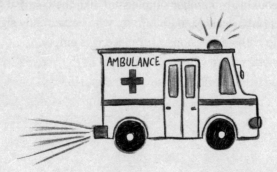

Trevor

By the time we got home from the hospital, it was close to midnight. I felt like I was the one who'd been hit on the head. It's crazy how exhausted you feel after your nerves have been on edge. I almost didn't check the video camera tape, because I was beat. Besides that, I didn't expect to find anything—not on Halloween. But if you stop and think about it, Halloween's actually a great time to steal something, because you don't look suspicious approaching a house dressed in all black. It was also a good time to rob our house because all three of us had been at the Halloween dance. After a successful date night, Dad had decided to join Mom, who had already signed up to help with concessions. Our place was empty.

The moment I saw his face flash across the screen, I went from dead tired to wide awake. I had him. He was done.

BRIEF #11
November: The Day After

Mother and I took the next afternoon to visit Scott and his family at their house. Mother brought a dish of her homemade lasagna and I carried a copy of *To Kill a Mockingbird,* in case Scott wanted me to read.

When we arrived, we were greeted by Mrs. Mason and Mrs. Woods, who was just leaving. Mrs. Mason led Mother inside so that she could put her lasagna in the refrigerator, but I stayed back to ask Mrs. Woods a question. Randi had seen two boys coming out of the locker room, only she didn't have a description, and Gavin, Trevor, and Mark seemed certain that Scott didn't slip and fall on his own.

"Mrs. Woods, would you agree that the right article in our school newspaper might help Mr. Allen get to the bottom of what happened?"

"That's my girl." She patted my arm. "Send it to me tonight

so I can read it. You need to move fast on this, Miss Kurtsman. We go to print in the morning."

"I will."

I watched my teacher walk to her car and drive away, and then I turned and headed into the house.

"How's he doing?" I heard Mother asking when I entered the kitchen.

It was a simple question that anyone would ask, but Mrs. Mason had reached her breaking point. She closed the refrigerator and slowly turned around. And then she started crying. Instantly Mother walked over and hugged her. "I feel so bad for him," Mrs. Mason said through her tears.

"Natalie, pull a chair out," Mother said, nodding toward the table.

I did, and Mother helped Mrs. Mason sit down. I found a mug and poured Mrs. Mason a cup of coffee.

"Thank you, Natalie." Mrs. Mason said, and took a sip.

Mother sat down with her, and I went to pour a second cup.

"He's got a long road ahead," Mrs. Mason began. "He needs to be kept out of school and all activities, which means no football, newspaper club, or Senior Center visits until his symptoms are gone. He can have no screen time and do no reading. If he does anything that causes a headache, he must stop immediately. Nobody can predict how long this will take."

Mother reached across the table and held Mrs. Mason's hand. Part of being a great lawyer was knowing how to squish the bad guy, but there was another part for knowing when to comfort and console your client, or in this case, a friend.

I placed the second cup in front of Mother and excused myself. It was time for me to go check on *my* friend. I found him on the floor in his bedroom, building with LEGOs.

"Hi, Scott."

"Hi," he said. I noticed that he didn't say my name. Was that because he couldn't remember it?

"What're you building?" I asked.

"Nothing, really. I'm just sticking bricks together without thinking. Thinking gives me headaches."

"Oh." I sat down across from him and picked up a red and a yellow and stuck them together. "I know you were doing an article on the Halloween dance for our newspaper, but I'll take care of that for you. You don't need to worry."

He stopped building and looked at me, confusion evident in his face. "What newspaper?"

I wanted to hug him right then, but I held it together. I explained things to him, speaking slowly, and while I was talking, I spotted the notebook I'd seen him using in school—the same one he'd had with him last night at the dance. I picked it up and thumbed through it to see if he had started the article, thinking that might help him remember. I didn't find many sentences, but I did find a bunch of calculations.

"Do you remember what you were doing here?" I asked, showing him the pages.

He squinted at his notes. "Estimating how much money the dance raised for the booster club."

I smiled. Numbers made sense to him even when he was confused. "You also have a list of sports written down here. Do you remember why?"

Scott looked puzzled. He shook his head. "I don't know."

"I think you wrote the word 'interview' over here, but it's hard to read your writing."

"Oh yeah. I wanted to talk to different teams and find out how the booster club's money had helped them in the past."

"What a great idea!" I exclaimed. "Do you mind if I take your notebook, so I can use it to write the article you wanted?"

"Sure."

"I'll show it to you when I have it written."

He shrugged. "My head is hurting. I need to lie down."

"I'll leave you alone so you can rest. Feel better, Stats Man."

He waved, but he didn't smile. Indeed, it was going to be a long road to recovery.

GOALS

- Resolve the strained relationship between Mrs. Woods and Mrs. Magenta. (Baby steps.)
- Keep our plan secret, which requires keeping Scott and the rest of the Recruits quiet—but mainly Scott. (Sadly, this will be easier now.)
- Teach Mrs. Davids how to read—and keep our work secret. (Steady progress.)
- Nail the bad guys responsible for Scott's injury. (I'm on it.)
- Finish the article on the booster club for Scott. (Coming soon.)

I'll tell you now, accomplishing the last two goals was easy. What was difficult—and scary—was everything that came after that.

Trevor

I watched the tape three times that night to make sure I wasn't missing anything. I couldn't capture everything with the one camera I'd installed, but I had enough. I had a perfect shot of Chris's pretty face.

It wasn't until later the next afternoon that I finally got the courage to show Dad the tape. I didn't say much. I just told him I had something I wanted him to watch. I had Mom sit in front of my computer, and Dad stood behind her. Then I clicked play and let the film do the explaining.

Mom gasped when she saw Chris on the screen. Dad's hands squeezed the back of her chair. He leaned forward, glaring at our thief.

When the tape ended, my parents didn't move. Neither did I. It can take a few minutes for shock to wear off, so I was patient. When Dad finally spoke, I felt the pain in his voice.

"Trev . . . I'm sorry. I never should've blamed you. It's

just . . . I failed your brother, and I thought I'd failed you, too. I'm sorry. I made a mistake."

"Your mistake was having me," I muttered.

"Trevor, no—" Mom started.

"It's true," I said, cutting her off. "I know you never wanted me in the first place. I was a mistake. I'll always be a mistake."

Mom covered her face with her hands. She was crying.

"That's more crap you heard from your brother, isn't it?" Dad fired at me.

I didn't answer.

"You're better off forgetting anything he ever told you. Yeah, it's true your mother and I weren't trying to have another baby, but we also weren't *not* trying, so you can't be considered a mistake. What you were was a surprise. Sometimes surprises are bad; sometimes they're good. And you were the best surprise we could've asked for. Don't you ever forget that." He jabbed me in the chest with his finger and then walked out of my room.

Dad's fiery temper hadn't startled me, but his words had. Mom was still crying, but she got up from her chair and pulled me into a hug.

"We love you, honey," she whispered. Her arms relaxed, and she stepped back and wiped her face. Then she looked at me. "We love your brother, too, which is why it's so hard to see him struggling and making poor decisions. Your father blames himself because he wasn't around enough for Brian. He's trying hard not to let that happen with you. He might not always be right, but remember what he just told you. It's the truth."

My throat tightened.

After she left, I sat on my bed. Sharing feelings and saying hard stuff out loud can be more exhausting than a football game. I'd cleared my name and nailed Chris. But what about Brian? I wanted to help my brother so Dad could see he hadn't failed.

9

THE FINAL GAME

Randi

Mom drove Gav and me over to Scott's house on Sunday afternoon so that we could see how he was doing. Mom had made a casserole, and Gav and I brought a tin of chocolate chip cookies. Mrs. Mason appreciated the food, and Mickey squealed when he saw the treats—there was no mistaking that he was Scott's brother—but we didn't stay long because Scott was sleeping. Mrs. Woods and Natalie had visited him earlier, and he was wiped out.

"The doctor said he would be very tired for the next week or more, and that rest is the best thing for him," Mrs. Mason explained. "I'll tell him you were here."

Gav and I were disappointed, but we understood.

"I'm sure you could use some rest yourself," Mom said. "We'll get out of your hair, but let us know if you need any-thing—or if Scott does. We're here."

"Thank you," Mrs. Mason said.

Our visit was short and sweet, but I'd wanted Scott to know we were thinking of him.

On Monday the talk of the school was the dance. Nothing about Scott. Most people still didn't even know that anything had happened. The ambulance had swooped in from the back and disappeared just as fast. It felt like no one cared about my friend—but Natalie took care of that.

Mrs. Woods had spent all morning printing copies of the first edition of the *Lake View Times* so that we could spend our lunch period distributing them throughout the school. "Nicely done, Miss Kurtsman," she said when she dropped the papers off to us. "Couldn't have said it any better myself."

"I just hope it helps," Natalie said.

"It will," Mrs. Woods assured her. "I have no doubts about that. Now get those papers delivered," she urged the rest of us. "It's important. I'd help, but I have to rush off. I'm parked illegally."

I watched her leave, and then I looked down. My eyes popped when I saw Natalie's editorial front and center. OUT FOR JUSTICE blazed across the page in big bold letters. She detailed Scott's accident and asked for anyone with information to report it to Mr. Allen. Her piece closed with a warning to the guilty: *You can run, but you can't hide.* It was cheesy, but it was fantastic.

Mrs. Woods was right. Come Tuesday, the talk of our school turned to our paper and to Scott. Mr. Allen made a special morning announcement, publicly thanking Natalie for her reporting and urging anyone with information about the incident to come and see him, like her article said. If students hadn't known about Scott getting hurt, they did now. I wanted to believe we'd catch the kids responsible for his accident, but as far as I knew, I was the only person who'd seen the boys come out of the locker room—and it wasn't like I'd gotten a good look at them. I'd gone to Mr. Allen on Monday and had done my best to describe them, but I had no idea who they were.

"I can't wait till football practice tomorrow," Gav said at lunch. I thought this sounded odd, because I knew football wasn't going well for him.

"Why?" I asked.

"'Cause I'm not letting Nicky and Adam get away with this. Mr. Allen can do his investigating, but I'm gonna make sure those two pay the price, even if it means running till I drop."

"I'm right there with you," Mark said.

Gav snarled.

"Who're Nicky and Adam?" I asked

"They're the ones who hurt Scott," Gav replied.

"Wait, you know who did it? Why haven't you told me? And how can you be so sure?"

Trevor plopped down across from Natalie and me, interrupting the conversation.

"Dude, where've you been?" Mark asked.

"With Mr. Allen. He wanted to talk to me about the dance. He wants to see you now. The guy's been meeting with students all morning. Natalie's article has got everyone buzzing." Trevor smiled at her, and she looked away.

"Nice work, Kurtsman," Gav said.

"Mr. Allen wants to nail those jerks as much as we do," Trevor said.

"Did you tell him Nicky and Adam were the ones who did it?" Mark asked.

"You bet. I've had enough of those punks. They're going down."

Mark stood. "Good. Mr. Allen's going to hear the same thing from me." He took his tray and left us sitting there.

"How do you guys know Nicky and Adam did it, whoever they are?" I asked.

Gav looked at me, then at Natalie and Trevor, then back at me. "'Cause they wanted to get even," he said.

"Even for what?" Natalie asked.

Gav sighed. "Scott was being Scott, trying to do everyone on the team a favor by cleaning our helmets before our first game . . ."

After learning about the Stickum story, I had to go back to Mr. Allen. "Water Boy's getting what he deserves," one boy had said. It wasn't much, but I wanted to do everything in my power to help. And once I finished with Mr. Allen, I was getting Gav to talk, because I was beginning to realize how little I really knew about the football team and all that he'd been dealing with.

NATALIE KURTSMAN
ASPIRING LAWYER
Kurtsman Law Offices

```
BRIEF #12
November: A Fly on the Wall
```

There are instances when a trial lawyer needs to become an investigator. The same can be said for a journalist. I was both a trial lawyer and a journalist, and my time to do some digging had arrived. That was not what I'd had in mind when I'd started, but things took a turn and put me on a new path, where nothing was what I'd expected.

Originally I had planned on including three short interviews with Scott's article: one with the field hockey coach, one with the girls' soccer coach, and one with the boys' soccer coach. I was trying to decide if I also wanted to examine gender equality at Lake View Middle School, but I soon discovered that we had a much bigger issue on our hands.

At the conclusion of my interviews, I'd learned that the field hockey and soccer programs (both boys' and girls') hadn't received any support from the booster club in the last three years, meaning no new equipment, uniforms, warm-ups . . . nothing.

Curious and perplexed, I decided on my next move. Objective: to share my findings with Mr. Allen.

I trusted that my principal would be able to provide additional information and perhaps a possible explanation. Instead, when I arrived at his office, I found Mr. Allen in the midst of a conversation with someone else. It was well after school hours, so no one else was around. I decided to take a seat and wait. The exchange I overheard was alarming.

"Mr. Holmes, thank you for coming in so that we could meet. I know you have practice to get to, so I'll try not to take long, but this is something that couldn't wait. After conducting a thorough investigation into the incident involving Scott Mason at the Halloween dance, we have reason to believe your son and Adam Frazier were responsible."

"Oh yeah? Where's your proof?" Mr. Holmes challenged.

That was not the response I'd been expecting, but I didn't know Mr. Holmes like the guys did. I slid into the chair closest to Mr. Allen's office, but with the way things escalated, I could've heard them from the hall.

"Mr. Holmes, I was hoping you'd approach this situation in a cooperative manner," Mr. Allen responded, maintaining his calm demeanor. "I understand that this news about Nicky has to be upsetting."

"My son hasn't done anything wrong," Mr. Holmes growled.

"I've had numerous students come to me to report differently. There's even a witness—someone who saw two boys leaving the locker room just before Scott was found—who heard them refer to Scott as 'Water Boy.' Does that ring a bell?"

"Those kids are lying," Coach Holmes argued.

"Mr. Holmes, we are obviously not in agreement. I have mounting evidence and even a confession that says otherwise. Your son and Adam Frazier need to be held accountable for their actions. Therefore, we are suspending them from school for five days and from football for the remainder of the season."

"What!" Mr. Holmes roared. "I never should've let that little sissy be a part of my program. I don't care about any confession; this is all his fault. I was trying to be nice, and look at what's happened. That kid belongs in a skirt, not on my sideline."

"Mr. Holmes, please do not talk about a student that way. Scott Mason is a terrific person and representative of our school. You should consider yourself lucky to have him involved with the football team."

"Lucky? Ha! The only kid worse than him is that Davids. No Mexican is playing for me, I can tell you that. If you really want to help the situation, then you should tell that dirty half-breed and his loser sidekick to join a different program."

"Mr. Holmes, you have crossed the line!" I heard Mr. Allen's hands slap on his desk and his chair fly back. I pictured him on his feet, glaring across at Mr. Holmes. "What you just said is completely offensive, racist, and unacceptable from anyone within our school community. You and Coach Frazier will sit out this last game. And we'll have to see if your futures include coaching at Lake View Middle after this season."

"You just killed the best program at this school," Mr. Holmes countered. "It's people like you who're ruining this country."

Stay or go? Stay or go? My indecisiveness left me trapped. Mr. Holmes came charging out of Mr. Allen's office.

"Who're you?" he barked, spotting me in the chair.

I sat up straight. "I'm Natalie," I said, finding my firm voice. "Natalie Kurtsman. I'm with the school newspaper. I'm here to talk to Mr. Allen about an article I'm writing."

"Oh yeah? Here's a headline for you: FOOTBALL PROGRAM GOES TO MEXICO ALONG WITH OUR JOBS."

A lawyer can't allow herself to get agitated by the witness. I maintained my composure, but it was not easy. I wanted to tell this horrible man that the headline was going to read: FOOTBALL PROGRAM SAVED BY MEXICAN SUPERSTAR, but I held my tongue. Mr. Holmes yanked the door open and stormed out of the office.

"Hello, Natalie," Mr. Allen said. "How much of that conversation did you hear?"

"Enough," I said.

"That's what I was afraid of. Natalie, I do not believe that Mr. Holmes is a racist man, but he is an angry man. Let me explain something to you. Several years ago the factory where he was working shut down and moved to Mexico. He, along with many others, lost his job. Unfortunately, Mr. Holmes seems to be taking his anger out on anything and anyone Mexican, which I gather has included Gavin."

"But that's totally unfair."

"For whom?"

"Gavin, of course . . . and Mr. Holmes."

"Life can be complicated, Natalie."

I nodded. "It's not always black-and-white," I said, thinking back to last year. I acted like I knew what I was talking about, but I didn't know the half of it. Things were going to get extremely complicated before the end.

"So, what did you want to see me about?" Mr. Allen asked.

I told him about the article I was writing, and he provided me with the names and emails of all the coaches for Lake View's sports program. I made it quick because he was on his way to football practice, where he had news to share.

I thanked Mr. Allen and left with the information, unaware that I was one step closer to uncovering a bombshell.

Trevor

"Holmes" and "Frazier" happen to be the names of two very famous old-time boxing legends—Larry Holmes and Joe Frazier. Both were former champions who fought against the greatest, Muhammad Ali. But you would've thought my football coaches were the same Holmes and Frazier, the way they went after each other before practice that day.

I was putting on my pads when Coach Holmes came storming into the locker room. "Frazier! Where are you?" he yelled.

Coach Frazier and Adam stopped what they were doing. Was Coach Holmes searching for the dad or the kid? Or both? It didn't take long to get answers.

Coach Holmes never slowed down. He lowered his shoulder and tackled Coach Frazier. Their tangled bodies bounced off the lockers and benches and hit the ground, but they didn't stop there. They continued rolling and wrestling and throwing punches.

"Dad!" Nicky screamed.

"Dad!" Adam screamed.

The team jumped into action, half of us grabbing Holmes and half of us grabbing Frazier. It wasn't easy, but we managed to pull them apart.

"What's wrong with you?" Coach Frazier yelled, wiping blood from his mouth.

"We've been sacked because your wuss of a son went ahead and ratted on Nicky," Coach Holmes said, rubbing the egg that was bulging over his eye.

"You told?" Nicky said, turning and looking at Adam, his voice full of disbelief.

When Adam didn't respond, Nicky's stare hardened. I was ready for those two to go at it next, but before that happened, we got another surprise.

"Gentlemen, is everything okay here?" Mr. Allen asked, entering our locker room in the nick of time. A few seconds later and he might've arrived to an all-out bloody battle royal.

No one answered.

"Gentlemen?" Mr. Allen repeated.

"Let's go, Nicky. We're outta here," Coach Holmes said, bumping Mr. Allen on his way out. Nicky hesitated, still staring at his old friend.

"Scott got hurt, Nick," Adam said. "I'm sorry."

Nicky spit on the floor near Adam's feet. Then he threw his helmet in his locker and stormed out behind his dad.

Coach Frazier put a hand on Adam's shoulder. Together they left quietly, following Mr. Allen outside. The second they were gone, the entire locker room started breathing again. And then erupted in talk.

"Holy crap! Did you see that?"

"That was awesome!"

"Dude, they dented the lockers."

Something as crazy and unexpected as what we'd just witnessed gets you excited. We replayed the action blow by blow, stretching it and making it better, until Mr. Allen came back to give us the lowdown.

"Have a seat, boys," Mr. Allen said. "I'm here to tell you that today's practice is canceled." No surprise there. "Moving forward, you will be without Nicky Holmes and Adam Frazier. They have been suspended from football for the remainder of the season for their involvement in Scott Mason's accident at the Halloween dance." Mr. Allen glanced around the room while he let this sink in. "In addition," he continued, "you will be without Coach Holmes and Coach Frazier. They have been sidelined for their inappropriate conduct as coaches. I'm not going to elaborate any more on that subject, but you should know that we will work to find a replacement coach as soon as possible, so that you can begin preparing for your final game."

"Mr. Allen, I know the perfect person to be our coach," Gavin said.

"Excellent. Send them to me."

I knew exactly who Gavin had in mind. I hoped it worked.

After Mr. Allen finished talking, we took off our stuff and closed our lockers. Talk about a crazy afternoon. Even though the future of our team was uncertain, uncertain was way better than Coach Holmes and his precious Nicky.

Just when I thought I finally had lots to talk about at our usually silent family dinner table, something else I wasn't expecting happened. My father never showed up for dinner. No explanation. So much for trying. By the time he got home, his food was ice-cold. I wasn't in the mood for talking at that point. Neither was Dad. He didn't only come home late. He came home angry.

GAVIN

"Valentine, things like this have a way of working themselves out," Coach had told me. "That's one of the beauties about sports. Good things happen to people who work hard."

I don't think I ever coulda predicted the way things worked out, but it felt like a brand-new season. For the final game, football became everything I'd dreamed about and wanted. I was so happy.

Too bad that Holmes's being gone from football didn't mean being gone for good, though. I hadn't heard the last from him.

SCOTT

Sleeping and resting were the only things I was allowed to do. That was what Dr. Pirani recommended if I wanted to get better, and I did a good job. I did so much sleeping that I don't even remember November. I almost slept the month away.

Thanksgiving was right around the corner, and I still wasn't back to school yet. My headaches were getting better, but the doctor said if I rushed it, I would only make things worse, and then I might not return to school at all. My brain still needed rest if I wanted to fully recover. Those were the rules. But sometimes there are what my Mom called "extenuating circumstances," at least that's what she told Dr. Pirani when she called to tell her I was needed on the sideline at our final football game. Mom explained the situation to her, and Dr. Pirani gave me the green light—but just for the game. That was all I wanted. I was super-happy.

Finally, during our last game of the season, I got the chance to be Stats Man. Even better, I was Stats Man alongside Coach Woods and his two assistants, Mrs. Woods and Mrs. Magenta.

I didn't know how all that got sorted out, but if you asked me, it couldn't have been any better. Gavin led the way as our quarterback. Coach was right when he said that things have a way of working themselves out.

My memory of events before the accident still wasn't perfect, but I knew the answer when Coach turned to me for advice. "You know these boys better than I do, Junior. What should we call to start the game?"

"Onside kick," I said. "Let's catch them Titans sleeping."

And that was exactly what we did. We recovered the opening kickoff and showed the undefeated Titans of North Lake that the Warriors meant business. They hadn't see the likes of Coach Woods or Gavin all year.

Late in the fourth quarter we were trailing 32–28. Gavin had already thrown for four touchdowns and more than three hundred yards, breaking a school record. The only thing left for him to do was lead the team on a game-winning drive. Coach Woods had called a time-out and had the offense huddled around him by the sideline.

"Junior," he said, "what do you see out there?"

I swallowed. This wasn't only Gavin's moment but mine, too. "We've been doing better running to the right all day . . . so their defensive backs on the left are getting overaggressive. They're attacking the run and leaving our guys open. I think we should try a toss right, quarterback throw-back on the left," I said.

The faces around me lit up. "Yeah! Let's do it!" the guys cheered.

Gavin slapped me five. "Great idea, Junior."

Coach called the play and sent the offense out to run it,

but not before he grabbed Gavin by the pads and held him back for a final word. I didn't hear what he said, but whatever it was, it jolted Mrs. Woods and Mrs. Magenta. They gasped and looked at each other like I'd never seen them do before. Gavin jogged onto the field and took his spot behind our center. He yelled the cadence, and the ball was snapped.

I held my breath.

Gavin turned and tossed the ball to Mark, who ran right. Gavin spun back and took off down the left sideline. The defense swarmed in pursuit of Mark, and when he had them sucked in, he stopped, planted his feet, and threw the ball back across the field to our wide-open quarterback. Gavin caught the pass and scampered down the far side of the field. He scored the winning touchdown as time expired.

The celebration that followed was better than a birthday party. We ran around the field, yelling and high-fiving. Gavin and I found each other, and he picked me up in a bear hug.

"Great play call, Stats Man."

"Great game, quarterback. You did it."

He put me down and looked me in the eye. "We did it."

I smiled. "Can coaches get inducted into the Hall of Fame?" I asked him.

Gavin grinned. "C'mon," he said, "we've got to shake hands."

My head was hurting, but I'd rest later. I had to do some more celebrating first.

GAVIN

Maybe I owed Coach Holmes a big thank-you. If he hadn't made me do all that running, there's no way I would've outlasted number twenty-five sprinting down the sideline. That kid almost caught me. Almost.

My teammates swarmed me in the end zone, yelling and cheering, smacking me on the pads and helmet. My nightmare season had a storybook ending like that one in *ECHO*. Me and Coach Woods got to smile when shaking hands, 'cause we'd won. Our smiles wouldn't last forever, though, 'cause there was something much bigger than football at stake—I just didn't know it yet. I would soon, but for the moment everything was perfect.

When I walked back to our sideline, Kurtsman and Randi were waiting for me. Randi gave me a huge hug.

"You're the best, Gav. You were awesome."

"Thanks for always passing the ball with me," I said. "You helped make today happen."

She squeezed harder.

"Nice home run, Davids," Kurtsman said, winking at me. She'd managed to learn a few things about America's game—finally. I smiled, but then she quickly moved on to more important stuff. "What did Coach say to you during that last time-out? It seemed important. It seemed to rattle Mrs. Woods and Mrs. Magenta."

"Really?"

"Yes, so what did he say?"

"Gavvy!" Meggie cried. My little sister came running over. "You did it!" She wrapped her arms around my waist, and I went soft inside.

Mom and Dad joined us. Dad patted the back of my neck, and Mom kissed me on the cheek. "I'm so proud of you, *Niño*."

"Thanks," I said. "I've got to get to the locker room, so I'll see you in a few minutes."

I took off at a jog toward the school.

"Gavin," Kurtsman called.

"I'll tell you later," I yelled over my shoulder. I had to keep going. I was the last one leaving the field. After you score the winning TD, everyone wants to congratulate you.

I got to the locker room right as Coach was getting ready to give us his postgame speech. Grandpa was nearby, just in case, 'cause Magenta and Woods couldn't come in. I'd heard many of Coach's talks at the Senior Center, but here we were, for real. We grew quiet, ready to hang on his every word.

"Gentlemen, how about a hand for our Stats Man, for calling that last play of the game?"

"Woot! Woot!" we cheered.

I'd never seen a bigger smile than the one stretched across

Scott's face. He beamed, but he also covered his ears. Head-ache. He was a lucky kid and a poor kid at the same time.

"Gentlemen," Coach continued, "I want to thank you for giving me the opportunity to lead you today. It's the best pres-ent I've received in a long, long time. Go home and celebrate with your families. You've got reason to be proud and happy, and you've got much to be thankful for."

I stood and started clapping, and it only took another sec-ond before everyone joined me. I was the last one to leave the locker room that day. I was in no rush. I savored the memory, replaying the highlights of the game in my head. I clung to and remembered every detail about my dream game, but in the end the one thing that wouldn't leave me alone was the same thing Kurtsman had asked about. The moment when Coach had pulled me aside during our final time-out.

I thumbed the letters on my quarterback towel.

Randi

With Gav's incredible football game and Scott's great work on the sideline, and the moment when Mrs. Woods and Mrs. Magenta stared deep into each other's souls, and then with Scott leaving with a headache after it was all said and done, I had a lot on my mind. Mental exhaustion can be worse than physical exhaustion, which explains why I felt wiped out, like I'd just completed a gymnastics workout, and why I forgot to grab the mail when we got home.

I was sitting at the kitchen table with a glass of seltzer water when Mom came walking in, carrying the day's stack of envelopes. She dropped the pile onto the counter—all except for the one she held up. "Do you know what this is?"

I almost died. "No," I croaked.

"It's an invite to your first national competition—the Elite Stars Festival!" Mom exclaimed. "I'm going to call Coach Andrea. This is it, Randi. Your big chance."

Mom gave me a quick hug, then took the phone and slipped into the other room. She was excited to the point where I wondered if a little Jane was coming out, but I could deal with that later. I was excited, too. A national competition would be amazing. But first things first. I had to check the rest of the mail.

I rose from my chair and snuck over to the counter. I sifted through the envelopes and found one from Kyle sitting on the bottom. What were the chances? That had been a close call. Way too close.

I snuck the letter under my shirt and scurried up to my room. I closed my door and sat down. Then I tore open the envelope. *I found this,* Kyle wrote. *Also, we'll be at the Elite Stars Festival. If you go, it could be your big chance.*

This was a photo of toddler Kyle and his dad. There was no doubt about it anymore. Kyle was my half brother.

"Randi," Mom called up from downstairs. "I talked to Coach Andrea. We're going!"

My big chance. Destiny, I hope you know what you're doing.

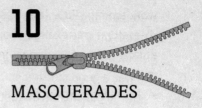

10

MASQUERADES

NATALIE KURTSMAN
ASPIRING LAWYER
Kurtsman Law Offices

BRIEF #13
December: Accident

My meetings with Mrs. Davids had been going extremely well. I'm confident in saying that was partly because I was a good teacher but mostly because Mrs. Davids was a quick learner. She was a smart lady. I found myself wondering more and more why she hadn't already learned how to read English. But as much as I wanted to ask, I knew it wasn't my place. I kept my questions to myself and focused my attention on the work before us. If I pushed for too many answers, I feared our lessons would end.

As stated, we were making great progress. During one of our lessons in November, Mrs. Davids had been able to take a picture book and read it to Meggie for the first time. Watching them cuddled together was one of the best feelings I've ever experienced. Especially because Mrs. Davids and Meggie were hatching their own secret plan. It was going to come to fruition on Christmas Eve. I wished I could be there to see it unfold, but I relied on Meggie to tell me all about it afterward; she was a good storyteller.

At the conclusion of another successful session, I checked out the books Meggie had selected, which had become part of our normal routine. Why Mrs. Davids still hadn't obtained a library card of her own was beyond me, but that was another one of those questions I kept to myself. It was no problem for me to check the books out using my card, so that's what I did.

Mrs. Woods didn't force the issue when she was around, either. She never said a word on the matter. I was quite certain my old teacher was fully aware of my extracurricular activities and what Mrs. Davids and I were doing, but she chose to stay quiet about that, too. I also had the inkling Mrs. Woods knew I was aware of her situation with Mrs. Magenta, and that I was keeping that information to myself. We seemed to have ourselves a silent agreement: *I won't say anything if you don't say anything.*

When we finished checking the books out, I grabbed my things and walked with Mrs. Davids and Meggie to the exit. Mother was waiting for me in our car at the end of the street. It was cold and spitting snow, but I stood on the sidewalk and watched little Meggie and Mrs. Davids climb into their car. Mrs. Davids pulled away from the curb, and I turned and hurried along toward Mother.

I'm not a scout, nor will I ever be, but I pride myself on being prepared. This is precisely why I work hard. But the fact remains, there are some things you simply can't prepare for—what happened next is a case in point.

First I saw the look of horror that spread over Mother's face. Then came the terrible sound of metal smashing into metal. I stopped dead in my tracks, fearing the worst, and slowly turned around.

GAVIN

I had to stick around after school to turn in my equipment and clean out my locker. Since we were without coaches, Mr. Allen was there to give us a hand. The season was over. It hadn't come close to what I'd dreamed about all my life, but it couldn't have ended any better.

"Next year, Gavin," Mr. Allen said. "Next year will be your time to shine from start to finish. Don't lose faith." He patted me on the shoulder.

How much did Mr. Allen know about the way Holmes had been treating me? I didn't know, but something told me I could count on him looking out for me.

"Thanks," I said.

"You bet."

I left the locker room more determined than ever. I *was* going to make my mark next year. I was done with Holmes. Things were going to improve from here on. Turns out, I was dead wrong—about both of those things.

I walked out and hopped in the truck with Dad.

"Everything go all right?" he asked.

"Yup," I said, and I wasn't lying this time.

"Good." He put the truck in gear and drove out of the parking lot—and all was good, for a little while.

When we made it home, Dad pulled into the driveway and parked.

"Where are Mom and Meggie?" I asked.

"I don't know. Musta stepped out for somethin'. I'm sure they'll be back soon. I hope so. I'm starvin'."

"Maybe we should make dinner?"

"Eat your cookin'? You tryin' to kill me?"

I laughed and punched him in the arm. We went inside, and I got started on my homework while Dad got busy cleaning the house. I guess he figured if he couldn't cook, he could at least clean. When Mom and Megs still hadn't shown up after a couple of hours, I began worrying. So did Dad. He called Mom's cell but only got her voice mail. We tried to stay calm by making up excuses for them. Too bad we weren't even close.

The second we heard tires crunching stones in our driveway, me and Dad rushed to the door. It was Mom and Meggie all right, but not in Mom's car. Mrs. Kurtsman got out of the driver's seat, and Natalie climbed out of the back with Megs. She held Meggie's hand. Megs had been crying. I could see her red eyes all the way from the porch.

"Carla, what happened? Are you okay?" Dad asked, jumping off the porch and hurrying out to her. I was right behind him.

Mom didn't say anything.

"Gloria?" Dad said, turning to Mrs. Kurtsman for an explanation.

"Let's go inside," she said. "There was an accident. Everyone is fine, but there is much to explain."

I sat down at the kitchen table with Mom and Dad and Mrs. Kurtsman, and the first thing Mrs. Kurtsman said was, "Gavin, I need a few minutes to talk to your father alone. We'll fill you in afterward."

"I . . . I . . ."

"Go check on your sister," Dad said. "Read her some books."

What was going on? I'd never seen Mom like this. She hadn't said a word. She wouldn't even look at me!

"Just a few minutes, Gavin," Mrs. Kurtsman said. "Thank you."

I got up and left the kitchen. I felt like a zombie. My brain and body were numb. I shuffled my feet along the floor and into Meggie's bedroom. My frightened little sister came over and hugged me as soon as I walked in. "Megs, what happened?"

She shook her head hard and buried her face in my shirt.

"Don't make her talk about it," Kurtsman whispered. She motioned for me to sit next to her on Meggie's bed. "There was an accident," she explained. "A driver ran a stop sign and crashed into your mother and Meggie."

"Where? And how do you know this?" I asked, my voice rising.

Meggie covered her ears.

"Shhh," Kurtsman said, reaching out and rubbing Meggie's back.

"Sorry," I mouthed.

"It was outside the public library," Kurtsman whispered. "I was there. I saw it."

"Did anyone get hurt?"

"No. Like my mother said, everyone is okay."

"I don't get it. Why are you all acting so funny, then? Was our car totaled or something?"

Kurtsman nodded. "But that's not all."

I was confused. "What, then?"

"Gavin, your mother was arrested. . . . She doesn't have a driver's license."

NATALIE KURTSMAN
ASPIRING LAWYER
Kurtsman Law Offices

BRIEF #14
December: Too Many Secrets

Naturally, by the end of the next school day, the entire student body and faculty knew about Gavin's mother being arrested. At this point the arrest was nothing more than a quick local news story, but word traveled fast. It was only a matter of time before the rest of the story came out, and when that happened, well . . .

I was in the know on all of this because Mother was the legal counsel representing Carla Davids—that was a no-brainer—and Mother had decided to share all the details with me when we got home from Gavin's. Yes, one could argue that was a breach of the lawyer-client confidentiality contract, but Mother knew that everything she was telling me was going to become public knowledge, and when it did, things were going to get messy, so she wanted me informed. Prepared. Of course I was sworn to secrecy, but I was getting good at keeping secrets. Besides, I didn't need to stay mute for long. As expected, the rest of the story blew up three days later.

Coincidentally, three days later also happened to be Gavin's first trip back to school. There were silent stares and whispers—among students and teachers—all day long. *Wait until they get the full story,* I thought. It was weird; even we, his friends, didn't know what to say or how to act around him—me especially, since I was holding my breath, waiting for all the news to break. We needed Scott to kill the tension like only he could do.

I didn't know whether to expect Gavin at our newspaper meeting that afternoon or not; I was surprised he had even come to school to begin with, so I'd understand if he didn't show, but he was already waiting in the classroom when I arrived. Soon after me, Mrs. Woods entered, then Trevor and Mark followed by Randi, and last but not least, Mrs. Magenta. With our team assembled, I decided that carrying on in a normal way would be best—but I was wrong, which doesn't happen very often. In my defense, I'm not certain there was anything I could've done to prevent Gavin's outburst.

"Okay, everyone," I began. "Our first printing of the *Lake View Times* was a major success. Job well done. Now our school community is looking forward to our next release, so the pressure is on. Are there any ideas? What do we want to include?"

"How do you do it?" Gavin said.

I braced myself. "Do what?"

"Go along pretending everything's okay when you know it isn't? How do you do it?"

Here it comes, I thought.

Gavin turned and looked squarely at Mrs. Woods, then at Mrs. Magenta. "How do the two of you do it?" He didn't wait for their response. "We know all about your secret," he continued, his voice rising. "The mom and daughter who aren't talking because of some buried past. Coach is running out of time, and all he wants is to see you two together again. You think he doesn't know, but he does."

Mrs. Magenta gasped, and quickly covered her mouth. She was visibly shaken. Mrs. Woods, who could normally hold eye contact even longer than I could, turned away and gazed out the window.

"All these secrets we're keeping are only tearing our families apart," Gavin finished.

Tears streamed down his face—and Mrs. Magenta's, too. The anger and pain and sadness Gavin harbored had exploded from inside him. He bolted out the door, leaving the rest of us stunned. Stunned and speechless.

The word "masquerade," a verb, meaning "to go about under false pretenses or a false character," popped into my mind. Gavin had just called out Mrs. Woods and Mrs. Magenta for their masquerade. Our grand secret was a secret no more. And why? Because Gavin's mother had been living her own masquerade for his entire life. Imagine learning that one of the closest persons to you is not whom you had thought them to be. I couldn't blame him for his outburst.

Randi started to go after him.

I stopped her. "Randi," I said, grabbing her by the arm. "There's a lot going on with Gavin that you don't know about." I realized it would hurt her saying that, because she'd been his best friend for his whole existence.

224

"There's more? And you know about it?" She made no attempt to hide the pain in her voice. Her shoulders dropped.

"Yes, but not because he confided in me," I quickly explained. "I just happened to be there. It's complicated, but it's you he needs right now, not me. Go."

She looked up again. "We've been keeping too many secrets. Gav's right." She pulled the door open and left.

Randi

I'd never seen Gav like this. He'd just blown up. He was crying before he even got out of the room. He was hurting so bad, and I didn't know why. I was supposed to be his best friend, and I didn't know what was going on. But Natalie did, and that just made me feel worse. It made *me* angry. This is going to sound ridiculous, but I was jealous that Natalie knew what I didn't. Now I was one angry person going to find another angry person. You don't need psychic powers to know that that was the ingredients for a fight.

He was where I expected, sitting in the bleachers, staring out at the football field. It didn't matter that it was freezing out; football was Gav's sanctuary. The ball, the field, the game—they made him feel better. Or at least they used to. What did I know anymore?

I climbed the benches and sat next to him. I shivered when the metal seat touched my butt. "Gav, what's going on? Please tell me."

He slid away.

That was all it took. "So your girlfriend, Natalie, is allowed to know what's going on, but you can't tell me? I thought I was your best friend." I was out of there. I got up and started down the bleachers.

"Kurtsman's not my girlfriend. And you can go and cry on Kyle's shoulder."

I froze. How did he know? Slowly I turned around. "Who told you about Kyle?" I asked, the fight gone from me.

"You left your backpack sitting in the cafeteria and Scott kicked it over by accident. Kyle's picture fell out. But don't worry, no one else saw it, and I haven't told anybody about your stupid boyfriend. Is he the real reason you didn't come to my first game?"

"No. . . . No!" I said, shaking my head. "I told you why I didn't come. Gav, Kyle's not my boyfriend. He's my brother."

"What? What're you talking about? You don't have a brother."

"I didn't know I did, not until destiny had me meet him."

"You're making no sense."

"Gav, you're right, we've been keeping way too many secrets." I walked back up the bleachers and sat next to him. And then I told him everything about camp, and Kyle, and our dad.

"You should've told me," he said.

"Like I told you at the dance, I knew football wasn't going well, so I felt bad about sharing my good news. And I haven't told you about Kyle because . . . I don't know why. I'm sorry."

"What I dealt with during football was nothing compared to . . ."

"Compared to what? What's going on?"

"Let's just say you're not the only one who's discovered something about your family."

My face scrunched. "You mean about your mom not having a driver's license? Was it expired or something?" I rubbed my hands together, trying to warm them.

"No. She's never had one. She never even tried getting one."

"Why?"

Gav sighed. "'Cause my mom's an illegal immigrant."

I didn't get it. "What do you mean?"

"My mom's an illegal immigrant," he said again. "She's not a US citizen. She couldn't risk people finding that out. It's why she doesn't have a driver's license."

"An illegal immigrant? But how is that possible?"

He shrugged. "She just is."

"But why didn't your dad help her, then?"

"'Cause he didn't know she was illegal, either."

My mouth fell open. I couldn't believe it.

"Yeah, tell me about it," Gav said. "Surprise."

I stared out at the empty field, trying to wrap my head around everything he was telling me. I took a deep breath of cold air and asked the scary question. "Gav, what happens to illegal immigrants? They can't deport your mom, can they? I mean, she's married and has you and Meggie."

"Ready for the next whopper? . . . My parents aren't married."

"What!"

"They never got married. Neither one of them had the money for a wedding, and my dad says my mom didn't like the idea of going to city hall. Too unromantic. Truth is, she didn't want to 'cause she was worried they'd find out about her being illegal and deport her back then. My old man didn't know about her immigrant status, and he didn't make a stink about getting married. He said he didn't need to tie the knot to love my mother any more than he already did. My parents are more in love than most married people, for crying out loud, but now the government might take her away from us. How's Meggie supposed to be okay if that happens? Tell me that."

Tears ran down Gav's cheeks again. I cried with him. It was just like him to be thinking of Meggie. There was nothing I could say, so I just slid closer and hugged him.

We stayed that way, our bodies pressed together and warming each other, until Gav rubbed his eyes and wiped his face. "What happened with Woods and Magenta after I stormed out?" he asked.

I let go and sat back. "I don't know. I rushed out after you before they said or did anything."

"We'd better go check on them." And just like that he got up and started climbing down the bleachers. Apparently he was done with feeling sad. I followed him, happy to go inside where at least there was heat.

"Randi, what did your mother say when you told her about Kyle?" he asked over his shoulder.

When I didn't answer, he stopped and turned around. I couldn't look at him. I stared at the ground.

"You haven't told her, have you?"

I shook my head.

"You need to. You said it yourself, we need to stop with all these secrets. It just causes problems." Gav spun around and continued his march back to the school.

I stood there for a second before following him. I wanted to tell Mom, but it was going to be hard.

SCOTT

I still wasn't allowed to return to school. In hindsight Dr. Pirani decided the football game hadn't been a good idea. I'd been having a relapse of headaches ever since. It was too much too soon, but I told Dr. Pirani it had been worth it. My headaches were happening less again now. The thing I didn't like was that I couldn't remember everything about the game, but I didn't tell anyone that.

So I was at home with Mom again. Mickey was at preschool for the morning, which normally was Mom's chance to get some work done, but not that day. She was glued to the TV. I wasn't supposed to do screen time, but I walked into the living room to see what had her so interested. I saw Coach Holmes standing in a parking lot outside an empty factory. He held a sign that said DEPORT DAVIDS. There were other people holding signs, too. The reporter asked Coach Holmes to explain what was going on.

"I'll tell you what this is about," he said. "This factory behind me"—he thumbed in its direction—"used to be the place where I worked. It was the place where all of us worked. But now it's closed and our jobs are someplace south of the border, where those Mexicans will work for less money. And if that's not bad enough, we've got other Mexicans sneaking up here illegally and taking our jobs. They're nothing but trouble. That Davids lady is one of those illegals. She got caught, and now she needs to be sent back where she belongs. It's time to clean this country up."

"Did you know that Mrs. Davids is a mother? She's been here for seventeen years," the reporter said.

"Doesn't matter," Coach Holmes barked. "Just because she snuck over here and got pregnant doesn't mean she gets to stay. We've got laws. She broke them, and now she needs to pay the price."

Mom huffed in disgust and clicked off the TV. When she turned around, she was surprised to find me standing there. "Scott!" she exclaimed.

"What were you watching?" I asked.

"Just the news. Nothing much."

"Was that Gavin's mom that Coach Holmes was talking about?"

"You've been standing there for a few minutes?"

I nodded.

She sighed. "Yes, he was referring to Gavin's mother, Mrs. Davids. She was in a car accident with someone he knows, and it was discovered that she not only was driving without a license, but it seems she is also an illegal immigrant."

"What does that mean? How can she be illegal anything?"

"You need to fill out forms and apply for citizenship when

you come to our country. For some reason, it appears Mrs. Davids never did that."

"But why?"

"I don't know."

"Can they really kick her out and make her go back to Mexico, like Coach Holmes was saying?"

"I don't know the answer to that, either. Immigration laws are complicated. I hope not, but I don't know."

"Mom, the Recruits are meeting after school for the newspaper. I need to go. I need to be there. I have to check on Gavin. He checked on me."

Mom gave me a weak smile. Then she nodded. "Okay," she said. "Okay."

Trevor

After Randi hurried out the door, Natalie got down to business. Even though Gavin had just spilled everything to Mrs. Woods and Mrs. Magenta, there was no time for cleanup.

"I need to tell all of you what's going on," she began, "because Gavin's going to need us now more than ever."

Natalie gave us the down and dirty, the true hard facts and none of the baloney that was flying around school. I couldn't even move when she got done explaining. Things were way worse than any of us had realized.

"Gavin's going to need us," Natalie repeated.

I can't say if what happened next was a result of Gavin's explosion, Natalie's speech, or something else, but when Natalie finished, Mrs. Woods got out of her chair and started across the room. Mrs. Magenta met her halfway.

Mark and I always make stupid jokes and say dumb things during the sappy parts in movies, be we didn't do any of that when Mrs. Woods and Mrs. Magenta hugged. There was nothing funny about this special moment.

"I'm sorry, Olivia," Mrs. Woods whispered.

"Me too, Mom. I'm sorry, too."

It was a long hug that was long overdue, and before it ended, things got even better. Out of nowhere the one and only Scott burst into the classroom. When he spotted Mrs. Woods and Mrs. Magenta holding each other, he got so excited that he ran over and wrapped his arms around both of them.

"You did it!" he cheered. "You've forgiven each other. You're all better."

Now Mark and I laughed, and so did everyone else. Mrs. Woods and Mrs. Magenta squeezed him tight.

It was only then that I began to wonder what Scott was even doing there. He was supposed to be home, resting. Before I got the chance to ask him, the classroom door swung open again, and this time it was Randi and Gavin. They froze in their tracks when they saw the three-way hug. I bet they were full of questions, but as soon as Scott saw them, he hit Gavin with the latest news.

"Coach Holmes was on TV with a bunch of people who want to send your mom back to Mexico because she's an illegal immigrant," he blurted.

And just like that the whole Gavin thing got worse still. Talk about a punch in the gut. Talk about adding fuel to the fire. This was a staggering blow. The whole thing was getting so hard to believe that it didn't seem real, or even possible. Gavin had dealt with unfair treatment all through football, and now Coach Holmes was going after his mother. I always thought having one of your parents die when you were a kid had to be the worst, but having your mom taken from you when she was still alive was a close second.

Gavin's knees buckled. Randi caught him by the arm, and I jumped up and helped her get him to a nearby chair. He sagged forward and buried his face in his hands. Randi stood next to him rubbing his back.

"I told everyone what was going on," Natalie confessed. "I'm sorry, Gavin."

"It's okay," Randi assured her. "No more secrets."

The girls reached out and grasped hands. And the next thing I knew, the rest of us were holding hands and standing near Gavin.

"No more secrets is right," Mrs. Woods said. "You kids have been trying to help Olivia and me all along. Your hearts have shown through no matter how much you tried hiding it."

"Thank you for not giving up on us," Mrs. Magenta said.

"Mr. Davids, you're not alone," Mrs. Woods told him. "We're here for you. All of us. Together."

BRIEF #15
December: The Story Comes to Us

Mrs. Woods and Mrs. Magenta finally appeared ready to move forward—together. Inside I was ecstatic. This major victory would've been cause for celebration under normal circumstances; sadly, "normal" wasn't in our description. I still had so many questions for my teachers, but Gavin and his mother were our concern now, not my wonderings. This was not the time or the place—unless, of course, you were Gavin. He was the exception.

He was looking at Mrs. Woods. "Who's Eric?" he asked, wiping his face. "Coach called me Eric during the last time-out."

"He was my son," Mrs. Woods answered.

"My twin brother," Mrs. Magenta replied.

"The quarterback towel Coach gave me was his, wasn't it?" Gavin said.

Mrs. Woods nodded.

"You're a lot like he was," Mrs. Magenta said.

The word "was" hung in the air.

"What happened?" Scott asked. It was the question on all our minds.

Mrs. Woods squeezed her daughter's hand. "The story will come to you on its own, when it's ready," Eddie had said. This was it.

"After all these years the pain is still with me every day," Mrs. Woods said. "The pain and also the shame." She glanced at Mrs. Magenta.

"You're not alone in this, Mom," Mrs. Magenta said.

Mrs. Woods responded with a weak smile, then turned to us. "You kids deserve an explanation after all you've done for us—and Coach." She took a deep breath, and then she started letting the past out. "Eric was a remarkable boy. He excelled in the classroom and on the field. He was a smart player. When your husband is the head coach and your son the star quarterback and captain of the team, you live and breathe football in the house, and Olivia was not to be left out."

"Dad was great at including me," Mrs. Magenta said. "We had our special time every day that he called 'visiting hour.' We did more than talk football, but that was when he shared plays with me and taught me the game. I became his first official stats woman."

Scott grinned from ear to ear. Yes, figuratively, but he came close to making it literally.

"Coach was great with Olivia, but I wasn't," Mrs. Woods admitted. "Growing up, I wanted to be a journalist, but my mother wouldn't hear of it. That was no place for a woman. End of discussion. I hated her for that, and yet . . . I became her.

The apple doesn't fall far from the tree, I thought. *People might say the same about Mother and me.*

"Olivia was good with numbers, but her passion was for art, which was something I didn't want to hear about," Mrs. Woods continued. "Art wasn't a reliable profession. She was talented, but I was so scared that she'd fail, that she'd be struggling for work. I wasn't going to let that happen, so I tried to squash her dream. I told her she was foolish and that she wasn't good enough. And I kept reminding her of that, hoping she'd change her mind. But the more I pushed, the more she resisted and withdrew—like I did with my own mother. Olivia and I were constantly fighting. I knew better, but I couldn't help myself, and then—"

Here Mrs. Woods paused; I could sense this was where things got difficult.

"I applied to several art schools my senior year without Mom knowing." Mrs. Magenta took over. "I didn't expect to get in. I did it out of spite. I wanted to prove her wrong. The day my first acceptance letter arrived, Mom and I had our biggest fight. I was so upset, I made Eric drive me to my friend's house so that I could stay there. On his way home—" Mrs. Magenta's voice dropped. She had to stop.

"On his way home Eric was hit head-on by a drunk driver who crossed over into his lane," Mrs. Woods said. "He was killed instantly. Taken from us at the young age of seventeen."

Silence. Randi gripped my hand. The room was heavy with pain and loss and sadness. Trevor nudged Mark, and the two of them pulled over chairs so our teachers could sit down. The rest of us took seats near them.

"Coach was devastated," Mrs. Woods suddenly continued.

"He pulled away from us and sank into depression. I became terrified of losing Olivia next. I needed her close, where I could keep her safe. Those art schools were all so far away. I did the most terrible thing. I threatened not to pay for any of her schooling if she chose to attend one of them."

"Losing Eric hurt so much," Mrs. Magenta said. "I blamed myself. I needed to get away. I had to go where I wouldn't be constantly reminded of him. I chose a school far from home. I went and studied education like Mom wanted—and I never came back."

"Never?" Scott asked.

"Not until last year."

"Well, you're here now, and that's what's important," Scott said.

"You're right, Mr. Mason," said Mrs. Woods. "It's time to live in the present. I've got my daughter with me now."

The two women leaned and grasped hands again.

"I love you, Mom."

"I love you, Olivia."

"Coach needs to know that his wife and daughter have forgiven each other," Gavin said. "It's all he's wanted."

"We'll take care of that, Mr. Davids. Don't worry," Mrs. Woods said. "You do know what he'd say to you right now?" she asked.

Gavin nodded. "Keep fighting," he whispered.

"That's right. Keep fighting."

It's safe to say that was our most memorable newspaper meeting of the year. Not only did we accomplish our collective goal—the thing we had all set out in July to achieve—but we also took on a new challenge. Something just as important—except this was no secret. After the holidays, we were going to be ready to fight.

GOALS

- ✓ Resolve the strained relationship between Mrs. Woods and Mrs. Magenta.
- ✓ Keep our plan secret, which requires keeping Scott and the rest of the Recruits quiet—but mainly Scott.
- ✓ Teach Mrs. Davids how to read—and keep our work secret.
- ✓ Nail the bad guys responsible for Scott's injury.
- • Finish the article on the booster club for Scott.
- ♦ Save Miss Carla Davids!

Randi

I got a ride home with Mrs. Kurtsman after our newspaper meeting. My head was still spinning from all that had happened, but Mom was waiting for me when I walked in the door.

"Randi, I saw the news. How's Gavin? Was he in school today?"

Suddenly I felt exhausted. There was so much to tell that I didn't know where to begin. I dropped my bag and fell into Mom's arms. She held me close and rubbed my back. She made me feel safe—like only a mother can do. Just thinking that made me ache for Gav and Meggie.

I headed into the living room and collapsed onto the sofa. Mom brought me a cup of hot tea and sat next to me.

"Sorry about the wet spot on your shirt," I said.

Mom rubbed the area where my runny nose and tears had touched. "It'll dry."

"Can they really force her out of our country?" I asked.

Mom sighed. She cradled her teacup. "I don't know, honey. I'm not an expert at this stuff."

"Natalie's mom is handling the case," I said.

"That's good to hear. She'll fight for Mrs. Davids."

The word "Mrs." reminded me of how much Mom didn't know. "It's 'Miss,' not 'Mrs.,'" I said. "Gav's parents aren't married."

"What? You're kidding me."

I shook my head. "It's true. Imagine how Gav must've felt when he found out."

"Ohmigoodness. But why?"

"Gav said they didn't have the money for a wedding and his mom didn't want to go to city hall. Mr. Davids didn't push it. He told Gavin he didn't need to tie the knot to love his mother any more than he already did."

"Smart man. Sometimes we trick ourselves into thinking getting married will make us love one another or fix what's broken."

"Is that what happened with you and Dad?"

"Yes," Mom was quick to answer, "but we don't need to get into that. That was a long time ago, and it doesn't matter."

I took a deep breath. "Actually, it does sort of matter."

Mom's face scrunched.

"Miss Davids isn't the only one who's been keeping secrets," I said. "I need to tell you what happened at camp."

"Did you get hurt? Did somebody do something to you?"

"No. Nothing like that."

Mom shifted on the sofa. She placed her cup on the coffee table and folded her hands in her lap. "Then what?" she asked.

"I've got to get something first." I found my bag and grabbed the pictures I had hidden inside. Then I came back and sat down next to her again. "I've been afraid to tell you, and I don't know why. Gav's situation has given me a different perspective. What his family is dealing with is awful. What happened to me at camp wasn't bad. Just unexpected. I've been acting silly."

"Randi, will you please just tell me? You're making me nervous."

I handed her Kyle's school photo. "I met this boy at camp. His name is Kyle."

"Did you do something with this boy that you want to tell me about?"

"No, Mom! Jeez!"

"Just asking. He's cute. Is he your boyfriend?"

"He's my brother."

Her mouth fell open.

"His name is Kyle Cunningham, and he's my half brother. We met at camp." Her mouth still hung open. "I know. We couldn't believe it, either. When he got back home, he sent me this picture." I handed her the one of Kyle posing with his dad at a wrestling tournament. "After I got it, I scoured our house, searching for a picture of Dad so that I could compare the two. I found this." I handed her the shot of baby me and Dad making cookies. "And then Kyle sent me this one." I showed her the picture of toddler Kyle and Dad. Mom just sat there staring at the pictures. She didn't say anything.

"Are you okay?" I whispered.

"He sure didn't take long to move on and find somebody else, did he?"

The same thought had crossed my mind. I didn't know how to respond.

"So you're a star gymnast and your brother's a star wrestler.

I used to like to pretend your talents came from me. Guess now we know that isn't true. Your father was your better half."

"Mom, stop it! I'm more than just a gymnast, you know. I also happen to be a good student and a loyal friend. And I know Dad hasn't helped me become either of those. And he definitely didn't help me develop as a gymnast."

"Yeah, well, I wasn't always very good at helping with that, either," Mom said. She peeked at me and gave me a small smile.

It was my turn to pull her into my arms.

"How did I end up with such a wonderful daughter?"

"Do you really want me to explain the birds and the bees?"

"Ugh!" she groaned, sitting back.

We laughed. I watched her study the photos some more.

"Mom, Kyle is going to the Elite Stars Festival. Dad will be there."

"I haven't seen your father since he left all those years ago. Just talking about him brings back all sorts of emotions. I can't even imagine what seeing him will do."

"I'd like to meet him," I said.

Mom grew quiet. "He is your father. I can't be upset with you for wanting to meet him. Just know it might not be as pretty as you're imagining. We didn't exactly part on good terms—not at all."

"I know. But I'm ready."

Trevor

If Gavin was going to keep fighting for his family, I was going to keep fighting for mine, too. When I took my place at the dinner table, I was ready to do some talking. I'd told Mark I was going to. This wasn't gonna be one of those quiet meals. *No more secrets.*

"Did you know Brian was at my last football game?" I started.

"He was?" Mom said. "Really?"

"I saw him. He was standing on the visitor's side, wearing a cap."

Obviously Mom had had no idea. She turned to Dad, and he didn't say anything. I took that to mean he knew.

"He was at my game but not with us for Thanksgiving dinner," I said. "Why?"

I was talking to Dad, and he knew it. Truth be told, I wasn't sure I wanted my brother around, but Mom was still worrying about him and I had questions.

"I gave you the tape," I said. "And you called the police about Chris."

Mom looked at Dad and stiffened. She seemed ready for him to explode. Dad put his fork and knife down. He wiped his mouth with his napkin and sighed. I'd seen my father mad before. This wasn't it. He was something else. Distraught? What in the world had happened? Mom leaned forward. She sensed something different in him as well.

"Honey, what's wrong?" Mom asked, her voice full of concern. "What is it?"

"It's time I tell you both what took place," Dad said, pushing his plate away. "Remember the night when I came home late?"

We nodded.

"I got a call from Police Chief Daniels that afternoon. He asked me to stop by the station on my way home. That's why I was held up." Dad looked at Mom and then at me. "The police found Chris at Brian's apartment . . . and they found everything that he'd stolen there as well. All of it. They had to arrest Brian, too."

"Arrest Brian?" Mom said.

"Yes . . . my own son. Stealing from me. I failed him even worse than I'd thought."

"No, *we* did," Mom rasped. "The two of us." She got up and left the room. Dad pushed back his chair and followed her down the hall. Even though we'd hardly eaten, none of us was hungry. I cleared the table and loaded the dishwasher. I put our leftovers in some of Mom's Tupperware and went to my room.

Being mad kills your appetite, and I was mad. Mad that Dad hadn't told us this when it had happened, and mad at my brother. His problems weren't my fault or my parents'. Brian was to blame for being a loser. He'd made his bed, and now he had to lie in it. I didn't care anymore. I was mad that I'd ever cared. I cranked my music and plopped down on my bed. I grabbed *Sports Illustrated* off my nightstand and flipped through the pages. I tried reading a few articles, but I couldn't concentrate. I threw the magazine across my room and rolled over on my side. I stared at my speakers and headphones, and I thought back to that day at Best Buy and the look on Brian's face after Chris had stolen the video games. The police were wrong. I knew what I had to do.

I was up way early, before Mom or Dad. I'd barely even slept. And by the looks of Dad when he came into the kitchen, I knew the same was true for him.

"Trevor? What're you doing awake?"

"Couldn't sleep," I said.

"Me neither. Your mother is zonked out, though, thank goodness. Want some coffee?"

I grimaced. "Okay," I said. I wasn't a coffee drinker, but maybe Dad thought I could use some. Or maybe he wanted my company?

He filled two mugs and took a seat across from me at the kitchen table. He passed me the cream and sugar.

I copied what he did. Then I swished the spoon around in my cup. "Dad?"

He sipped his joe and looked at me. "Yeah."

"I'm up early because I wanted to talk to you."

"I figured," he said. "You didn't get the chance last night, and you should be able to ask questions."

"I don't know about questions, but . . . I just think . . . don't give up on Brian."

"Trevor, I know it's hard to hear what your brother did, but the fact is that he stole from us—from his own family. He turned his back on us. He quit on us."

"No, he didn't," I said. "You don't know what I know."

My father put his cup down and stared at me. "What don't I know?" There was a sudden edge to his voice that hadn't been there a few seconds before.

"I should've told you this when it happened over the summer, but I was afraid. I didn't want to make more trouble for Brian. I hoped things would get better on their own."

"What should you have told me?" He leaned forward.

I took a sip of my coffee and started explaining. I told him about running into Chris at Best Buy and what he did to Mark and how Chris stole the video games. "When I looked for Chris out in the parking lot," I said, "I saw Brian waiting for him in his car. The look on Brian's face told me he had no idea what Chris was up to. And I don't think he knew about Chris stealing from us, either. What I can't figure out is why he's still hanging with that loser. I think he needs help, Dad. And I bet he doesn't know how to ask for it—like me last year."

Dad got up and walked over to the sink. I watched him standing there with his back to me, rinsing out his cup. I'd said way more than I'd expected. Once I'd gotten started, all the things I'd had bottled up inside came pouring out.

"You still believe in your brother?"

"I want to. People can change, Dad."

He nodded. "I'll go and talk to him."

He put his cup in the sink and walked out of the kitchen.

11

'TWAS
THE NIGHT
BEFORE
CHRISTMAS

SCOTT

My very favorite Christmas movie is *Elf*. Mickey and I have tried and tried to burp like Buddy does after he drinks that two-liter bottle of soda, but my longest belch is only three seconds. We got Grandpa to try one time, and he made it to three, too, which was impressive for an old guy, but Mickey held our record. He made it four seconds once, but he pushed so hard, he left Hershey squirts in his underwear. Buddy's burp goes on forever!

Mom and Dad don't mind *Elf* because it's a funny movie. "Stupid funny," Dad says. But their favorite is one called *It's a Wonderful Life*. They watch it every Christmas Eve. I always thought that movie had to be dumb and boring because it's so old that it's in black and white, so I never watched it. But I decided to give it a try this time because I hadn't been allowed to watch much television since getting hurt and I was ready to watch anything. Maybe Mom was right about all the proper rest she'd made me get, even though I didn't like it, because something got the great-ideas part of my brain working again that night, like it used to.

At the end of *It's a Wonderful Life* the main character, George Bailey, gets a book from his guardian angel friend, and there's an inscription that says, *Remember no man is a failure who has friends.* It's George's friends who come to his side when he needs help most.

"We need to go over to Gavin's house tomorrow," I announced. "The whole family. Even Grandpa."

"But, Scott, tomorrow's Christmas," Mom said.

"I know. We can go after opening presents so Mickey has a new toy to bring with him, but we need to go. My friend needs us right now, like George Bailey did."

Mom and Dad looked at each other and smiled.

"Your brain might've gotten hurt," Dad said, "but your heart is as big and strong as ever."

Trevor

It was Christmas Eve. Mom was in the kitchen, throwing something together for dinner, when the doorbell rang. I ran to answer it. It was already dark outside, and our front light was blown, so I couldn't see through the window. I twisted the knob and pulled the door open.

"Hey, Trevor."

I stood there, frozen, and not because of the cold.

"Nice game against the Titans."

Still nothing from me. My brain had gone numb.

"It's freezing out here. What do you say you let me come in?"

I stepped aside.

"Who is it?" Mom called from the kitchen.

When I didn't answer, she poked her head around the corner to see for herself. Her dish towel fell to the ground.

"Brian!" she cried out.

"Hi, Mom."

She hurried over and grabbed my brother in a huge hug. "You're staying for dinner," Mom said. She unzipped Brian's coat and started pulling it off his shoulders. She wasn't asking. This was more of an order. "It's just about ready. Your father should be home soon. We'll sit down and have a real family meal."

I didn't know if Dad had had anything to do with this, but Mom had just gotten the thing she wanted most for Christmas.

"Sounds terrific," Brian said. "Let me help you."

We followed Mom into the kitchen. "Had I known you were coming, I would've made something special," she said. "I'm sorry."

"Don't worry about it," Brian said. "I'm just happy to be here."

At that, Mom turned around and hugged us both.

Brian and I helped by setting the table and carrying out the different plates of food. Mom was right. We weren't having anything too special, just some mac-n-cheese, green beans, and chicken patties.

We got everything ready, and then we sat down. "I don't know where your father is," Mom apologized. "If he makes us wait much longer, the food will be cold."

"He's not coming," Brian said.

Mom stopped. "How do you know that?" she asked. "Have you seen your father?"

"He came and found me last week."

"So he knows you're here, but he's choosing not to be?" Mom said, sounding sad.

"Yes," Brian answered. "But things are better now. Can we eat, and I'll explain everything?"

Mom sighed. "Okay."

We made our plates and dug in. Brian ate a ton. *Must be living on your own doesn't feed you well,* I thought. He polished off his seltzer water and put his glass down. "I wish I could tell you I was completely innocent in all of the stuff with Chris," he started, "but I can't."

I glanced at Mom. Her smile faded.

"I had the feeling that Chris was stealing. I'd seen him do it before," he continued, "but I didn't ask. I definitely didn't know he was stealing from us—from you—so I let it go. I didn't do anything about it."

"Why?" I asked. "Why did you keep hanging with him when you knew he was a loser?" It was the first thing I'd said to my brother all night, but I needed this answered.

"It didn't turn bad until Chris guaranteed he had a fast way for me to make some cash. He had these connections and assured me that if I gave him some money, he'd place a couple of bets and I'd make a pretty penny. It worked—the first few times."

Mom gasped. "You were gambling?"

"I was desperate. I came home from college with tons of credit card debt. That stupid piece of plastic helped me party my way out of school. Reality didn't sink in until I found myself working nights at the lousy service station."

"I didn't know," Mom choked.

"Dad kept the debt a secret so you wouldn't worry. He was trying to help me, but I was an idiot. I tried taking the easy way out instead of working harder, and I ended up losing big. I needed Chris's help paying. I should've wondered where he got the money, but I only cared that he had it for me. After that I was trapped. I owed him."

Things got quiet while Mom and I tried to let all this digest. "So now what?" I asked.

"The good news. Dad talked to the police, and they're giving me a second chance. He was able to strike a deal with the judge. The charges against me were reduced so I won't have a felony record or go to jail, but I'm on probation. I need to log two hundred and fifty hours of community service."

"Your father did that?" Mom said.

"Yes. He even helped me find a new job working the night shift at a warehouse, which is better money and gives me a fresh start. No more lousy service station. No more Chris."

Mom swallowed against the knot in her throat. I could see that this news about Dad and Brian had her on the verge of tears.

"Dad told me to come here tonight," Brian said, "but he still needs time. I've got to prove myself by doing the right things. I can't blow this chance."

"I've got to prove myself, too," I said. They looked at me like I had three heads. "Mark and I don't want to sit back and watch them take Gavin's mother away without a fight. We want to help, but we don't know how."

"I've seen the news," Brian said. "That's a bad situation. I can take you guys over there tomorrow. You and Mark, so Gavin knows his buddies are with him. That's a start."

I liked that idea.

"But tomorrow is Christmas," Mom reminded us.

"We won't stay long," Brian said. "Just enough so Gavin's family understands they aren't alone in this fight. Trust me, it makes a difference when you know you've got people on your side." He looked me in the eyes then. "Dad told me you were the one still believing in me, Trev."

I swallowed. I hadn't been expecting that.

"I've made a lot of mistakes," Brian went on, "but the way I treated you was the biggest. I'm sorry. I'm sorry I was never a good big brother. I'm sorry I let Chris bully you and that I ganged up on you, too."

I nodded. That was all I could manage. I swallowed again, fighting the lump in my throat. Then Brian flicked a mac-n-cheese noodle at me. I dodged it and sent one flying back at him.

"Boys!" Mom squawked.

We laughed. I laughed because for Christmas I'd just gotten the big brother I'd never had.

GAVIN

I used to think my dad was kinda wimpy 'cause he was always doing whatever he could to make his customers happy. I was wrong. He wasn't being wimpy; he was providing great service. Even though my old man didn't walk around with his chest puffed out like an angry linebacker, I saw firsthand that if you threatened to harm his family, or take something away from him that he loved, then my dad became a fighter. If I'd let him know about Coach Holmes during football season, he woulda gone to bat for me, and maybe then Scott wouldn't have gotten hurt and none of this terribleness with Mom woulda happened. Maybe being a man actually meant knowing when to ask for help? It was too late for that, though. But like I said, Dad was ready to fight, and I felt good about that. Unfortunately, I also knew the law was the law—no matter how good and tough you were.

Mom, on the other hand, wasn't so focused on the fight, but on us—me and Meggie, especially. She was determined to still make Christmas special for us. We were behind schedule 'cause of all that had happened, but it wasn't too late.

"Get your stuff on," she told me and Megs on Christmas Eve. "We're going to get our tree."

We bundled up and piled into Dad's truck and went and cut down the best-looking Douglas fir you've ever seen. Me and Dad carried it into the house and got it standing straight in the corner while Mom and Meggie got to work making home-made pizza. We ate, and then Mom brought the ornaments and decorations down from the attic. Dad put on Bing Crosby, and then we trimmed our tree. We laughed at the different decorations as we pulled them out of the boxes, like the ugly gingerbread man I'd made back in kindergarten. It was covered in glitter and glue and had a picture of booger-nosed me on its face. On the back I had written the words "for Mom." . . . I stopped laughing. What was real wasn't funny.

Mom kissed me on the forehead. She took the ornament and hung it on a branch in the front. After the last snowflake went on, Dad lifted Meggie in the air and she stuck the star on top. Then we took a step back and admired our work.

"Is it time for our surprise now?" Megs asked Mom.

"Not yet," Mom answered. "First we need to bake cookies."

"Yay!" Meggie cheered.

Dad looked at me and shrugged. We followed them into the kitchen and did our best to help, even though Dad was better with a wrench and I was better with a football. When it came to the decorating part, I was pretty good, though, 'cause that was close to art, just with frosting instead of a pencil. I made a snowwoman for Meggie, but she told me it looked so good that it had to be for Santa. And then she showed me the cookie she had made for Santa.

"It was supposed to be a reindeer," she said, "but I broke off his horns so he could be a dog instead because I want Santa to know that a dog is what I really want for Christmas."

"A dog would be nice," I said, "but I don't know if Santa travels with pets in his sleigh." There was no way she was getting a dog, so I was trying to prepare her for that. I didn't want her to be let down in the morning. Mom and Dad shoulda squashed that idea of hers a while ago—but they'd had their minds elsewhere.

"Yes, he can," Megs said. "Santa can bring you anything you want."

I wanted to believe her with all my heart, 'cause I knew what I wanted—and it wasn't anything I would find under a tree. "I hope you're right," I said.

Dad squeezed my shoulder and messed Meggie's hair. She looked up at us and flashed her smile. She had frosting on her nose and cheek. We laughed.

"Is it time for the surprise *now*?" Megs asked Mom.

"Okay, *mija*. Ready!"

What surprise? I'd had enough surprises.

Meggie directed me and Dad into the living room and made us sit on the couch. Then she carried one of our kitchen chairs out and put that across from us. "You sit here, Mommy." She scurried off and came back a few minutes later with three picture books. She was going to read to us, my little kindergarten sister who was so smart. I was proud of her.

But she handed the books to Mom and came and sat in between me and Dad on the couch. I was confused. Mom took the first book, *The Polar Express,* and opened it. She never stumbled or stopped or goofed on the words. The sentences flowed from her lips. If there'd been a silver sleigh bell in our house that night, I woulda heard it jingling.

"But, Carla . . . how? . . . When?" Dad asked, just as dumbfounded as me.

"That's why we were at the library!" Meggie exclaimed. "Natalie's been meeting with Mommy and teaching her how to read. And me too sometimes. She's a good teacher."

"And a loyal friend," Mom said, looking at me.

I nodded. This was an amazing surprise. I just wished Kurtsman could fix what was broken with Mom now, like she had fixed Mom's reading. "I'm proud of you, Mom."

"It was you and Meggie who inspired me, *Niño.*"

I rubbed my eyes.

"Off to bed now, *mija,*" Mom said. "Otherwise Santa won't be able to make his stop here."

Megs hugged Mom and Dad, and then she grabbed my hand. It was my job to tuck her in at night. That was how it'd been ever since I'd started reading to her last year. Maybe Mom would start doing this sometimes now—if she was still with us.

"Gavvy, is Santa going to come tonight?"

I wanted to tell her yes. I wanted to tell her yes so bad, but I didn't know, so I told her the truth. "I don't know, Megs." I was done with the lies.

"But I've been a good girl."

"You've been the best," I said. "But maybe instead of

delivering presents, Santa will help make sure Mommy gets to stay with us. Wouldn't that be better?"

"But how will we know if he does that?"

I sighed. "We won't. Not right away. Time will tell. We're gonna have to believe in what we can't see."

"Like in *The Polar Express*?"

"Just like that."

"You're the best big brother, Gavvy."

I hugged her so she wouldn't see my eyes getting wet. "Love you, Megs."

"Love you, Gavvy."

I turned her light out.

BRIEF #16
December: A Surprise Ceremony

The holidays can be a complicated time. Many families get together and share in love and warmth and happiness, but for others it can be a sad reminder of who or what has been lost—or in Gavin's case, who might not be around much longer. Given all that had happened, even with his family together, I imagined they might still feel alone.

"Natalie, let's get dressed. We should go and visit Gavin's family."

I was not surprised by Mother's suggestion, even if it was Christmas. After all, Carla was her client, so of course Mother wanted to check on her. (Mother's commitment to her clients was just one of the many things that made her exceptional at her job.)

"I've been thinking about them, too," I said.

"Dress nicely," Mother added.

Now, that did surprise me. When didn't I dress nicely? I always looked professional. Perhaps with the holiday she thought I might get lazy—but I never lowered my standards.

We got ourselves ready—Father, too—and then we departed. The moment we arrived, I saw that the Davidses were anything but alone.

"Looks like some other friends had the same idea," Father remarked.

Mother and I smiled. "Looks like it," I agreed.

I stepped out from the backseat, and the first thing I heard was a booming bark. I didn't recall meeting a dog the last time I'd been there. As we climbed the porch steps, the barking intensified. Then Mother knocked, and the beast hiding on the other side almost lost his head.

Ruff! Ruff! Ruff!

"Otis!" Mr. Davids yelled. "Otis!"

"Otis, be a good boy." That was Meggie.

Things grew quiet, and then Mr. Davids opened the door.

"Hi, Natalie," Meggie squealed. "Look at my new puppy. His name is Otis. I got him for Christmas."

"Did you say p-puppy?" I stammered. The dog was bigger than she was; the string of drool hanging from his jowl was almost as tall.

"Yes, he's only a puppy," Meggie said. "He's gonna get bigger. He's a bull master." She wrapped her arms around his neck and squeezed him. Her head was a peanut next to his massive skull.

"She means 'bullmastiff,'" Gavin corrected her.

"Oh," I said. Whatever he was called, the bull part was very fitting.

"Sorry about the barking," Meggie said. "Otis gets excited."

I nodded.

"Merry Christmas," Miss Carla cheered, rushing in from the kitchen. (I'd settled on referring to her as "Miss Carla" because if she wasn't married to Mr. Davids, then I wasn't positive that "Davids" could be her last name; never mind the "Miss" versus "Mrs." dilemma.) "Come in. Can I get you some coffee? Natalie, would you like anything to drink?"

"No, thank you," I said.

Mr. Davids and Gavin took our coats. Then Mother and Father followed Miss Carla.

I spotted Randi and walked over to her. She was standing near Scott. He was eating a Christmas cookie—naturally—and by the looks of his shirt, it wasn't his first.

"What's everyone doing here?" I whispered. And by "everyone," I meant *everyone*. Not only had I shown up with Mother and Father, but Randi and her mom were there. Scott was with his family, including his grandpa. Even Trevor and Mark had come, and they'd brought someone I didn't know. Gavin's house was packed.

"We're here for our friend when he needs us," Scott said, crumbs falling from his mouth. "Gavin is George Bailey."

I raised an eyebrow. "Excuse me?"

Randi shrugged.

"Remember no man is a failure who has friends," Scott replied.

I didn't get the George Bailey reference, and while the last thing he'd said made sense, I found it hard to believe that all these people had coincidentally arrived on that same premise. Nevertheless, it felt good, and I was happy for Gavin and Meggie.

Ruff! Ruff! Ruff!

"Otis!" Meggie squealed, covering her ears.

There was a knock.

Ruff!

Who could it possibly be? I wondered. Everyone was already present.

Gavin opened the door. It was Mrs. Woods, with Coach and Mrs. Magenta—who was holding on to a gentleman's arm.

"Merry Christmas, Valentine," Coach said. "Got my family with me. The new guy's not a quarterback, but he's okay."

The gentleman chuckled. "I'm Olivia's husband, Matthew," he said, introducing himself. "Good to meet you."

"You too," Gavin replied. "Merry Christmas. And Merry Christmas, Coach. I'm really happy you got what you wanted."

"You will, too. Keep fighting."

I squeezed Randi's hand.

Mr. Davids and Miss Carla welcomed Mrs. Woods and company and took their coats. Mrs. Magenta spotted Randi and Scott and me and came over to us. "I'd like you to meet my husband, Matthew," she said.

"It's nice to finally see you all in person," Mr. Magenta said. "I've heard so much about each of you."

"We haven't heard anything about you," Scott blurted.

I elbowed him.

"You can expect to see Matthew more often now," Mrs. Magenta said, "thanks to all of you."

I smiled, while inside I wrestled with a new set of questions. I sensed there was still more to Mrs. Magenta's story, but I reminded myself to let these things come on their own.

Ruff! Ruff! Ruff!

Incredibly, there was yet another knock on the front door.

Mr. Davids answered it this time. "Hello, Ellen. Please, come in."

In stepped a plump, middle-aged woman.

"Ellen!" Miss Carla exclaimed. "Thank you for coming."

"Happy to be here. Are you ready?"

Ready for what? I wondered.

"Yes, I think so," Miss Carla replied.

"Merry Christmas, Ellen," Mother said, approaching the woman and shaking her hand.

"Merry Christmas, Gloria."

Do they know each other?

"If I could have everyone's attention," Mother announced. "I'd like to share some exciting news. This is Ellen Leone, a friend of mine from the courthouse. Ellen's here to help Mike and Carla make things official."

What? I was confused. *What does Mother mean "make things official"?*

"I've asked for Carla's hand in marriage," Mr. Davids explained, "and she's accepted." *Applause.* "Ellen is here to perform the ceremony."

"Wow!" Scott exclaimed. "This is like a surprise-wedding party."

"Can just anyone perform a wedding?" Randi whispered.

"No. She must be a celebrant," I explained.

"A what?"

"A marriage official," I said. "Someone who can legally perform a wedding."

"Oh." She nodded.

I'd heard of eloping before—"elope," a verb, meaning "to

run off secretly and get married"—but this was different. Scott was right; this was a surprise wedding right in the Davidses' house. And somehow, whether by miracle or destiny—Randi and I could argue over that later—they were surrounded by friends who could serve as witnesses.

And witness we did, a simple, yet beautiful, ceremony. I realize that this may sound out of character for me, but I daresay it was even a bit romantic. What was going on with me?

Natalie, do you see how he keeps looking at you?

Stop. I'm not interested.

Meggie hugged her mommy after her daddy kissed his bride. It was official. Miss Carla was now Mrs. Davids. The big question: Now that they were married, did that suddenly make Carla a legal immigrant? Could she still be deported?

I hoped Mother could give me answers when we got into the car, starting with: How had she kept this a secret?

Randi

When Mom and I made it home from Gav's, we got into our pj's and settled down to open presents, sticking with our tradition of exchanging gifts at night rather than in the morning. It was an especially small Christmas this year because Mom had sunk her money into our upcoming trip to the Elite Stars Festival. I wasn't complaining.

I had two things to open, so I went first. I started with the smaller package. I tore through the paper and pulled out a brand-new gymnastics bag. It was black with blue and orange lettering. Mom had had my name embroidered on it. It was perfect. The second gift was a new suitcase, just in time for our big trip.

"Thanks, Mom. These are great."

"You're welcome, honey."

"Your turn," I said.

She picked up the rectangular box. It wasn't much, but I was excited because I liked what I'd gotten her. Coach Andrea had taken a great picture of Mom and me at Regionals, and I'd been able to get it framed.

"Oh, Randi. I love it. Thank you."

We hugged and then went into the kitchen to make hot chocolate. We carried our steaming mugs into the living room and snuggled under blankets. Mom flipped on the TV. "Oh, let's watch this," she said. "This is one of my favorite Christmas movies."

I shrugged, but by the end of it I was smiling. I'd just learned who George Bailey was.

Mom and I enjoyed a lovely evening, but there was no doubt the best part of the day took place at Gav's house. Natalie was suspicious of her mother's role, but I didn't want to know. I liked Scott's theory. Of course, I also liked believing there was a bit of destiny mixed in there.

Still, I wasn't naïve. When I closed my eyes that night, I understood that Gav and his family weren't out of the woods yet, but I was so glad they'd gotten to spend the day in the clouds.

12

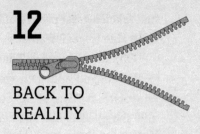

BACK TO REALITY

GAVIN

The holidays provided a short break from reality, but come January and the New Year, the fear of losing Mom was back to haunting me. We still didn't know what was gonna happen to her. Good thing we had Otis. That blockhead dog helped me get through each day by giving me something to think about other than Mom's fate. Otis was everything Meggie had wanted for Christmas, but trust me, there was enough of him to go around for the whole family—and we all needed his help. He was way better than that big red I-like-to-lose dog.

At nighttime Otis slept with Meggie and kept the bad dreams away from her. The haunting came for me every night, though, as soon as I closed my door and climbed into bed. Coach Holmes was still out there making noise, calling for Mom's deportation, stirring up people's anger. Mom and Dad never said anything, but I had the feeling they knew more than they were letting on. The not knowing was killing me.

School was no escape. My friends and a few others, like Mr. Allen and some of my teachers, were openly supportive.

Another pack ignored me, which I was fine with. And then there was the group that stared at me like my mother was a murderer. Their eyes stabbed me in the hallways, the classrooms, the cafeteria—all day long I struggled to breathe.

The worst was when I came across the "I have a dream" sentence strips that were hung in the hallway in celebration of Martin Luther King Jr. Day. Randi saw me coming and tried to turn me around.

"Let's go this way," she said.

But it was too late. I saw the ones that dreamed of cures for cancer and world peace, and I saw the one that somebody musta stuck up there when no teachers were looking, the one that said, *I have a dream that all illegal immigrants will be captured and kicked out.* Those words hit me harder than a blind-side crackback block, but I'm gonna tell you, they were nothing compared to when the haunting came for real.

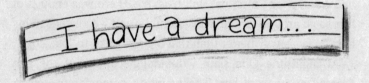

Randi

Mom and I flew out on a Thursday morning. We had an early flight, so we dropped in on Gav and his family before heading to the airport. "Don't worry about me. You've got to focus," Gavin said. "This is a big weekend for you. You've got your dad *and* the competition."

I half smiled. "Thanks, Gav." I stepped forward and hugged him.

"You're gonna do great," he whispered. "It's your destiny."

I squeezed him harder, and then I let go fast and turned and hurried out the door, before the knot in my throat gave way.

What Gavin had said was true—this was a big weekend for me. I'd been to a lot of gymnastics meets, but I'd never flown to one before. I was on my way to compete against the best gymnasts in the country—and to meet my father. I was scared, nervous, and excited all rolled into one. When Mom asked our flight attendant for wine, I realized she was feeling anxious, too.

"What?" she said when I looked at her. "I'm not driving, and this is a special occasion."

I wasn't buying the "special occasion" bit, and when she ordered a second wine, I knew her nerves were even worse than mine.

I'd planned on us meeting Kyle and my father after my meet and after we had agreed upon a time and place. But that's not what destiny had in mind.

We landed safely, and once we deplaned and used the restroom, Mom and I found the baggage claim area. I grabbed my suitcase off the carousel. When I turned around, there they were.

"Kyle!" I exclaimed.

"Randi!"

I froze. Slowly my eyes moved to the man standing next to my half brother.

"Randi?" the man croaked.

I nodded. My throat had gone dry.

He wiped his brow. "Gosh. I—I—didn't expect to meet you here . . . now. . . . I'm not sure what to say. . . . You've grown a lot since I saw you last."

"Duh," Kyle said.

My dad turned red. I chuckled. What was I worried about? He was just as nervous as I was. It was Mom who took command of the situation.

"Hello, Tom," she said, stepping beside me and wrapping her arm around my shoulders.

"Hello, Jane. . . . You—you look terrific," Tom stammered, turning redder.

"Thank you," Mom replied, as cool as they come. She looked to Kyle. "Hi, Kyle. I'm Jane, Randi's mother. It's nice to meet you." They shook hands. Must have been that the wine had worked, because Mom was kicking butt. "Where are you guys staying?" she asked them.

"Um . . . we're . . . um . . . ," Tom stumbled.

"We're at the Marriott," Kyle answered.

"Us too," Mom said. "Shall we plan on having dinner tonight in the hotel restaurant? Say seven o'clock?"

"Sounds good," Kyle said.

"Will your mother be joining us?" Mom asked.

"No, she's at home with my little brother."

"Okay. I'll make the reservation for four people, then. We'll see you tonight." Mom took our suitcases and started toward the exit.

My father looked at me and shrugged, apologizing for his embarrassment.

"Bye," I said, waving. I hurried to catch up to my awesome mother.

"Where did that performance come from?" I asked her.

"Maybe you get your ability to rise under pressure from me?" she said.

I smiled. Then we hopped onto the hotel shuttle—and I was still smiling. I smiled all the way there.

Dinner that night was nice. Both Mom and Tom ordered a martini to start, and after a few sips they both relaxed. It was strange to think that I suddenly had a dad, but we both did our best.

"How's school?" Tom asked.

"Good."

"Are you looking forward to competing tomorrow?"

"Yes."

It was all small talk, but it was a start.

A lot had changed for my mom and Tom; at least they were able to sit together and have a conversation without getting angry, and without bringing up old grudges, which was something Kyle and I had feared could happen. Like I said, it was a nice evening.

I had thought that it would be the least stressful for me to not meet my father until after I'd competed, but once we finished dinner and that part of our trip got checked off the list, I felt much better. I was able to clear my head and focus.

Friday came, and I did like Mom had done. I rose under pressure and delivered the best performance of my life. There were sixty girls competing, and I finished fifteenth on vault, twelfth on bars, sixth on floor, fourth on beam, and in eighth place for the all-around. Eighth out of some of the very best girls in the country!

Afterward, at Mom's insistence, I spent the night celebrating with Kyle and Tom . . . my dad. Mom went out with Coach Andrea, who had arrived earlier that morning to coach me. Kyle had a great day, too. As destiny would have it, he'd finished in eighth place in his weight class. I got to watch one of his matches on the TV in his hotel room before we went to dinner. I'd never seen a wrestling match before, so it was confusing, but exciting, too. Kyle was losing with seconds to go when he grabbed his opponent in some hold and did a back arch, throwing the other boy to the ground and scoring two points right before time ran out. My half brother was good, like Gav was good at football. They would like each other, I decided.

Mom was very happy on our way back home the next day, and I thought that was because of how well things had gone—with Tom and with my meet. I'm sure that was part of it, but it'd be a while before I found out what else had her smiling. Unfortunately, our good cheer came to an abrupt end when we stopped by Gav's and found out what had happened while we were away.

The instant I saw that Natalie and Mrs. Kurtsman were there, I knew it couldn't be good.

BRIEF #17
January: Part I: Taken; Part II: Emails

Mr. Davids phoned Mother when it happened, and we were out the door in a flash. Now was when Gavin's family was really going to need us.

Mother and I were still there when Randi and Ms. Cunningham stopped by on their way home from the airport. Mother was with Mr. Davids in the kitchen, and I was sitting with Gavin out in the living room; Meggie and Otis were passed out on the couch beside us.

Randi must have sensed something was wrong, because she hurried over and wasted no time in asking, "What happened?"

"While you went and found your father, they came and took my mother," Gavin responded.

"Wait. What? Who took your mother?" Randi said.

Gavin sighed. "You explain," he said, turning to me. He looked beat.

"Immigration police," I said, talking softly. "They came and took Mrs. Davids into custody." Randi didn't move. "They'll be holding her in a detention center until her court date," I continued, "at which time her case will go before a judge and her fate will be determined."

Randi glanced at Gavin and swallowed. She looked back at me. "When?" she whispered.

"We don't know yet, but hopefully within a couple of weeks."

"What does your mother think?"

"She's hopeful," I said, doing my best to sound optimistic. The truth was that Mother didn't know what to expect; she wasn't an immigration lawyer. It was a very good thing that Carla had been paying taxes for the past seventeen years, and it was terrific that she and Mr. Davids had gotten married—doing so could help change her status to legal immigrant—but that didn't change the fact that she'd been breaking the law for all those years beforehand. If you rob a bank but then return the money a day later, it doesn't erase the crime; you're still going to face jail time.

"How'd the meet go?" Gavin asked, obviously needing a change of subject.

"It went well," Randi said.

"How well?" Gavin pressed. "Did you place?"

Randi sighed. "Yeah. I finished eighth in the all-around."

"Eighth!" I exclaimed, unable to contain my excitement. "Against the best girls in the country? Randi!"

She nodded.

"Told you," Gavin said, which actually made her chuckle a little. "How'd everything else go?"

Suddenly I started hearing about a half brother, Kyle, and

about Randi meeting her dad at the baggage claim, and about her mom, and dinner, and more. "Wait. What!" I said, sounding exactly like she had earlier, when she was the one who was confused.

Gavin laughed at me, and it was the best feeling. He and Randi filled me in on everything I didn't know, and then Randi finished telling us about her incredible weekend. The change in subject was a welcome break. But it lasted only so long.

We stayed until late that night, but eventually we had to leave. Mr. Davids and Gavin thanked us and told us they'd be all right. I had promised myself I'd be strong in front of them, but I almost lost it when Mr. Davids put his arm around Gavin's shoulder. They were far from all right.

For me, the most frustrating part was the fact that there wasn't anything more I could do. I felt helpless, and that does not sit well with a take-charge girl. There had to be something—and lo and behold, there was. The answer was waiting for me when I got home.

My experience working alongside Mother and Father in the office had taught me that people don't always respond to messages in a prompt manner. There are times when this requires a follow-up call or email—to subtly encourage a reply. Experience had also taught me that people often fall behind on such matters during the hectic holiday season. So you need to exercise patience and let people catch their breath.

In my case, the teachers and coaches I'd emailed requesting an interview to discuss the booster club and what support their programs had received belonged to the post-Christmas responders. But this didn't test my patience, because thanks to the whirlwind happening around me, my article on the booster club had completely slipped my mind. I had forgotten I'd even sent emails. And because Lake View Middle School was upgrading servers during the holiday break, our student accounts were down. It wasn't until the technology upgrade was complete, and our accounts were activated again, that I received the messages. They all came across at the same time and were waiting in my inbox when I came home from Gavin's that night.

I wasn't planning to read all of the messages before going to bed, but after opening the first email, I had to read a second, and then a third, and a fourth. Essentially, each person wrote one of two things:

> My program has never received any financial support from the booster club.

Or:

> My program received one small contribution in the amount of [X] dollars to help us purchase [fill in the blank].

Everyone concluded by saying they'd be happy to meet with me if I felt it was necessary for my article.

After doing some simple math, it was easy to see that the amount of money Holmes had given out didn't come close to what he had likely earned from the Halloween dance over the past three years.

Embezzlement (noun): *the misappropriation of funds (money) for one's own use*
Synonyms: *theft, larceny*

This was the word that immediately came to mind, and it frightened me. This wasn't a small-time thing. Let me be clear: it was beginning to look as if Mr. Holmes were quite possibly taking most of the money he was supposed to be raising for the booster club and was padding his own pocket instead. If this was the case, the man was a crook.

I hoped I was wrong. I hoped that when asked to provide a booster club bank account statement, he would have one that showed all of the fund-raised money sitting right there where it was supposed to be. Then the conversation would be about Mr. Holmes being a bad booster club president rather than a criminal. If, however, the money didn't show up in the account, there would be real trouble.

I didn't like Mr. Holmes. He was a rotten man. But accusing a person—even one you strongly dislike—of such a despicable offense required proof. I suppose that's why lawyers get paid the big bucks. But I wasn't officially a lawyer—not yet—so I didn't officially know what to do. I could have consulted my mother on the situation, but she had plenty to worry about with Carla Davids—and I wanted her focused on that, because saving Carla was priority number one.

I had to slow down and think. It was still possible that Mr. Holmes was innocent. Remember, innocent until proven guilty.

What is my next move? I wondered.

SCOTT

I was so excited when I finally returned to school, but things weren't the same. School had never been hard for me, but I couldn't remember everything from before. All the information that used to run around in my brain at high speed got stuck in slow motion. I needed more time to process and think. Some of my teachers understood and gave me extended deadlines on my makeup work, but a couple were as flexible as iron and didn't want to hear my excuses, because they didn't get it. Mom told me to do the best I could and not to worry about it. She said that me slowing down wasn't all bad, that there was a hidden silver lining in that—but I wanted to be back to normal.

It wasn't just me not operating like normal. Lake View Middle wasn't the same, either. It used to be noisier, with more shouting and craziness—in the halls, especially. But lately the halls were full of whispers and stares.

"What's going on with everyone?" I asked the Recruits at lunch. "I don't remember it being like this."

"You mean all the whispering and staring?" Trevor said.

"Yeah."

"It's me," Gavin mumbled. "Everyone is whispering about me . . . and my mom," he added.

I wanted to help, but my brain wasn't working fast enough. I didn't know what to do.

"It'll stop soon," Randi said. "After your mom is set free."

"Hang in there, dude," Mark encouraged. "It's just going to take a little time, that's all."

"It doesn't have to," Natalie countered.

She had our attention.

"This nonsense in school doesn't have to last," she said. "Not if we give everyone something else to talk about."

Natalie had something up her sleeve. But what?

The bell rang, and the cafeteria burst into a sea of bodies pushing toward the exit. "What do you mean?" Randi asked, yelling above the noise.

"Just what I said," Natalie replied. "You'll see." She got up from our table and marched off to her next class. Sure enough, we found out exactly what she meant the next day.

Natalie Kurtsman gave our school something else to whisper about. Something I'd started and had forgotten all about.

Trevor

I didn't get many of the details, except that Chris got a more severe punishment than Brian, but I didn't care. All I knew was that Brian started coming to my basketball practices and helping out every afternoon, earning his community service hours—and it was great. Brian had been a good player back in high school, but he was an even better volunteer coach. He was everything Coach Holmes wasn't, starting with fair. Even though I was his brother and Mark was my best buddy, he pushed us just as hard as the rest. The only favor he did us was give us a ride home after practice.

It was when we were leaving the gym that I spotted Natalie down the hall. It was late for her to still be hanging around. Usually we never saw anyone after practice. What was she doing? I stopped and watched her.

"Dude, are you coming?" Mark said. He and Brian were standing at the exit doors, waiting for me.

I glanced back at Natalie. She had one of those boxes the

printer paper comes in, and she was shoving it across the floor with one foot. It must've been filled and heavy.

"What's she up to now?" Mark said, suddenly standing next to me. He'd come over to check out what I was staring at.

"I don't know."

"Let's go, fellas," Brian called.

"C'mon, dude," Mark said. "We'll find out tomorrow."

"You guys go on. There's something I've got to do," I said. "I'll call Mom for a ride later."

"Whatever," Brian said.

Mark caught my arm. "No way! You like her, don'tcha?" he squawked.

"What? No! Shut up, you moron," I scoffed, playing it cool. Then I turned and quickly started down the hall, taking long strides so I could get away from Mark before he made any other stupid comments.

Natalie was all the way at the other end. She had her back to me, so she didn't see me coming, and I guess she didn't hear me, either.

"What're you doing," I said when I got close to her.

"Ahh!" she screamed, tripping over her box and falling backward. Luckily, I was there to catch her. She twisted around in my arms and glared at me. "You scared me!" she said, punching me in the chest.

"I'm sorry. I didn't mean to." She stared into my eyes. Our bodies and faces had never been this close. I quickly let go and took a step back. "I came to see if you needed help. Do you?"

"You can't tell anyone," she said.

"Tell them what?"

"Just promise."

"Okay. I promise."

She glanced around, and then she bent down and pulled a single paper from the box. She handed it to me. It was a one-sheet special of the *Lake View Times*. The headline read: CROOKED COACH, OR BOOSTER CLUB BUST? I scanned the story and saw Coach Holmes's name. I started reading from the top. When I finished, I looked up.

"Well? What do you think?"

"Natalie, this is some serious stuff."

"I know. Mrs. Woods said the same thing when I showed her what I'd written."

"Is it true? I mean, the booster club really hasn't done much to help our athletic programs, even after all the fund-raising?"

"Of course it's true," she exclaimed. "I wouldn't fabricate a story like that. I'd lose all credibility as a journalist. I'm not saying Coach Holmes is guilty. I'm just raising the question of, where has the money gone?"

"Here's what I know," I said. "This story is going to be the talk of the school tomorrow, not Carla Davids."

She smiled. "Told you I had a plan."

Natalie was the bravest person I knew. She'd gone toe-to-toe with that lawyer lady in our classroom last year, and now she was going after Holmes. "I'm glad I'm on your side," I said.

"You're lucky I like you."

"Do you?"

Silence. It got awkward real fast. My heart pounded inside my chest. *Why did I say that?* I was hot all of a sudden. I could feel my armpits sweating. I stared at the floor.

"Maybe," she whispered.

My eyes widened. *Really?* I looked at her and smiled. Then I bent down and hoisted her box onto my shoulder, feeling like Popeye after eating his spinach. "Okay. Now what?" I said.

We walked up and down the halls, slipping a copy of her special report through the vents in every locker and underneath every classroom door. This story was going to hit Lake View Middle first thing the next morning. When we'd finished, we returned the empty box to the main office and stuck the last paper inside Mr. Allen's mailbox.

"I've got to go," Natalie said when we were back in the hall. "My father is waiting for me."

"Okay."

"Thanks for helping me," she said.

I nodded. And then Natalie gave me a smile I hadn't seen from her before. Or maybe it was her eyes that were different. I didn't know, but I was feeling something I hadn't felt before. I didn't start breathing again until she was out the door.

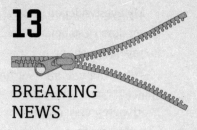

13

BREAKING
NEWS

SCOTT

I opened my locker, and books and papers spilled out on the ground around my feet. I'd only been back a few weeks, and already my locker was a war zone. Between the old work, my makeup work, and current work, there was too much for my deluxe clipboard to hold, but now was not the time to try fixing that. I scooped up the mess and stuffed it back inside. I had one giant pile of everything crammed on the bottom—except for my clipboard. My top shelf was a reserved space for that.

I hung my backpack and jacket and reached up to grab my clipboard, and noticed there was something lying on top of it. It must've been slipped through the vent in my locker door and had landed there. I pulled it out. It was a special edition of our newspaper.

I still couldn't read as fast as I used to, but it didn't take me long to get through it, and holy smokes! This was the kind of story Grandpa watched on those *Law & Order* shows.

"What do you think?" a voice behind me asked.

I turned around. It was Natalie. "You talked to all those coaches?" I asked her.

She nodded.

"How did you find out how much money was made at the dance?"

"I didn't. You did."

"What?"

"You don't remember, do you?"

I shook my head.

"Scott, it was your idea to do an article on the dance and the booster club in the first place. You kept track of all the ticket sales and money earned at the concessions that night. Your calculations couldn't have been exact, but they were very detailed. I know you; I know they were close. Anyway, after you got hurt, I took over the article. We talked about it."

"I don't remember."

"It's okay. I never expected it to unravel in such a huge way, but it did."

I glanced around and saw that everyone else was reading the article, and whispers were flying. Natalie had been right. Gavin's mom wasn't the hot topic anymore. It was all about Coach Holmes this morning—and Nicky didn't like that. I spotted him shoving people out of his way, stomping toward us. I shrank back against my locker. Natalie twisted around when she saw my face.

"Are you the stupid girl behind this?" Nicky growled, holding up the paper.

Natalie stood tall. "I'm not a stupid girl, and yes, I'm the author."

Nicky dropped the paper. His fingers curled into a fist and

he pulled back his arm. I saw it in his eyes. It didn't matter that Natalie was a girl. He was going to flatten her, and he would've if Trevor hadn't gotten there first.

Seconds before Nicky let his knuckle sandwich fly, Trevor grabbed ahold of his arm and threw him. Nicky's body bounced off the lockers next to me. He fell to the ground, but he didn't stay down long. He sprang to his feet and went right back at Trevor. I was ready to see my first fistfight, but Nicky stopped when he saw that Mark was standing there, too.

"Smart choice," Trevor growled. "You don't want to do anything stupid. Everyone is watching you now."

Nicky glanced around and saw that Trevor was right. Everyone *was* looking at him. "This isn't over," he hissed. Then he took off running down the hall.

I watched him until he disappeared. I didn't want to, but I felt bad for him. I didn't like his father, but I still wanted to believe there was some good in Nicky. I'd never met anyone that was all bad.

I was about to say something to Natalie and Trevor, when I saw them walk off hand in hand. My eyes popped.

Had I missed that much in school?

Trevor

"Dude, that was awesome!" Mark cheered, grabbing me around the back of the neck after catching up to me.

"Get off me," I said, shoving him.

He was laughing. "Seriously, that was awesome. Everyone's still back there talking about it. You freaking tossed Nicky against those lockers, bro. That was sick."

I shrugged.

"I thought he was going to come after you, but then he chickened out. I had your back. I was ready."

"I know."

Mark danced around, shadowboxing. "So you gonna tell me what's going on with you and Kurtsman?"

"What're you talking about? Nothing."

"Dude, you got in a fight to protect her. Then you walked her to class, holding her hand. But you're gonna tell me nothing?"

"Nothing."

"You're lovestruck, bro."

"Shut up!" I said, shoving him again.

"Lover boy," he jeered. He skipped ahead of me into his first period, still reliving the story.

He was ready to replay the fight with anybody who'd listen, and he was right, that was all anybody was talking about. Not me. The only thing I could think about was what had just happened with Natalie. I could still feel her hand in mine.

Natalie Kurtsman
ASPIRING LAWYER
Kurtsman Law Offices

```
BRIEF #18
Late January: Fists, Hands, and Interviews
```

I didn't need protecting; I'm a strong young woman who can handle herself. But Nicky Holmes wasn't playing by the rules. He wasn't interested in a battle of wits and words. He was mere milliseconds away from clobbering me. I'd never been trained on what to do in such a situation. My life flashed before my eyes.

I won't lie. What Trevor did left me feeling like one of those girls from the movies—not the airhead but the smart one that you root for who ends up with the hunk in the end. Trevor saved me. He took care of the bad guy, and then he took my hand and led me away. His fingers and palm were quite sweaty, but oddly, I didn't care. I did begin to worry that maybe it was my hand that was sweating. My mind raced and my heart pounded. As we neared my first-period classroom, Trevor gave my hand a reassuring squeeze before letting go.

"I'll be back to get you after class," he said. "You don't need to worry about that jerk."

"Thanks," was all I could manage in reply. I had to look away. For the first time in my life, I failed to keep eye contact. Only after I reached my seat did I finally start to breathe normally again—too bad nothing else was normal after that.

The first van pulled up outside our school fifteen minutes into class. It had the letters *WGBTV* written on the side. A second van with *ARDTV* showed up right behind it. And a third from BSZTV. When I saw the people with video cameras hopping out, my heart began pounding again. How had they found out? And so quickly?

"Miss Kurtsman, this is first-rate journalism," Mrs. Woods had told me after previewing my report. "Don't be surprised if this story catches the attention of people outside Lake View Middle School. Are you ready for that?"

"Yes," I said.

"That's my girl."

Here was my chance. I watched the different men and women as they walked across the parking lot and into our school. And then I waited. It didn't take long. Mr. Trammel's phone buzzed, and he paused his lesson to answer it.

"I'll send her right down," he said.

I was on my way before he'd even managed to hang up. Books in hand, I walked to the main office, where Mr. Allen stood waiting for me. He met me in the hall and whisked me into his office through the back door. "Natalie, did you contact these reporters?" he asked, not hiding the urgency in his voice.

"No," I said.

Mr. Allen sighed. He sat on his desk and rubbed his brow. "Well, someone did, and now they're hoping to interview you. When I first got here this morning, I didn't see what you had written because I had to finish some other work. I just got off the phone with Mrs. Woods, and she told me to check my mail. Natalie, this is serious. If what you wrote is true, and I have no doubt it is, because it's you we're talking about, then the question you raised about Mr. Holmes and the missing money will be investigated."

"As it should be," I said.

"Yes. Yes. You're right." He slid off his desk and began pacing the room.

"Mr. Allen, relax. I can handle these reporters. You don't need to worry."

He stopped and looked at me. "It's not you I'm worried about."

I understood his concerns, but I wasn't backing down. It isn't always easy to do the right thing. Hadn't we learned that last year? I waited.

"You're sure you want to do this?"

"Absolutely," I replied.

"I've already spoken to your mother. She's fine with you doing the interview, but I'm going to stay with you. You may not need me, but it'll make me feel better."

"Okay."

"You ready?"

I nodded.

He sighed. "Let's go."

I followed Mr. Allen out to greet the reporters. They quickly cut to the chase. "We'd like to talk to you about your story," one of them said. "And if it's okay with you, Mr. Allen, we'd like to set up in your office."

"Sure, fine," he replied.

Back to his office we went. It didn't take long for the crews to have their lights and cameras situated. I sat in the chair, where they positioned me and placed my hands in my lap. The interview began.

As promised, Mr. Allen stayed with me while the reporters asked their questions. In the beginning they mostly wanted to know about me, who I was and how I'd come upon this information. The fact that Mr. Holmes had already made a name and face for himself on TV by attacking Carla Davids made for an even juicier story; the reporters were eager for my answers. They soaked up what I said. I sat tall and looked proud. I gave confident responses.

I had thought I was in control, but all the lights and attention clouded my vision. The more the reporters swooned over the young, impressive girl—me—the more I lost sight of what was truly important. The moment started to get the best of me, and it's quite possible I would've missed my opportunity had one reporter not asked the right question.

"Natalie, why did you do this? What were you hoping to accomplish?" she asked.

I repeated her question inside my head. *Why did I do this?* And then the high-and-mighty Natalie disappeared and the real me—the one who knew what mattered—came back.

"Thank you for your question," I said, "because this isn't about me. It's about Carla Davids. Yes, she broke the law by carrying on as an illegal immigrant, but she poses no threat. Carla's been in our country, working hard and paying taxes, for the past seventeen years. She is a wonderful person, friend, mother, and member of our community who has been unfairly attacked by Mr. Holmes. Well, guess what? When that happens, the first thing you want to do is check the credibility of the source; that's Lawyering 101. So I did a little digging—and it took only a little—and this story is what emerged.

"I want to remind our viewers that Mr. Holmes is innocent until proven guilty—that's also Lawyering 101—but more important than that, I want to encourage our community to rally behind Carla Davids. I ask all of you watching: What possible good could come out of deporting Carla and tearing her family apart? The answer is 'none.'"

I stopped talking. I had accomplished what I wanted. So why was I feeling bad?

GAVIN

After Kurtsman's special report and TV interview, things changed. There was still whispering about me and Mom, and there were stares, but it was different. More people were talking about Holmes now. I appreciated that Kurtsman was trying to help, but she was no Super Bowl MVP. None of this won the game and brought Mom home. Whispers or not, my mom was all I could think about—all through school and after. And especially at night. There was no escape.

Dad was busy working long hours 'cause now he was the only one earning money for us. We'd become what they call a single-income household. That meant it was up to me to get home after school so someone was there for Meggie when she got off the bus, which also meant missing Magenta's program, on top of everything else—but it didn't matter. Even talking football with Coach wasn't gonna make me forget Mom.

So in the afternoons it was me and Megs—and Otis. That dumb dog's special talent was being a royal pain in the you-know-what, but by running that play he always made sure we weren't sitting around, moping and feeling sorry for ourselves.

If me and Megs played Monopoly, the dog would grab our money or the dice and run, so we'd have to chase him. If it was cards, he'd grab those and run. Otis was so darn big, he could grab things right off the table. Then he'd barrel his way through the house. It was a miracle that he'd only broken one lamp so far.

Me and Megs dealt with Otis, and we played our games and counted our way around the boards, but it was the days until Mom's court date that we were really counting. I'd thought waiting for football to start was hard. That was nothing compared to this. I'd thought losing a stupid game was something I could never smile about. That was nothing compared to what I might lose now.

It was torture, and I'm pretty sure time did crawl, but the week of Mom's court case finally did arrive. When Mrs.

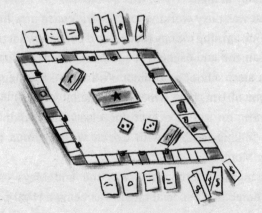

Kurtsman showed up at our house without Mom, my stomach dropped. I feared the worst. But the news she gave us was not anything we'd been expecting. Mrs. Kurtsman came to tell us that the immigration judge assigned to Mom's case was sick, down and out with kidney stones.

"What's that?" Meggie asked.

"The guy has little stones in his bladder that he has to pee out," I grumbled.

"Does that hurt?" Megs asked next.

"I've heard it's the closest thing a man can experience to deliverin' a baby," Dad answered.

"Oh," Meggie said.

"What's this mean for Carla's case?" Dad asked Mrs. Kurtsman. "How long do you expect the judge'll be out?"

"I can't say. Hopefully, it won't be too long. But they won't reschedule Carla's date until he returns."

Meggie and Otis got up from the table and walked into the living room. I stayed with Mrs. Kurtsman and Dad, but I was done listening at that point. Was I ever getting my mom back? She'd been gone for almost four weeks now. The longer this dragged on, the more the community seemed to forget about her—everybody except for us.

"Can me and Meggie see her?" I asked. We hadn't seen Mom since she'd been taken. With Dad working extra-long hours and her being more than two hundred miles away, it had been too hard to figure out a visit. I knew it'd be impossible to arrange a way for me to go without Megs, so I asked for both of us. It was worth a shot.

Mrs. Kurtsman turned to my father, but he didn't say anything. He wore the same glossed-over look that I'd seen on

Coach so many times. "Gavin, I don't think that would be a good idea for Meggie," she said. "She's handling this remarkably well, and I'd hate to disrupt that by taking her to see your mother in a federal detention center. That is not a glamorous place."

I nodded. It was true Megs was doing great. Probably 'cause she was convinced Mom would be coming home soon. I wished I could be positive like that.

"Hang in there, Gavin. It'll be over soon."

"One way or another," I said. I pushed my chair back and went to check on Megs. I found her sprawled out on the floor, coloring a picture she'd drawn.

"Whatcha doing?" I asked.

"Making a card for Mommy's judge," she said. "Knocking down fences by being nice. Remember, Gavvy?"

Even with everything else that was going on, Megs made me smile. That was her superpower. Leave it to her to think of somebody else, even in a time like this. I wished all people could be as nice as my little sister.

Randi

It was our first trip to the Senior Center since Natalie's story had hit the news, and as you'd expect, Eddie and Agnes had plenty to say about the situation.

"Here she is, our very own Angela Lansbury," Eddie started in as soon as we sat down.

Angela Lansbury? I'd heard of Nancy Drew, but who was Angela Lansbury?

"Who's that?" Natalie asked, beating me to it.

"Who's that!" Eddie shrieked, getting excited. "She's the star on *Murder, She Wrote*. Agnes and I have been watching those old episodes ever since your boyfriend got us that fancy TV."

"Excuse me. Trevor's not my boyfriend," Natalie clarified. "Thank you very much." Her neck and ears were turning red.

"You need to play more poker," Eddie suggested. "You're not very good at bluffing. I saw the way you two were looking at each other. You're not fooling fast Eddie."

"Ugh," Natalie groaned, growing increasingly flustered. I'd seen Natalie keep her composure during the toughest times, but Eddie had her rattled just by mentioning Trevor. Wow, she had it worse than I'd thought.

"Leave her alone, Eddie," Agnes scolded. "She's been through a lot."

Eddie winked at me, and I snorted.

"How're you feeling about things, Natalie?" Agnes asked. "You're on quite the roll. First you help Pearl and Olivia, and then you catch Bad Man Holmes red-handed."

"Bad Man Holmes is innocent until proven guilty," Natalie the lawyer reminded us, "and I'm not feeling particularly great. I'm thrilled about Mrs. Magenta and Mrs. Woods, but I haven't done much to help Carla Davids. In fact, the only thing I've managed to do is create a mess for a different family."

"You didn't create the mess for Mr. Holmes and his family," Agnes said. "He did that on his own."

"Let's talk about something happy," Eddie suggested. "Agnes, go ahead and tell them what we've been thinking about."

What they'd been thinking about? These two had a plan? Uh-oh.

"You're right," Agnes said. "We should tell them." She straightened in her chair and leaned forward, placing her hands on the table. "Did you know Eddie and I have coffee with Pearl and Olivia almost every morning now? I've got to tell you, it's so nice having those two together. Coach is happy as a bee in honey. That old man might get confused, but he knows."

Natalie and I smiled.

"We have fun visiting," Agnes continued. "Pearl and Olivia are good at sharing stories and keeping us in the loop."

"Gossip," Eddie said, telling it like it was.

We chuckled.

"Well, after Christmas, Pearl and Olivia had plenty to tell us about Carla and Michael Davids getting hitched," Agnes went on. "What a surprise that was! They thought it was beautiful."

"We met Mr. Magenta there," Natalie mentioned.

"Oh, we've had the pleasure of meeting him, too," Agnes replied. "Now, he's a fella who's easy on the eyes. Don't you agree?"

I giggled. Agnes never talked like that, but she was right.

"So we got to talking about weddings and such," Eddie took over, too excited to wait. "And I mentioned to Agnes about how I'd seen some story about renewing vows on *Good Morning America*. I'm telling you, if you ever want the world to know something, put it on that show. Apparently, renewing vows is a popular thing to do these days."

"I've heard about it," I said.

Eddie leaned forward and said this next part in a hushed voice. "We've decided that having Coach and Pearl renew their vows would be a great thing. We think it would help Coach."

My eyes grew wide. I looked at Natalie, and she had the same expression.

"That does sound like a great idea," Natalie said.

"We're not just two old biddies, you know," Agnes said, sitting back in her chair, smiling.

"When should we do it?" Natalie asked. "Have you already talked to Mrs. Woods and Coach and Mrs. Magenta?"

"Talked to us about what?" Mrs. Magenta asked. She was making the rounds and had come to check on our group at just the right time. Natalie had her sit down. When we got done explaining, Mrs. Magenta looked lost.

"Are you okay?" I asked her. She was totally zoned out. "Mrs. Magenta?" I touched her arm.

"What? Oh, sorry," she murmured. "I was just thinking. Usually parents watch their children get married, but it'll be nice for me to see Mom and Dad renewing their vows. It's a splendid idea."

"Your parents missed your wedding, didn't they?" Natalie said.

"Yes, unfortunately. I invited them. It was going to be my first time seeing them since I'd left home, but they didn't make it. Dad had suffered a stroke, which was the onset of his problems, and they didn't want me to see him like that, not on my special day. They never told me, because Dad didn't want me worrying. He was supposed to get better, but that's not how these things work sometimes."

"I thought you came back because of him," I said. "If you never knew, why did you?"

Mrs. Magenta paused. Eddie and Agnes reached across the table and each took one of her hands. Whatever the reason, it wasn't easy.

"You don't have to tell us," I said. I felt bad for asking.

"It's okay," Mrs. Magenta whispered. "Matthew and I moved back to town after I had a miscarriage. It was late in my pregnancy, and we were heartbroken. It was then that I began to understand how much my mother had lost and was suffering. I wanted to be near her again, to start over, but when I got here, I discovered what was going on with Dad. I was so angry with her for not telling me that our silence never stopped. I only stayed for Dad."

I glanced at Natalie and saw that her eyes were wet like mine. I glanced at Eddie and Agnes. They gave me a slight smile. Now I understood why they hadn't wanted to tell Natalie and me everything. There was so much.

"Mrs. Magenta, I'm so sorry for your loss," Natalie said. "I'm sorry about your brother and baby and everything you've had to go through."

"Me too," I said.

"Thank you, girls."

There was a brief moment of quiet, until Eddie came up with the perfect idea. "I've got it," she said, slapping her hand on the table. "Olivia, you and your hubby need to renew your vows alongside your mother and father."

My face broke into an instant smile.

"Matthew and me?" Mrs. Magenta asked.

"Yes!" Eddie exclaimed.

"Yes!" Natalie and I repeated.

"Edna, don't let this go to your head, but that's about the best idea I've ever heard come out of your mouth," Agnes said. "What do you say, Olivia?"

Mrs. Magenta shrugged.

"Great," Eddie said. "It's final, then. We'll fill Pearl in the next time we have coffee. Now let's get started. There's no time to waste. We've got us a joint ceremony to plan."

And just like that, Eddie's perfect idea was set in motion. By the time we had to leave, Natalie and I were way beyond feeling sad. We were giddy with excitement because we had something double special to look forward to.

Trevor

The cheerleaders were using the gym after school to get ready for their big February competition, so we had a later practice time. Brian picked me up at home, and then we were going to grab Mark. Before we did, and before Mark could start busting on me nonstop with his relentless jokes about how I was in love with Kurtsman, I was glad to have Brian all to myself. This was my chance. A big brother was supposed to be there to give you advice. We were still feeling our way to being brothers, but I was getting comfortable around Brian. He was no Romeo, but he knew more about girls than Mark and me combined.

"What do you do when there's a girl that you like?" I asked, staring straight ahead, trying to play it cool.

"What did you just ask me?"

"You heard me. Don't make me say it again."

Brian laughed. "Well, you grab her butt and plant a big one on her lips."

"Shut up! I'm being serious."

"My little bro, in love. How about that."

"You know what, forget I asked. You're a jerk."

"Simmer down," Brian said. "You've got to let me have a little fun. Who is it? Tell me about her and what's happened so far."

"It's Natalie. You might remember her from when we went to Gavin's house on Christmas day."

"Oh yeah. Hey, she's cute. How'd you pull that off?"

I took a breath and kept talking. I told him everything, even though it sort of felt like nothing had really happened.

"You're flipping out over hand holding? You've got to chill, Trev. Don't go getting all crazy, trying too hard, because then you'll be moving too fast and mess everything up. That'll freak her out, especially this girl, by the sounds of it. So relax."

We *were* going slow, and it was already freaking *me* out—never mind her. But I listened and nodded.

"Maybe you should get her a little something for Valentine's Day," Brian said. "That's coming up, you know."

"I thought you said go slow? Now you want me to get her a present?"

"I didn't say buy her a ring, doofus. Something small," he emphasized. "If you do nothing, then it looks like you don't really care. Something small, and you're taking it slow and you care. It's the perfect move."

I shrugged. I could do that. "So, what do I get her?"

"Jeez, Trev! Do I need to do everything for you? I don't know. Figure it out."

We pulled into Mark's driveway, and that meant we

were done talking about Natalie. But I wasn't done thinking about her.

Mark hopped in the back. "What's up, losers."

Brian chuckled. "What's up with you, pukeface."

I shook my head and laughed. With our greetings out of the way, Brian put the car into reverse and backed out of Mark's driveway.

"I've got one pit stop that I need to make before we go to practice," Brian said.

"Where?" I asked.

"You'll see. It'll be quick."

I didn't like his answer. Brian and Mark were yapping away about something they'd seen on *SportsCenter,* but I was quiet. I worried that Brian's pit stop could mean trouble, and I had myself thinking bad things until we pulled into the elementary school and parked.

"This is your pit stop?" Mark asked. "Kids Klub?"

"Yeah. I'm doing some of my community service hours here. I need to go and see the person in charge real quick, so I know when I can start."

"Kids Klub!" Mark exclaimed. "Yo, Trev, remember those days?"

"Yeah," I grumbled. Kids Klub was an after-school program where little kids could go and hang out until their parents were able to pick them up. I remembered it well. I always hated it.

"C'mon, dude. Let's go check it out and see if it's changed."

"I don't care what you buttheads do," Brian said, "but we're gonna make this quick."

Mark was all about seeing if any of the counselors we'd had

311

were still there. I didn't really care, but I went in because it beat sitting in the car.

"Whoa," Mark said. "That dude is still here."

I saw the guy he was talking about. He was older now, less hair, but I recognized him. "That was the one guy I liked," I said.

"Me too. He was always so cool. I can't believe he's still here."

"Maybe he likes the job."

"Let's go say hi, see if he remembers us."

I was down with that, but then I spotted a little boy who was sitting by himself. The kid looked sad. "You can go say hi," I said. "I'm going over here." I left Mark and walked over to the kid. "You okay, little man?"

He wiped his nose on his shirtsleeve and glowered at me with duck lips.

I almost laughed, but I held it in. I sat down across from him. "I used to come here when I was your age," I said.

Bigger duck lips.

"I hated it."

"I like Kids Klub," he said. "I hate the older boys who pick on me."

"Where are they?" I asked, looking around, ready to take care of them.

"They're not here today."

I wasn't buying that, but I didn't push it. "Have you told anyone? Your teacher? The counselors? Your parents?"

"I can't," he said.

I nodded. I understood way more than this little boy realized—and way less than I realized.

"Yo, Trev, let's go!" Mark yelled.

I stood. "Hang in there, little man. It'll get better."

He shook his head and sniffed. He didn't believe that—not one bit. I didn't move. I wanted to find the right words for him, something to make him feel better. But Mark yanked me away before I had the chance.

14

VALENTINES

GAVIN

When you're in kindergarten, Valentine's is a special day. It's a big deal to decorate paper bags or tissue boxes that will collect your silly cards, and an even bigger deal to go around passing your notes out.

I thought it was the dumbest holiday on the calendar. But it gave Meggie something to do for a few afternoons. She took her time making these fancy homemade cards. I liked hers a whole lot better than the cartoon and movie ones they sold in the stores, but I felt bad for her 'cause I knew she'd end up with a bunch of those in her box. Megs didn't care. The making part was what she liked best anyway.

When her big day finally rolled around, Meggie was up early. I figured it was 'cause she was excited, but turns out she wanted to see Dad before he left for work. She had a card for him, too. Call me soft, but I thought that was so sweet. And then I found out the card wasn't from her.

"Mommy wanted me to give this to you on Valentine's Day if she wasn't here with us."

Dad took the envelope and held it. "Thank you," he said, and gave Megs a kiss on the head. Then he put his coffee cup on the counter and walked off without a word.

We stood there and watched him go down the hall and into his bedroom. I turned to my sister. "What was on the card?"

Meggie shrugged. "I don't know. Mommy had it sealed in the envelope."

I groaned, frustrated.

"Let's go see," she said, taking my hand and pulling me along. We tried being quiet so Dad wouldn't know we were coming, but Otis and quiet didn't go together. The dog's excited breathing was louder than our footsteps. There was no way to shut him up, so I pushed him to the back of our line. That was the best I could do. When we got to the end of the hallway, we stopped and slowly peeked in on Dad. I wasn't ready for what I saw.

He was on his hands and knees, hunched over something on the floor. He had his back to us, and his body was shaking. I didn't need to see his face to know he was crying. I'd never seen my old man cry before. It scared me.

Otis didn't like waiting or being left out, so the next thing I knew, he was knocking us out of the way and plodding into the bedroom. It was too late. There was nothing I could do to stop him. I watched our dog stick his big blockhead in Dad's face and start licking him. When Dad wrapped his arms around Otis and squeezed, I had to fight back my own tears. Me and Megs weren't the only ones missing Mom.

Then, just as suddenly as everything else that had happened so far, Dad got up and came walking toward us. He didn't even care that we'd been spying on him. He threw his arms around me and Meggie. "That's from Mom," he whispered. He held us tight, and in another sudden move he let go and walked out of the house. I didn't know if he had an early appointment or if he was going for a lonesome drive, but he was gone.

Otis barked. I tried ignoring him, but that didn't work. *Ruff! Ruff!*

"What dog? What!" I yelled.

"He wants to show us something," Meggie said.

I followed her into Dad's bedroom. Otis got down next to the thing on the floor that Dad had been looking at.

"Okay, boy. Okay," I said, patting his head. "What is it?"

I looked. It was an album full of sketches from Mom. She had given Dad a homemade Valentine's Day card for every year they'd been together. They were all there. It was a secret tradition of theirs that I'd known nothing about. Suddenly Valentine's Day wasn't so dumb anymore.

Mom was really good at drawing. I'd seen some of her quick sketches before, but these were serious. I smiled. Guess I knew where my talent came from.

Meggie turned the pages until we found this year's card. Mom had sketched a bunch of fancy letter people, and they were hugging. The letters *R, E, A,* and *D* were together. It was cute. The part that got me—and Dad, too, I was sure—was her written message. *You'll always be with me, no matter where I am. Hug Gavin and Meggie. I love you.*

An album full of cards, and this was the first one where she'd written a note. If only she'd learned to do this sooner. Maybe then . . . I shook my head. Those thoughts weren't gonna help.

"Don't worry, Gavvy. I sent the judge my card," Meggie said.

"It was a Valentine?"

"Yup. I had Mrs. Kurtsman deliver it for me."

I pulled her into a playful side headlock. "C'mon," I said. "We've gotta get breakfast. And don't you worry. I'll take your bus to school so you don't have to be alone this morning. I can walk to the middle school from the elementary building."

"Thanks, Gavvy," she said, and smiled.

So I'd be late. I didn't care. I owed Megs. She'd just given me newfound hope, 'cause if there was one thing I knew, it was that Meggie's superpower was her ability to melt hearts.

NATALIE KURTSMAN
ASPIRING LAWYER
Kurtsman Law Offices

BRIEF #19
February: Happy Valentine's Day

I stopped paying attention to February 14 after kindergarten. Back then I was mildly amused by the exchanging of cards, but I quickly outgrew that. How my first-grade classmates could continue to find ninja turtles, superheroes, and princesses exciting was beyond me. I did appreciate the effort of handmade cards as a nice gesture. But after second grade, I stopped participating in the event altogether. To be frank, it was quite simply far too childish for me.

Needless to say, Valentine's was a day of no significance, a day I gave little thought—until this year, when I opened my locker and a red card fell off my top shelf and floated to the ground. I picked it up and read it.

I hope you rot in hell for what you've done!

I took a deep breath, trying to calm myself. I reread the message written inside. I'd heard of lawyers on high-profile cases receiving threats before, but I'd never thought much about it. Why would I? Mother and Father had never been threatened. The notion of that happening to me had seemed ridiculous, if not impossible.

I read the sentence several more times. While alarming, it was not threatening. Instead I decided that it qualified as harassment, which did nothing to make me feel any better, but I want to be clear. Keep the facts straight.

I looked down the hall, first to my left, then to my right. I glanced over my shoulder, checking behind me. I was ready to find Nicky Holmes charging at me with his fist raised in the air, but there was no sign of him. I rubbed my hands on my pants; they were sweaty. Disgusting. If I was going to make it in this business, I needed to grow thicker skin.

I placed the note back on my locker shelf. I wanted to tear it to pieces, but I refrained, knowing that if things were to escalate, I might need it as evidence. By using my brain, I'd regained control of the situation—but not for long.

The sudden touch on my shoulder took years off my life. "Ah!" I screamed. I whipped around, my arms covering my face and head in a protective guard. I squeezed my eyes shut and shrank to the ground, ready to absorb Nicky's punches.

"Natalie. It's me."

I peeked and saw Trevor. He was squatting in front of me, asking me if I was okay. Before I realized it, I had my arms around him.

Thinking back on this now, I can only imagine how shocked

and confused Trevor must have felt, but I'd like to believe that part of him was more than happy to have me hugging him. And to be clear, I was holding him tight because he'd scared me half to death.

"I got you something," he whispered into my ear.

I sat back and brushed the hair out of my face.

He pulled a small teddy bear from under his hoodie. "Happy Valentine's Day," he said.

I smiled and took the bear from him. "I love it," I told him. And I did. It wasn't one of those specialty ones with a heart or bow and arrow, but a simple, straightforward, classic teddy bear—who smelled like strawberries!

Trevor helped me to my feet and walked me to my first-period class. I hope it's understandable when I tell you that the rest of my morning became a blur; for goodness' sake, my heart was aflutter. February 14 had catapulted to the top of my holiday list.

"What's gotten into you?" Randi asked me after lunch.

"Nothing," I was quick to say. She was onto me. I had to do better. "Just have a lot on my mind."

"Don't we all."

That comment snapped me to my senses. I put my guard back up—not literally but figuratively. I refused to carry on like one of those ditzy girls who fall hopelessly and madly in love, though I'll admit, that did have a hint of romance to it. Nevertheless, that was not happening to me in seventh grade! Pu-lease!

I pulled myself together for the remainder of school. Natalie Kurtsman was back—until Trevor stopped by my locker after school.

"Thought I'd walk out with you," he said. "Unless you don't want me to."

"No," I was quick to say. "I'd like that."

I closed my locker and swung my bag to my shoulder. We walked side by side, no hands, few words, but plenty of feelings. I tried shutting them off when I got into the car with Mom, but try as I might, I couldn't hide my giddiness. She had me pegged before we made it out of the parking lot.

"Natalie, did you hear me?"

"What?" Wrong response.

"What has you so distracted? Did something happen today?"

"No." I giggled.

"Natalie Eugene Kurtsman, if I didn't know any better, I'd say a boy is behind this unusual behavior of yours."

I stared out the window, trying to hide my smile.

"Natalie!" Mother gasped. "Are you in love?"

"What!" I cried. "Mother! Heavens, no!"

"Okay," she said. "Just checking. You had me worried." She smirked. Mother knew best.

"What was it you were telling me?" I asked, pulling the change-topic strategy before she dug any deeper into my love life.

She sighed. "I'm not sure I want to repeat it now. You've had such a good day."

"What is it?" I said, seriousness in my voice. I sat up straight and fixed my seat belt. Giddy Natalie was gone, and lawyer Natalie was back.

"I received official notification of Carla's court date this afternoon," Mother began. "She is scheduled to go before the judge in three weeks."

"Not till then? That seems like an outrageously long time."

"I agree, but that's how these things work."

We slowed for a red light.

"Well, at least she has an official date," I said. "That's good news. Why did you think that would ruin my day?"

"I didn't. There's something else."

Green. We were moving again. I braced myself.

"When your father was over at the courthouse this morning, he heard that Mr. Holmes is being arrested and charged with grand larceny. After your article and television interview, the journalists kept digging to unearth the full story. It's been all over the news. It seems Mr. Holmes started embezzling funds from the booster club after losing his job at the factory. He hasn't been able to find another job like what he had, and coaching football doesn't pay that much. His wife works as a hairdresser, but without his regular income they were strapped. He made some bad decisions. It doesn't look good."

No wonder Nicky wanted me to rot in hell. I'd always thought that seeking and finding justice would leave me feeling good inside, but here was another reminder that life wasn't always black-and-white. Life was messy. I didn't know how to feel.

"Natalie, you mustn't blame yourself for this," Mother said, reading my mind. "I know it's hard to believe, but by bringing this to light, you're not only going to help the school's extracurricular programs get the funding and support they deserve, but you're also going to help Mr. Holmes get back on the right track. Sometimes people need to fall before they can rise again. It might take a while, but it will happen."

I nodded, but it wasn't a very convincing nod.

"You've got to believe that, Natalie. Otherwise this job will tear you up inside." Mother reached out and took my hand in hers.

Later that night, as I lay in bed, I didn't know what I believed, but I knew what I hoped. I hugged my teddy bear so that I wouldn't feel so lonely, and eventually I drifted off to sleep.

Randi

Waiting for my gymnastics scores to get posted after completing one of my routines was always hard, but waiting to hear the decision about Gav's mother blew that away. The closer we got to the date, the longer the school days became.

Gymnastics was my escape. The worries of the world fell off my shoulders with a single back walkover on the beam. It had to be that way, or else I'd risk falling—or worse, getting hurt. Coach Andrea had me working extra hard lately, and I was loving it. Even though I had a solid bars routine, we were trying to add another element to my repertoire—one that would increase my difficulty level and give me a higher score to start.

After practice I changed out of my leotard and into comfy sweats, and then I went to find Mom. Usually she was ready for me, but not that day. I found her huddled in a corner of the lobby, talking on her phone and giggling. She acted like she didn't want anyone else to hear what she was saying, and that made me wonder if the call was about Mrs. Davids. I hurried over, but the second Mom saw me coming, she quickly ended the call.

"Practice is over already?" she asked, blushing.

"Yes," I answered, narrowing my eyes on her. "Who were you talking to?"

"Oh, nobody," she said, waving her hand and brushing off my question. "Now, where did I put the car keys?" She began digging through her purse, clearly flustered.

I reached into her jacket pocket and pulled them out. "Here they are," I said, jingling the set.

"Thank you," Mom said, taking the keys. "I must be losing it."

I nodded. Something was up, but I didn't push it. I was going to let the story come to me on its own. After all, that approach had worked once already. I just hoped it didn't take quite as long this time around.

SCOTT

We had a regularly scheduled newspaper meeting that afternoon, which was good because we needed to talk about ideas for our next issue. Natalie's special report had put our paper on the network news and made us the talk all over town.

It was exciting to be a part of something important, but I was fresh out of ideas. That part of my brain still wasn't working like it used to.

"Give it time," Mom kept telling me. "You'll get those creative synapses working again."

I'm terrible at being patient, but I tried my best to listen to Mom's advice because she hadn't ever steered me wrong. Even Grandpa agreed with her, and he knew I could do it because of all the chess we'd played, so I was trying. For starters, I walked into our meeting instead of running.

I smiled big because the first thing I saw was Mrs. Woods and Mrs. Magenta sitting together and talking.

"Hello, Mr. Mason," Mrs. Woods said.

"Hi, Mrs. Woods. Hi, Mrs. Magenta."

I took my seat, still smiling.

"Okay, everyone," Natalie called, bringing us to order.

She'd used the word "everyone," but that wasn't right. None of us had forgotten that we were missing Gavin.

"Natalie," Mrs. Magenta interrupted. "Would you mind if I shared some news before we begin?"

"Of course not," Natalie said. "Please, go ahead."

Mrs. Magenta stood. "I'll need to tell the others later, but I couldn't sit here and not tell all of you now," she began. "I received notification from the state this afternoon that we need to find a new project for our after-school program or I will lose my grant that funds it."

"Why?" Randi asked. "What's wrong with the Senior Center?"

"Nothing's wrong with it," Mrs. Magenta said. "It's just that when I wrote the grant request, I indicated that we would engage in a variety of community service initiatives, so we need to do something more than the Senior Center to prove we've done that. I'm sorry."

"Don't worry, Mrs. Magenta," I told her. "We'll keep going to the Senior Center even without the program. Right, guys?"

The Recruits agreed with me. This was a no-brainer.

"Scott, that concussion may have hurt your brain, but your heart is as big and strong as ever. You don't know how happy I am to hear you say that. You've just validated everything I believe in."

Dad had told me the same thing about my heart, so I knew I had a good one of those. If I could just get my brain back to normal, I'd be all set. I didn't know what Mrs. Magenta meant about validating anything, but I was happy.

"I know what we can do next," Trevor said. "For our next project, I mean."

"Really?" Mrs. Magenta asked. "I'm all ears."

Trevor spoke about Kids Klub and how he thought we could make it a better experience for the kids there by doing the same things we'd done at the Senior Center.

"Dude, that's actually a good idea," Mark said.

"Thanks, bro."

"That does sound like the perfect place for all of you to work your magic," Mrs. Woods agreed. "Well done, Mr. Joseph."

"Indeed," Mrs. Magenta replied. "I'll look into it. Thank you, Trevor."

"Hey, maybe our next article should be about our friends at the Senior Center," I blurted. "Like a wrap-up story."

"Brilliant suggestion," Natalie said.

I ran over and gave her a hug. She'd just made my day. Maybe my brain was starting to rev up again.

Trevor

It was our first day trying out my new idea for Mrs. Magenta's program—Positive Peers, Scott had named it, because the kid liked to name everything. I was nowhere near as nervous going to this as I'd been when we first went to the Senior Center, but I *was* worried. I hadn't stopped thinking about that little boy. He was the whole reason I'd come up with this idea. I didn't know what I was going to do once we got there and I saw him, but somebody else took care of that for me.

It also happened to be the first time Gavin got to hang with us after school since his mom had been taken away. She was still in custody, but Gavin got to bring his sister with him to Kids Klub. Mrs. Magenta arranged it. That was cool, but I didn't really pay attention to his sister. She was little. Before we got done, I was paying attention, because Meggie was the one who showed us what to do.

"Hey, there's Robbie," she said. We'd barely walked through the door at Kids Klub, and she spotted him.

"You know that boy?" I asked.

"Yup. Robbie's in my class. He's my friend."

He was sitting alone again and looked just as miserable as last time. Meggie skipped off in his direction.

"That kid looks like how I feel," Gavin said.

That was another one of those times when I felt like I should say something but had nothing. So we stood there and watched Meggie go and sit down at Robbie's table, and I swear, that was the first time I saw the boy smile.

"And your sister just changed that," I said.

"That's Megs for you," Gavin said, cracking a slight smile.

"C'mon, let's go join them."

We walked over and sat down. "Hey, little man," I tried again.

"Don't call me that," he snapped.

I pulled back. "Sorry."

"It's better than what the bullies call you," Meggie said.

"They're still bothering you?" I asked.

He wasn't talking to me.

"The older boys have been calling him Robbie the Robber," Meggie said.

"Are the bullies here?" I asked next.

Robbie shook his head. I didn't believe him, but I didn't push it.

"Let's play a game," Meggie said.

Gavin shrugged. "What game?"

"We'll get one," Meggie said. She and Robbie ran over to the game cart and came back with Chutes and Ladders.

"Man, I haven't played this in forever," I said.

Meggie and Robbie got the board set up. Robbie let Meggie go first because, "Girls before boys." No way I would have done that back in kindergarten. I had to wonder if this little guy already knew more about girls than I did.

Our game started out quiet, but after four or five rounds, Gavin and I started getting into it. We weren't necessarily hoping to beat Meggie and Robbie, but we were trying to beat each other. So when I hit one of the bigger slides and took a ride way down the board, Gavin started cheering, and so did Robbie. Seeing the two of them—Robbie especially—whooping and getting excited meant I'd already won. I smiled inside.

A couple of spins later it looked like Meggie was the one who would reach the top first, but then she landed on the space with the longest slide and slid way back to the beginning.

"Aww. That stinks," I said.

"It's okay," Meggie said. "I'll make it back to the top, just like Mommy is going to make it back home. Just a couple more days. Right, Gavvy?"

Gavin hesitated, but then he said, "That's right, Megs. Just a couple more days."

What was he supposed to say?

We took turns flicking the spinner, and wouldn't you know it, Gavin and I both hit the slides and fell back down to the bottom of the board. Meggie caught up to Robbie after climbing two ladders.

"Time to say goodbye," Mrs. Magenta announced.

"It's a tie," Meggie said. Her piece and Robbie's were sitting on the same square, way ahead of Gavin and me.

"We kicked your butts," Robbie said.

You did, I thought, looking at his happy face—but really we'd both won. "See you next week," I said.

"See you next week."

Leaving the elementary school, I thought about Meggie's bold prediction about her getting back to the top of the slide, and how she'd been right. I hoped she was right about her mother, too. We'd find out real soon.

15

A RETURNED
CARD

SCOTT

Mom had been right. There was stuff I still couldn't remember from before, but it was slowly coming back to me, and I was doing better at remembering what we were learning in school. My brain was getting closer to full speed again.

My biggest obstacle was going to be final exams because some of those were cumulative, which meant everything from the year was on them. I still had a lot of time before those tests, but I was already starting to review for them. I had to since preparing involved relearning the things I'd forgotten. But I was okay with that. After not being able to read for as long as I was sidelined, I was ready to read anything. And whenever we went to the Senior Center, Grandpa was great at quizzing me on history and science because he knew a lot about that stuff, and the quizzing helped his brain like it did mine. "You're keeping me young," he'd say.

The bad part was the stuff that was boring the first time around was still boring. It takes a special teacher to make the boring stuff interesting. I saw my special teachers after school, not during, which was why my newspaper project was the thing I was really excited about.

We decided that the best way to highlight our friends at the Senior Center was by getting their full names, dates, and places of birth and any other interesting personal information. And then we interviewed everyone. It was like taking a walk down memory lane, so they could share stories and words of wisdom.

I could've chosen Grandpa, but I already knew a lot about him, and since Gavin was spending afternoons with Meggie these days, interviewing Coach was left up to me. I knew the remembering part might be tricky for Coach, but I didn't care. I loved his stories. And Grandpa came with me in case Coach or I needed help.

Coach's brain was a lot like mine. He had a hard time remembering things. But he also got more confused in his stories than I did, which is where our brains were different. While my brain was getting better, Coach's wasn't. He had good days and bad days. Mrs. Woods, Mrs. Magenta, and even Grandpa seemed to always be saying, "You remember . . . ," and then they'd tell him who or what it was that he was supposed to remember. That worked sometimes but not all the time. Confused or not, Coach always made me feel like he knew what he was talking about, especially if it had to do with football, and especially by the end of his stories. This story time was different, though. It was something I won't ever forget.

Coach started telling me about one of his championship games. "I like this story, but I've already heard it," I said. "You told it to me last week." Really I'd already heard it four times, and each time it was different because Coach got mixed up, but I didn't tell him that.

"Is that right?" Coach said. "Then I should tell you about the time our bus was late."

I shook my head. "Heard that one, too."

"*Grrr,*" Coach gruffed. "I can't remember everything I've told you."

"It's okay," I said. "You've told me lots of your football stories, so is there anything not about football that you can tell me about?"

Coach got quiet. I waited in case he was thinking, but he stayed quiet. I worried I was losing him. It looked like he was spacing out on me, but he was reminiscing.

"Junior, there are a few things that happen in a man's life that are so special, they get lodged in your soul, not your head. No matter how bad my brain gets, I'll never forget the first time I met Pearl. She was working at an ice cream stand. My heart had never gone all irregular-beating like that. She handed me my cone, and I couldn't say anything. I couldn't stop looking at her, either, not even when I turned around. Stupid, because I wasn't watching where I was going and I tripped over a bench and fell in the dirt. Made a fool of myself, but she was smiling. I went for ice cream every day that summer." Coach laughed to himself.

I was the one smiling now. Even though this wasn't football talk, it was one of his best stories.

"The day we got married made the old ticker go even crazier," Coach continued. "Boy, she was something.

"The day my children were born was about the scariest time in my life. Eric came out first, but then Olivia started struggling, her little heart not beating like it was supposed to during the delivery. Hell of a thing when you can't do anything to help. I just stood there squeezing Pearl's hand and praying for our baby. And then she popped out hollering herself red, and I cried tears of joy."

I was still smiling.

"And I won't ever forget the bad feeling I had on the night my son didn't come home. I can't explain it, but I knew Eric was gone. I knew before getting the news. I felt it. A part of me died when he left us."

My smile faded. I looked at Grandpa, and he nodded. If pain were a sound, I'd have heard it in Coach's voice when he told me that memory. Not even I knew how to get us past that silence, and that's saying something. It was good timing that saved us.

"Time to go," Mrs. Magenta announced, suddenly appearing in Coach's room.

I jumped.

"I'm sorry. I didn't mean to scare you," she said.

"Ah, it's good for him," Grandpa said. "Keeps him on his toes."

Mrs. Magenta walked over and gave Coach a kiss on top of his head. "Bye, Dad," she whispered. "I'll see you later." She turned to me next. "Ready? The bus is waiting."

"Bye, Coach. Bye, Grandpa," I said, giving him a quick hug.

"You be good. Don't do anything I wouldn't do," he said. I grinned. Grandpa told me that every time.

"You tell Valentine that I expect to see him back here after his mother gets home," Coach ordered. "He's got plenty more to learn about football."

I glanced at Mrs. Magenta and then Grandpa before look-ing at Coach. I hadn't even mentioned Gavin. "Umm, Coach, we don't know if Valentine's mom *is* coming back," I said, my voice dropping to barely above a whisper because I didn't like to say that out loud.

"I know you don't know, but I do," Coach exclaimed. "I can't explain it, but I can feel it."

Did Coach know what he was talking about? How could he? It didn't matter. He had me believing. That's the power of a great coach.

"I'll tell Valentine," I said.

Grandpa winked at me, and I hurried out to the bus with Mrs. Magenta.

Natalie Kurtsman
ASPIRING LAWYER
Kurtsman Law Offices

BRIEF #20
March: The Sweetest Victory

Father picked me up after school that day. Every so often he did this to give Mother a break, especially when she was swamped with work, but this was not one of those occasions. He was my chauffeur because Mother was with Carla Davids; it was her court date.

There were several possible explanations for why Mother wasn't back yet, and I ran each of them over in my head: (1) the day's court proceedings were running behind schedule, or (2) they were stuck in traffic, or (3) the case had not gone well. I didn't like the last of those explanations, but it was a possibility that wouldn't leave me alone. I imagined that Mother was staying with Carla—and saying goodbye.

As you can see, this was a situation not in my control. Hence, it was the most nerve-racking afternoon of my life. Try as I might, I was futile in my attempts to silence any thought of a negative outcome. Carla Davids being deported was entirely possible—maybe even likely.

Give credit to Father; he did his best to comfort me. He brought me a cup of hot chamomile tea as I paced the conference room at the office. He assured me that Mother would be back soon, but we both knew he had no way of knowing that.

I tried distracting myself with homework, but that was useless, too, because I didn't have many assignments, and what I did have required next to no brain power. I plowed through it in a matter of minutes. There was the newspaper to work on, but that only made me think of my friends and Gavin. I settled on more pacing. Back and forth. Back and forth.

I'm not entirely sure when it happened, but at some point I began talking to myself. Yes, I do that in my head all the time, but presently I was doing it out loud. As a result I didn't hear when Mother opened the conference room door. I was walking away from her, but then I hit my designated turnaround spot and did an about-face.

I stopped. She was standing there—alone. Her face expressionless. Where was Carla? Mother walked to the nearest chair and collapsed into it, closing her eyes. Her body radiated defeat. Where was Carla? I was ready to scream. I was literally standing on my tippy-toes. Where was Carla!

Mother sighed. "Carla's home." She looked at me and smiled.

Tears sprang from my eyes. I rushed over and hugged her. She cried with me. It was what they call the sweetest victory.

Father joined us moments later. The hugging was wonderful, but I wanted the full story. Mother gave us the rundown.

Lawyer talk, so I won't bore you with the details. The bottom line: Carla Davids was home.

I had to let the others know. This called for the emergency phone tree.

GOALS

✓ Resolve the strained relationship between Mrs. Woods and Mrs. Magenta.

✓ Keep our plan secret, which requires keeping Scott and the rest of the Recruits quiet—but mainly Scott.

✓ Teach Mrs. Davids how to read—and keep our work secret.

✓ Nail the bad guys responsible for Scott's injury.

✓ Finish the article on the booster club for Scott.

✓ Save ~~Miss~~ Mrs. Carla Davids!

Randi

There had been so much happening lately that Mom and I decided that a quiet girls' night at home sounded nice. We ordered Japanese from a local restaurant and planned to watch a movie. When we sat down with our food, Mom brought up the topic of April vacation. That was still weeks away, and we never did anything during that break, so I was surprised when she mentioned it.

"Got any plans?" she asked, dipping her sushi into the soy sauce.

"No," I scoffed. I thought she was trying to be funny, but she was being serious.

"I was thinking we could go somewhere."

I took a sip of my bubble tea. "Are you taking me to Disney World?" I was trying to be funny.

"Um. No."

I snapped my fingers. "Shucks."

She chuckled, but then she got serious again.

"Where, then?" I asked.

"Your father and Kyle want you to spend the week with them." She stopped eating and waited for my reaction. "You'll meet Kyle's mother and his little brother."

I finished chewing my noodles and swallowed. "What about you?"

Mom placed her napkin on the table. "Randi, I need to tell you something."

I put my chopsticks down and sat back. I never saw it coming. Not in a million years.

"I've met someone," Mom said.

Huh? It took a second for that to register in my brain. My face scrunched. "What do you mean?"

"Coach Andrea introduced me to a gentleman friend of hers when we were at the Elite Stars Festival. I had dinner with him on the night you spent with Kyle and your father."

"Why didn't you tell me?"

"I've been taking it slow. This is the first man I've been interested in since your father."

"'Interested in'?" I repeated. "What's that mean? Like boyfriend-girlfriend?"

"It means we've stayed in touch and I'd like to go see him during April break while you're with your father."

"Mom! Go see him? Doesn't sound like you're taking it slow. Who is he? Where does he live? What does he do?"

"Goodness. Who's the parent here?"

"Right now it's me. What's his name?"

"Jacob. He's a gym owner. He's a widower, and he's very nice," Mom answered.

"I can't believe you didn't tell me this!"

"I'm sorry. I was worried you'd be upset. Are you?"

"Upset? Mom, this is great!"

She smiled.

"Looks like we've got big plans for April," I said.

She smiled more. Then the phone rang, and I hopped out of my chair to answer it. Maybe it was Jacob.

"Hello?" I said into the receiver.

"Randi, it's Natalie."

"Hi."

She was talking fast. Really fast. But I heard her.

"Randi?"

I needed a second to let it sink in. I'm not sure if Mom's news or Natalie's shocked me more that night. This was big.

"Randi?"

"I'll call Trevor," I blurted. This was definitely a phone tree emergency.

"No, I'll call him," Natalie said, breaking her own rule. "Don't worry about it."

Good thing she couldn't see me over the phone, because I smirked. There was no doubt about it: Natalie had a crush on Trevor. "Okay," I said. I'd give her a hard time later. "Thanks." I hung up the phone.

"Ready for our movie?" Mom called from the living room. "I got us a chick flick."

I walked in and gave her a hug. Natalie's news was the kind that made you want to hold your mother. I filled her in, and then we cuddled on the couch and watched our movie.

Love was in the air, all around me, and I was happy. I just hoped destiny realized that I didn't need to be *in* love right now. I'd leave that to Natalie. I could wait. Give it time. Lots of time. Besides, he wasn't ready.

Trevor

Mom was in her glory, humming away, making trip after trip from the kitchen with different bowls and platters of food. We tried, but she didn't want our help. She ordered us to stay put. This was what she'd been waiting for, all four of us gathered around the table—together. This marked the first full-family dinner we'd had in a long, long time, and Mom was making a bigger fuss over it than she had over Thanksgiving. After what felt like her hundredth trip, we looked at each other and started laughing.

"What?" Mom said.

We didn't say a word. I'd bet Mom was moving slowly because she didn't want the night to be over too soon—not after waiting so long for it to happen—and that was fine by me, because neither did I.

"What?" Mom asked again.

"Nothing," Brian said.

"This looks delicious, hon," Dad commented. "Won't you sit down and join us so we can eat it now, while it's still hot?"

Mom studied the table, looking to see if she'd forgotten anything, and then she finally took her seat.

"Thanks for all this," Brian said.

Mom smiled. "Let's bow our heads." Now, this was something we never did, but we weren't about to gripe and spoil her special occasion. We kept our mouths shut and did as she asked. We even joined hands. Mom led us in a short prayer, which was really one giant thank-you because she had her family together again, and then we dug in. I don't know if Mom put something extra in the food that night, or if having everyone in good spirits just made the food taste better, but it was incredible.

There's no telling how long we would've stayed around the table, eating and talking, if it hadn't been for the phone ringing. It had turned dark outside, and none of us had seemed to even notice. I went to answer it so Mom wouldn't have to get up. After all the cooking she'd done, she deserved to sit.

"Hello," I said.

"Hi . . . Trev."

Hearing her voice on the other end made my heart start pounding and my throat go dry. I didn't say anything. I couldn't.

"Trev, it's Natalie," she said.

"I know," I croaked.

"I'm calling because I initiated our phone tree. I have good news."

"But Randi's the one who's supposed to call me, according to the phone tree," I said.

Silence. Not a word.

"Natalie?"

Nothing. I could hear Brian telling me I was an idiot for saying that.

"Natalie?"

Still nothing. Idiot!

"I'm glad you're the one who called," I said.

I waited.

"I told Randi I'd call you. I . . . I wanted to," she said.

I got hit with a second round of heart pounding and dry throat. There was silence on both ends. Slowly I recovered. "What's the news?" I asked after finding my nerve again.

She told me everything. It was the news we'd all been hoping for, but if I'm being honest, talking to her on the phone was my favorite part of that call. That was the first time I'd ever talked to a girl on the phone.

When we hung up, I made my call to Mark, and then I returned to the table. Brian took one look at me and knew.

"Who was that?" Mom asked.

"My friend. Gavin's mother is home," I said.

"Oh, that's wonderful!" Mom exclaimed.

"Took long enough, but I'm glad that judge put politics aside and did the right thing," Dad said.

"Your friend, huh?" Brian teased. "Don't you mean *girlfriend*, lover boy?"

"What?" Mom sang, cluelessness ringing in her voice. "Lover boy? Trevor, do you have a girlfriend?"

"No."

"Yes," Brian said, egging her on.

"Trevor?" Mom repeated.

"What?"

She smiled at me. "My baby."

Ugh! I glared at my brother. He wore a stupid grin spread across his face. He thought he was so funny. I sneered at him, but really I didn't care. But if he told Mark, I'd slice his tires. I told him that after we had cleaned up and he was getting ready to leave the house.

"I wouldn't do that," he said.

"I mean it," I warned.

"Okay, okay. Don't worry, bro." We fist-bumped. "Just let me know when you're ready to be coached on how to kiss her. You don't want to screw that up."

I shoved him, and he laughed.

"Thanks for dinner, Mom! See you later, Dad!" Brian yelled from the doorway.

"Bye!" they called from the kitchen. That was followed by giggling. "Stop," Mom squealed.

"Have fun with that," Brian joked.

"Yeah," I said, rolling my eyes. "Thanks."

As I watched my brother walking out to his car, it hit me that sometimes you've got to break things before you can put them together again. Like I'd done with that old TV room at the Senior Center. Like with our family. The good news is, if you do the fixing part right, then you can make it even better and stronger in the end.

"Sto-op," Mom squealed again. I heard them running down the hall.

I shook my head. Them carrying on like that was gross.

Wicked gross. But it was better than yelling and fighting. I'd take their grossness over the fighting any day. Besides, by the sounds of it, I didn't need to worry about their relationship anymore, which was music to my ears. It was time to focus on mine and Natalie's instead. *Shhh.*

GAVIN

That afternoon was more of the same. Me and Megs huddled over Monopoly, Otis on the side, ready to steal our dice any second. I wasn't in the mood for his nonsense, and I let him know that. I'll give the dog some credit, he wasn't all dumb, 'cause after one scolding he moaned, sprawled out on the floor, sighed, and closed his eyes. I'd won—for now.

A little while later Meggie said, "Gavvy, I'm getting hungry."

"All right. We can pause the game and I'll make us something to eat."

"Mac-n-cheese," Meggie insisted.

I nodded. It was an easy recipe, and it made enough for the two of us. Megs wouldn't eat that much, and I'd polish off whatever was left. Dad would take care of himself whenever he came home. I put the pot on the stove and cranked the heat. Megs grabbed me the butter and milk. When the water got close to a boil, I opened the box and dumped the noodles in. I took the white pouch of cheese mix and set it on the side.

Otis struck. He'd decided that if I wasn't gonna let him get the Monopoly pieces, our cheese pouch would do the trick. He snatched it off the counter and barreled into the living room.

"Otis!" I yelled, tearing after him. "Drop it!"

The chase was on.

"Drop it!" I yelled again. That never worked. Why did I even try? The only way to get something out of his mouth was to catch him and pry his jaws open. Catching him was the hard part. Once we did, our cheese pouch was guaranteed to be soaked in slobber. Super-gross.

"Drop it," I growled, inching my way forward. We stood, faced off in the middle of the living room, both of us in our stances, knees bent and ready to spring. For such a large beast, Otis could change directions on a dime. I was no match for his athleticism or his size, so I had to outsmart him.

I sent Megs in from the side.

"Ready, Megs?" I asked.

"Ready," she said.

"On three, you charge. One. Two—"

I never made it to three. All of a sudden Otis dropped the cheese pouch and bounded to the front door, no longer interested in me and Megs or his game of chase. *Ruff! Ruff! Ruff!*

"Otis, there's nothing out there, you dummy. Settle down."

"Gavvy, the water's boiling over!" Meggie yelled.

I ran into the kitchen and yanked the pot off the burner.

Ruff! Ruff! Ruff!

"Be quiet, Otis," I groaned.

I went to the front door and opened it to see why he was causing a racket. Megs was behind me, and Otis was still barking. The instant I stepped outside, I saw what had him going crazy. Otis wasn't an idiot. But how had he known?

Dad was parked in the driveway, and sitting next to him in the cab of the truck was the person I thought I'd never see again. Meggie ran toward them squealing, "Mommy! Mommy!"

I was stuck on the porch, frozen in place. I couldn't move. I was already crying. I watched Mom jump out of the truck and swallow Meggie in her arms. Otis couldn't take it. He bowled them over and covered their faces in slobbery slurps. Their giggles made me smile through my tears. It was the best sound I'd ever heard.

Dad joined me on the porch. He put his hand on my shoulder. "She's home."

I looked at Dad and saw that his eyes were wet like mine. In that moment I realized I was happier for him and Meggie than I was for me. Maybe that's what it means to be family.

"Hi, *Niño,*" Mom said, climbing the steps to the porch.

I found my legs and took three long strides and fell into her hug. I held her for a whole minute, maybe longer. I didn't want to let go. I was a little boy again, safe in my mother's arms.

"I'm sorry," she said. "So sorry."

"It's okay," I whispered. "It's okay." And it was.

"*Mija,* I have something for you," Mom said, reaching into her bag and pulling out a card. "The judge asked me to return this to you." She handed it to Meggie. I read it over my sister's shoulder. It was the Valentine's Day card she had sent.

> *Dear Mr. Judge,*
>
> *Sorry you have bad kidknees. I heard my daddy say peeing those stones out is like haveing a baby, and he says haveing a baby is like pooping out a watermellun. That doesn't sound plesent. I hope you don't hurt too bad. Please get better fast so I can have my mommy back. Happy Valentine's Day.*
>
> > *Your friend,*
> > *Meggie Davids*

The judge had scrawled a note for Meggie at the bottom.

> *Dear Meggie,*
>
> *Thank you for your thoughtful card. It made my day. I hope I've returned the favor.*
>
> > *Sincerely,*
> > *Mr. Judge*

Good ol' Megs. Told you melting hearts was her superpower. She had saved Mom. Little did we know, we'd need her to use her superpowers again in the not-so-distant future. But for now we were finally together again. Happy and safe.

Epilogue

NATALIE KURTSMAN
ASPIRING LAWYER
Kurtsman Law Offices

BRIEF #21
Spring: The Perfect Secret

Although spring signifies the beginning of the end when referring to a school year, it was quite the opposite for us. More like the beginning of the beginning.

After a whirlwind of challenges and unearthed secrets, seventh grade finally slowed down and stopped throwing surprises our way—well, except for a few. There were two events that merit my reporting.

The first of those took place during Mrs. Magenta's program, when we were busy at Kids Klub. I found myself sitting at a table playing UNO with Randi, Trevor, Gavin, Meggie, and Meggie's friend Robbie. Trevor had told me about this little boy; he had described the boy as sad and he wanted to do whatever he could to make him happy. It was things like this that made my insides go all funny around Trevor; he was sweet.

There was plenty of laughter and fun while we played. All involved were having a good time; none involved was paying attention to the time or to the person who had just walked in looking for his little brother. I had my face buried in my cards, planning out my sequence of moves, when the table suddenly went silent.

I peeked over my hand and saw Nicky Holmes standing there. He glared at us before turning to Robbie. "You ready?"

"Can I finish this game?"

"No. Mom's waiting."

Robbie scowled.

Nicky sighed. "We're going to see Dad, remember?"

"Oh yeah," Robbie said, suddenly excited. He hopped up and grabbed his bag. Then he gave Trevor a fist bump. "See you next time, Trevor. Bye, Meggie. Bye, everyone else."

"Bye, Robbie," we said.

The little boy hurried off, but Nicky stood rooted in place. He stared into our faces for several long seconds, and then he turned and left. No words were exchanged, but it felt like a lot was said. What exactly, I wasn't sure any of us knew. It could've been *I hate you*. It could've been *Watch your backs*. It could've been *Thanks for playing with my little bro*. For me it was, *I'm sorry*.

The second event I need to report takes the prize. It took place at the Senior Center. You may have guessed that, yes, it was the special double ceremony at which Coach and Mrs. Woods renewed their vows alongside Mr. and Mrs. Magenta.

In the weeks leading up to the grand occasion, we worked to get everything ready. This entailed giving the Community

Hall a thorough cleaning and adding decorations, since this was the spot where the ceremony and reception would take place. We did the usual: filled balloons and hung streamers; and then for a special touch, throughout the venue we displayed photos of Coach and Mrs. Woods from over the years, along with a few shots of Mr. and Mrs. Magenta, and a gorgeous sequence of her paintings.

The first time Mrs. Magenta walked in and caught sight of the pictures and her paintings on display, she froze. We watched in silence as she stood there, taking it all in. Then she turned to us and swallowed. "Thank you," she croaked.

We nodded. The fact that she didn't even try to say anything more said it all.

There were many highlights on the big day, starting with the moment when Coach and Mrs. Woods actually renewed their promise. Don't tell me Coach's memory is gone. Looking at his face, it was as if he were seeing his wife on their wedding day all over again. Maybe he didn't remember all the details, and maybe he couldn't tell you much about it, but his heart remembered.

The expressions he and Mrs. Woods wore as they watched their daughter with her husband were every bit as sweet. When the men kissed their brides, the Community Hall broke into applause, and those of us who could stood. Old and young were left crying and smiling. The only word to even come close to describing the moment would be "beautiful."

The reception got under way immediately afterward. Mrs. Ruggelli and Mrs. Magenta had made the wise decision to have it catered, knowing that would be nicer and easier than a buffet line. While the meals were being served, Mrs. Woods and Coach, and Mr. and Mrs. Magenta, took the opportunity to go around visiting and thanking people. All of us Recruits were together at our table when they stopped by.

"You dress up nice for a football player, Valentine," Coach said. "You too, Junior."

"Thanks," they responded. The rest of us chuckled.

Mrs. Woods was next to say something. "All of you, Olivia and I want to make sure you understand . . . you've given us something we will never be able to repay. Thank you."

"Thank you," Mrs. Magenta echoed.

The best we could do was smile and nod—except for Gavin. He knew what to say. "Keep fighting. Okay, Coach?"

"To the last play, Valentine. To the last play."

That exchange choked me up as much as anything else that afternoon. I actually had to look away.

They moved on to the next table, and we turned back to our plates. The food was truly delicious, but it was the dessert that Scott flipped over—no surprise there.

"Did you try the cake?" he cried. "I'm on my third piece." He stuffed his mouth full. There was frosting on his nose and in his hair, but he didn't care.

Randi and I shook our heads and laughed.

Indeed the cake was amazing, but the ensuing music and party were even better. DJ Duane for the Ages, according to the banner hanging off his table, knew how to play to his crowd; his playlist of old-time rock 'n' roll got our friends out of their chairs and onto the dance floor. And let me just say, these seniors knew how to boogie. Their generation was way ahead of us in that department.

"Don't look now," I said to Scott, "but your grandfather is twirling Eddie around."

Scott gawked. Cake fell out of his mouth, but he just shoveled it back in and ran out to join the excitement, entertaining us with his own wild dance. It looked like a cross between the headless chicken and the drunken goose, but it worked. He and his grandpa got the party started.

Next to join were Mr. and Mrs. Magenta, followed by Coach and Mrs. Woods, and then Mr. Davids and Meggie, and Gavin and his mother. I won't kid you—by then I'd gone from smiling to wiping my eyes and choking back more tears. Having everyone together, after all that had happened, was no small feat. It was an enormous achievement, a borderline miracle.

And then the unimaginable happened. "Natalie, would you like to dance?" Trevor asked, taking me by surprise.

"Um . . . I . . ."

Randi nudged my arm.

"Um."

She nudged me harder.

"Okay."

"Don't let Eddie see you," Randi whispered.

I shooed her.

This was my first-ever dance with a boy, and it was not romantic or graceful. It was awkward. Trevor had two left feet; he stepped on my toes repeatedly and sputtered apology after apology. Here's the funny thing—I didn't mind.

"Guess I still need more practice," he said.

"You've been practicing?"

"A little. My brother's been coaching me."

"Who've you been dancing with, your mom?"

He hesitated. "No. Mark."

I couldn't help it; I laughed. *What a sight,* I thought. *But how sweet.*

"Don't tell anyone," Trevor pleaded. "He'd kill me."

"Your secret's safe with me," I said.

We smiled and continued turning in a circle on the floor. More important than Trevor's feet were his arms and hands—the ones wrapped around my waist and placed on the small of my back. If he had even tried to slip them down to my butt like nimrod Mark was egging him on to do, that would've been the end of us—no question. But Trevor wasn't that foolish.

I maintain, I wasn't some hopeless romantic falling helplessly in love. We weren't even boyfriend-girlfriend—were we? I didn't know; I'd never done this before. This was new territory for my heart, so I had to keep control over the situation, which meant establishing rules and expectations.

I pulled Trevor aside. "Listen, we've got to get a few things straight."

He swallowed and nodded. I loved that I could still intimidate him.

"One: Occasional hand holding will be permitted, but the PDA stops there. Got it?"

More nodding.

"You do know what 'PDA' is, right?"

No response. He didn't. Unbelievable.

"'Public displays of affection,'" I said.

"Oh. Right. Of course."

"Two: No texting. We're not ready for that. Phone calls are acceptable, but you should be the one who calls me."

"When?"

"How about Tuesdays and Thursdays for now? Let's start slow."

"Okay," he agreed.

I could see that he was more nervous than I was when it came to us.

"And three: Let's not blab about us to our friends, i.e., Mark."

Trev sighed. "I was hoping you'd say that. The last thing I want is him ribbing me at every chance."

"Good," I said, satisfied. I held out my hand and we shook, which wasn't a very boyfriendy or girlfriendy thing to do, but it worked. For now, we were the perfect secret.

ACKNOWLEDGMENTS

It's no secret that a book is read by many eyes and touched by many hands before it is finally ready for the world. *The Perfect Secret* was no exception. My daughter Emma and my wife, Beth, were the first to read the manuscript and will forever be two of my most important and trusted readers. I couldn't do this without their feedback and support. I'm also extremely lucky that my daughters Lily and Anya made sure I got the gymnastics stuff correct—which wasn't the case until they helped me.

Thank you to Kevin McQuade, who dedicated his time and expertise and helped me answer complicated immigration questions. Thank you also to Amy Jefferson and Robin Rowe Bradley for helping me with my questions about filing income taxes, as it relates to the story.

Once again, Gavin's sketches are the work of Leslie Mechanic—and I love them.

I'm beyond grateful for my editor, Françoise Bui, who always makes me better than I ever could be without her insightful comments and questions and friendship. Thank you to my agent, Paul Fedorko. And to Beverly Horowitz, for the care you've shown me since the beginning. I will never be able to adequately express my gratitude.

Lastly, a huge thank-you to the entire team at Random House Children's Books for continuing to support me and make my books look perfect.

Turn the page for a preview of

THE PERFECT STAR

AUTHOR OF THE **MR. TERUPT** SERIES

ROB BUYEA

1

SUMMERTIME
BLUES

GAVIN

I'd said it before and I would say it again, babies popped out
looking uglier than a linebacker, but for some, that ugliness
turned into cuteness by the time the toddler phase rolled
around. It was a fact. Once you got 'em past the poopy dia-
pers stage, the baby started looking and smelling better. What
made me the expert on this stuff? My little sister, Meggie.

Megs was good and ugly in the beginning, but nowadays
it didn't matter where we were. As soon as people saw her,
the "oohs" and "awws" would start. And that was always followed by, "She's so cute." I would just laugh. If these people
only knew that my precious little sister was the same cutie-pie
who'd tried to eat cigarette butts off the ground in the Food-
land parking lot—granted, that was when she was three, but
still. And it wasn't long ago that Megs needed help wiping her
butt and a reminder to wash her hands after using the bathroom. Megs was the same peanut who shared her bed with
our very large and slobbery bullmastiff, Otis. By morning
she would have a mouth full of Otis hair and a soaking wet

pillowcase, but she didn't care, and neither did the rest of the world, 'cause here was the other thing about Megs. She was a little person with a great big vocabulary. She was only going into first grade, but she liked using grown-up words when she talked, and that just made her cute card even stronger. It was her whole package that gave her the superpower ability to melt hearts—and we were gonna need all of that to save our family this time around.

I was firing another pass through my trusty tire target when Meggie yelled, "Gavvy, Daddy needs your assistance!" *Assistance?* See what I mean? She scared me pretty good by yelling like that when I wasn't ready for it, so my throw sailed high. It was the first pass I'd missed all afternoon. Blockhead Otis ran and snatched my football and raced around with it in his mouth.

"Drop it!" I shouted. Fat chance. I had to go and grab one of his tennis balls from near the porch, and then he came bounding over and dropped my football. The stupid dog was smart enough to know I'd throw his tennis ball for him all day long if he captured my football first, so who was the dumb one? I chucked his ball across the yard, and he tore after it. Then I turned to Megs, ready to yell at her for scaring me like that, but instead I burst out laughing. She had grease and dirt smeared across her upper lip.

"What?" she whined.

"Nothing." I wasn't gonna tell her. Cute or not, she was still my little sister. "What's Dad need help with?" I asked.

She shrugged. "He didn't say."

I picked up my football and wiped it clean on my quarter-backing towel. "Let's go see."

Randi

The way seventh grade had ended had been terrific. I really couldn't have asked for anything more. We had Mrs. Woods and Mrs. Magenta together again, Mrs. Davids was home, and then I finished the year off by winning the gymnastics all-around title at Regionals.

The hug Mom and I shared when I met her on my way into the awards area was one of extreme happiness mixed with relief. After years of hard work, I was finally regional champ. "I'm so proud of you, honey," she said into my ear, squeezing me tighter. "You were amazing today."

"Thanks, Mom."

Coach Andrea and Mom hugged next. Then a man I hadn't noticed before stepped forward. "Congratulations, Andrea."

"Thank you, Jacob," she replied.

Jacob? Wait. What?

The man turned to face me. "Randi, this is Jacob," Mom said.

This is Jacob, I repeated in my head. *The man Mom has been talking to since Coach Andrea introduced them last year, and the man she went to see during April break. This is Jacob? The man Mom has feelings for?* He offered me his hand, and I shook it. He was tall—and good-looking.

"Congratulations, Randi. You were wonderful out there. Your floor routine was beautiful," he said.

"Thank you."

"Next up is the USA Summer Showcase," Coach Andrea said. "You qualified with your scores today."

I smiled. I'd had no idea.

"I'd love to have you come and spend time training at my gym," Jacob said. "We have a group of top-notch athletes getting ready for the event, and I know you'd thrive in that atmosphere."

"That sounds great," I said, because I didn't know what else to say. He'd caught me off guard. From what Mom had told me, I knew that Jacob owned a big gym, and I had loved training with other serious gymnasts at camp last year, but deep down I wasn't sure I liked his idea. I didn't like the way Mom was looking at him, either. Was she falling for this man?

Mom beamed. She grasped Jacob's hand, and he kissed her on the cheek. Then the four of us stood there, staring at each other.

NATALIE KURTSMAN
ASPIRING LAWYER
Kurtsman Law Offices

BRIEF #1
Summer: A Case of Things Coming in Threes:
     A Letter, a Talk, a Text

Unlike the big-announcement letters that had arrived closer to the start of school the previous two summers, this one came early. It was addressed to Mother and Father, but I was allowed to open it, since it was from Lake View Middle; that was our rule. I waited until I was at the law office, and then I found a chair in the conference room and began reading.

> *Dear Eighth-Grade Parents & Guardians:*
>
> *I hope this letter finds you well and that you've been able to enjoy the beautiful weather and time with your children. I don't want to rush away the summer, but I have news to share.*

The eighth-grade teachers and administration have been in search of something special for our students, and we believe we've found it. We'd like to send our eighth graders to Nature's Learning Lab this fall. Nature's Learning Lab is an overnight, outdoor-education experience roughly two hours northwest of here. This opportunity would enrich our curriculum and provide a wonderful community-building component. Students would live and learn together and gain a new appreciation for and perspective on our world and their place in it. We would leave school on a Monday morning and return the following Friday afternoon. You can read more about the facility and the experience on their website, www.natureslearninglab.org.

We are in the early stages of the planning process, but before getting too far into the details, we'd first like to gather your feedback. We ask that by the end of next week you kindly complete the short survey that can be found on our school website. Essentially, we need to know how many of our students would like to participate in this adventure.

Thank you for your time and your continued support of our children's education.

> *Go, Warriors!*
> *Albert Allen (principal)*
> *and the eighth-grade team*

An overnight outdoor learning experience? What did that mean? Was I supposed to sleep in a tent? Preposterous!

Trevor

My summer was a catch-22. What the heck did that mean? For one, it meant I was glad to be done with early mornings and homework and classes, but without school, I didn't get to see my friends. For two, it meant Mrs. Magenta was spending all her time with her mom and dad and husband now that we had helped fix their family feud—and I couldn't blame her for that—so her community service program wasn't happening. And for three, it meant Mark was around in the beginning, but then he took off on this month-long family vacation seeing relatives, leaving me with nothing to do. I wanted to hang out with everyone—especially Natalie—but I didn't know how to make that happen. How was Natalie supposed to be my girlfriend if I never got to see her? Basically, the catch-22 was, it was great that it was summer, but my summer sucked.

SCOTT

My little brother, Mickey, needed to get a physical before starting school this year. I didn't want to get dragged along to his appointment, because that would be worse than clothes shopping, so I made a deal with Mom that she would drop me off at the Senior Center to spend the afternoon with Grandpa when she took Mickey. I got Gavin to come with me because we weren't in Mrs. Magenta's program this summer and I was super-bored and missing the Recruits—and also because I knew Gavin would want to see Coach.

"Hi, Gavin," Mom said, greeting him when he got into our van.

"Hi, Mrs. Mason. Hi, Mickey. Hi, Scott," Gavin replied.

Mickey waved, but Gavin and I did a fist bump.

"How's summer going?" Mom asked.

"Pretty good. Just waiting for the school to hire a football coach."

"Yes, I've heard. I'm sure they'll find somebody soon," Mom said.

It didn't take us long to get to the Senior Center from Gavin's house, and that was good because I was starting to have a hard time sitting still. When Mom pulled into the parking lot, I unbuckled my seat belt before she even stopped.

"Have fun at the doctor's," I said.

Mickey stuck his tongue out at us and scowled.

"Gavin, I'm counting on you to keep Scott and his grandfather out of trouble," Mom said.

Gavin chuckled. "Sure thing, Mrs. Mason."

I pulled open the side door, and we hopped out and ran inside. We found Grandpa and Coach hanging out in Coach's room just like we'd expected. Mrs. Woods was there, too, which was an extra bonus.

"Hi, everybody," I sang when we walked in.

"Well, hello, gentlemen," Mrs. Woods replied in a cheery voice. "What a nice surprise to see you here."

"Hi, boys," Grandpa said.

Coach didn't bother saying anything. He was busy studying some kind of book.

"What're you doing, Grandpa?" I asked.

"Oh, nothing really. Just sitting here with my cat, farting around with this crossword puzzle until Coach decides it's time for our chess match."

I walked over and gave Smoky a scratch behind the ears, and his purring motor fired up. He loved a scratch behind the ears almost as much as he loved Grandpa's lap.

"What's Coach looking at?" Gavin asked Grandpa.

"Pearl brought him an old scrapbook to exercise his memory today."

"How's he doing?" Gavin whispered.

Grandpa shrugged and tried smiling, but it was a smile that said, *Not the greatest.* We watched Coach. Mrs. Woods was sitting next to him so that she could remind his memory when he needed it. I wondered if she'd been helping him a lot.

"Go have a peek," Grandpa said.

Gavin and I crept closer and saw the newspaper clippings, photographs, ticket stubs, and other things stuck on those pages.

"What's this?" Coach asked.

Mrs. Woods looked. "That's from a long time ago when you took me to a concert at the beach," she reminded him.

Coach flipped the page over. His face scrunched. "Who's that?" he asked, pointing to an old snapshot.

"That's you with your first football captains."

"Wow, that's Coach?" I shouted. "He's so young. Look at all that hair!"

Coach glanced up at Gavin and me and then turned back to his book.

Mrs. Woods chuckled. "Any word from the school about a new football coach yet?" she asked us.

"No, not yet," Gavin mumbled. "If we don't hire someone soon, we're gonna be in danger of missing preseason camp."

"We did get a letter about the eighth grade maybe going to a sleepaway camp!" I exclaimed. "An outdoor-education place. I hope we go."

"Sleepaway camp?" Grandpa repeated. "You let me know about that, because I've got a few tricks I can show you ahead of time."

"Mom said not to tell you because you'd say that."

Seven kids.

Seven voices.

One special teacher

who brings them together.

ROB BUYEA'S beloved

mr. terupt series

Delacorte Press